L. RIFKIN

THE NINE LIVES OF
Romeo Crumb

LIFE ONE

Stratford Road
Press, Ltd.

THE NINE LIVES OF ROMEO CRUMB
LIFE ONE
Copyright © 2005 by L. Rifkin. All rights reserved.
Illustrations, Copyright © 2005 by Kurt Hartman.
Reproduction of the whole or any part of the contents of this publication without written permission is prohibited.

The Nine Lives of Romeo Crumb is a trademark of L. Rifkin

Library of Congress Control Number: 2004096366

ISBN 0-9743221-0-5

Printed in the United States of America.

THE NINE LIVES OF
Romeo Crumb

Illustrations by Kurt Hartman

LIFE ONE

Chapter One

It all began on a dark, stormy Wednesday night in the alley behind Sal's Leather Shop. The rain was tapping on the torn awning above, and the glow of the cafe lights cast odd shadows across the alley walls. Beneath the cracked windows and thick fog, Mrs. Gamble lay anxiously on the only dry part of her soggy cardboard box which she and her husband called home. It rested between two overfilled trash cans and a pile of old, abandoned shoes. The others watched in a puddle and chewed their claws as Mrs. Gamble delivered a new litter of six healthy felines. All males. A piercing siren rushed down the street as the first faint hint of a meow escaped from one of the newborns. That was Romeo. He was the oldest.

Mr. Gamble knelt down next to his wife and and stroked her matted gray coat. He marveled at

Chapter One

his sons.

"We did it, Sarah," he said despite the growing lump in his throat. "We did it."

Sarah Gamble, who was quite weak, lifted her heavy head and smiled, "Yes George, we did."

Just as the six kittens reached for their first sip of mom's milk, a familiar, devilish shadow rounded the corner at the far end of the alley. A cold chill flowed through Mr. Gamble. He stood back shielding his wife, hoping it was not Fidel, the meanest cat around. Unfortunately, it was.

"Fidel!" hissed Mr. Gamble. His eyes were drawn to the tarnished ID tags Fidel collected and wore around his neck stolen off the cats he had killed. They clinked hauntingly with every step Fidel took. Other cats scattered in a frenzy after Fidel knocked one of them out of his way.

Fidel was not impressed by his poor welcome. He took a dramatic leap toward the new family. His eyes glowed hypnotically, and his deep, foreboding purr was louder than the horns of all the taxi cabs combined. Behind him, his pack of faithfuls stood like a dark prison wall. The 'silent five', they were called. Slowly, Fidel circled the Gambles, whirling a hint of panic into the air.

"Well, well, well," Fidel spoke with a smirk. "What do we have here? I believe....yes, I do believe I see six of them. And all males. How perfect for *me*. Good work Mr. and Mrs. Gamble."

Life One

A passing firefly caught the attention of one of the kittens, his yellow eyes barely open. With all his five-minute-old might, he swatted, knocking the poor bug to the ground. Mrs. Gamble, who didn't approve of violence, pulled him closer to her body all the while keeping a watchful eye on Fidel.

"No, no, Mrs. Gamble, leave him be," urged Fidel. "He'll be *just* perfect." Fidel reached down with his ratty paw and smashed the quivering insect into an oozy mess. He raised his paw and licked off the sticky bug.

Mr. Gamble shot his wife a look hoping she wouldn't speak up. It didn't work.

"Now look, Fidel," Mrs. Gamble said with her last bit of strength. "I will not sit by and allow you to... to groom my boys into some*thing* like *you*. They are going to have a good life, a privileged life, not one full of hatred and violence." As the words spit from her mouth, she shook, making it difficult for the thirsty kittens to continue.

Fidel, unaffected by such sap, took one last look at her through the fog and added sinisterly, "We'll see about that Mrs. Gamble. We'll see about that."

And with those fateful words, he slithered back around the corner, his shadow and entourage following close behind.

Certain that Fidel was gone, Mr. Gamble turned to his wife. "Don't worry about him, Sarah. Our boys will be fine. I won't let that wretch near them."

Chapter One

"I hope you're right, George," she added with doubt. "If Fidel gets a hold of them, they'll lead a life of crime and danger. Just think of the horrible things he's done in this city!"

Three days later as night crept in, Mr. and Mrs. Gamble came to a difficult decision. They'd give up their precious boys.

"It's the only way," Mrs. Gamble wept.

Mr. Gamble hesitated and said, "I know, Sarah. It must be done quickly before Fidel returns."

Every Monday at noon at the corner of 54th and 8th, the van from City Pound made its scheduled weekly inspection. For most cats it was a time to scurry and hide anywhere possible. The Pound was no place to be. For many cats it meant getting *fixed*, which slowed the alley cat population. Something which Fidel didn't like because it cut into his recruitment numbers. Not only was the surgery something to fear, but for the very cute, young cats, another fate awaited them at the Pound. Something so horrible in the minds of the alleys that there was nothing they wouldn't risk to avoid it. Getting adopted. The idea of adoption where you had to live under the rules and order of some person was unthinkable.

Freedom, the most important thing to alley cats, was nonexistent at the home of a human, or so thought the alleys. A cat who fell into this misfortune would forever have the stinging title of being called a *stick*, short for dome*stic*. And no alley cat with any amount of pride wanted to be one of those. However, to save their sons from the clutches of Fidel, Mr. and Mrs. Gamble, themselves alleys, would sacrifice their young children to adoption. Something they saw as hopeful, even if they were alone in their thoughts. They would not go with their sons for they could never get adopted out of alley life. Nobody ever wanted the older cats.

On Monday at noon Mr. and Mrs. Gamble would leave their kittens huddled in a box at the corner of 54th and 8th. They would try to find some sort of a blanket to keep them protected from the bitter chill in the air. It was most important that Fidel not find out about their plan. Mr. Gamble would station himself at the far end of the alley to keep an eye peeled for him, and Mrs. Gamble would stay closer to the street and her sons. If Fidel got wind of their plan, he would be furious. And he wouldn't hesitate to let the Gambles know just how furious he was. He wanted those males to join his growing alley cat army. A new generation was always enticing.

Once the van from the Pound took the kittens, Mr. and Mrs. Gamble would hop on the bumper of the 718 bus with their few ragged possessions and head straight out of the city. Surely *they* would be killed if taken to the Pound. At their advanced ages, losing a life was not an option. The kittens had a chance, and it had to be done right away before Fidel and his gang of terrors could recruit them.

5

Chapter One

Monday morning at eleven-thirty sharp, Mrs. Gamble prepared her babies for their long journey. With difficulty, she placed them into an old shoe box which her husband found in a nearby alley. It was hard for her to pretend all was well, very hard, though she knew it was for the best.

Nearly twelve o'clock, Mr. Gamble took one final look at his sons before backing away to the deep corner of the alley. Above, many gray clouds had formed and an increasing mist swept in. Mrs. Gamble kissed her husband on the cheek and watched as he crept into the darkness. When his shape was no longer visible, she too took a long, mournful glance at the six miracles that she birthed only five days earlier.

"Good luck, little ones." A single tear fell from her sad eyes matching the scattered raindrops. "I wish I could be with you, but you could never be safe here." She looked around at all the filth and garbage that lined the alley. She dreamed of a warm, safe home for her children full of love and good food. This thought fed her the strength she needed for her final goodbye as the rickety, gray van turned the corner. With a loud roar it charged up the street pouring mountains of thick, black smoke in its wake. With not enough time for even a kiss, she gazed for that last moment at her kittens and seared each of their young faces in her memory. "Goodbye my loves, goodbye."

With that, she forced herself under a pile of old, wet newspapers only two feet away, yet the longest

 6

distance she had ever known. Her eyes watched the van as it skidded and turned into the entrance of the alley balancing on only its two right wheels. She tried not to move for fear of being seen and caught, but the van splashed so much mud and slush her way that she had to wiggle. Luckily, they didn't notice her.

The earlier mist now changed into a heavy downpour as the van door opened. On it among the many rust deposits, the faded words *City Pound* sat directly in Mrs. Gamble's view. As the door opened wider, it creaked with the sound of the wind sending a familiar chill up Mrs. Gamble's back. A dirty boot stepped out causing a splash once again in her direction.

"Looky here," said a heavy voice. "Joe, come look at this. Jackpot!"

Mrs. Gamble knew it was over. Her children had been spotted by some underpaid city employee who had no idea of the pain one mother was feeling only inches away. She watched in horror as the man picked up the wet shoe box and dumped all six cats into an old, wire cage. The sound of the meows was unbearable. She covered her ears, though that didn't help what-so-ever. Her angels were crying, scared and confused. It was almost enough to make her heave forward and take them back, and somehow, someway, make a good life for them. Yet, with a strength she never knew was possible, she cowered back beneath the pages of soap adds and theatre reviews and

allowed herself to feel every bit of pain her body pro-
duced. Perhaps the hardest moment of all was when
she looked up and for one last bit of a second caught
the eyes of all her sons. The smallest one extended his
little, bare paw as if to wave goodbye. It was like they
knew through those cold bars where she was, and
what she was doing, and why. That second would
be the hardest of her life, for in barely a blink, they
were gone forever. It was over. All that remained of
her miracles was an empty shoe box which sat alone
in the gutter. The gray van and her unfortunate reality
spun out of sight.

 8

Chapter Two

Four weeks later, Dennis Crumb, a ten year old misfit, ran home from school. His baggy, brown pants were full of mud and tears, typical for a boy his age. However, being that it was his birthday, he knew his mother would overlook it.

Down the street he ran, passed the blocks and blocks of the homeless, passed the hotdog stands, passed the rats, and through the dark alleys. He ran faster and faster knowing his birthday present would be waiting for him. What it was he did not know.

Finally, he reached his building at 17 E. 58th Street. Dennis ran up the cracked stone stairs which were sternly guarded by two stone gargoyles perched above. When he got to the third floor he dashed across the maroon carpeted hallway to apartment B. The door was unlocked.

Chapter Two

"I'm home!" he yelled. "Mom, I'm home!"

The Crumb apartment was small, as were most in the city, but homey. A cozy living room greeted its occupants followed by a kitchen full of more smells than a bakery. The walls were decorated with faces and places of a life long ago. Plastic covered furniture carefully arranged sat comfortably inside the snug dwelling. Dennis' room was covered with toys, all of which sadly had once seen better days and were now ignored. Mr. and Mrs. Crumb were good, hard working people, though heartbroken that fate only handed them one child. Dennis was a miracle, something they reminded themselves of daily, yet they desperately wanted another face around the house, not just for them but for lonely Dennis. Dennis' birthday present would be just the thing.

Dennis found his parents in his room. They sat patiently on his cowboy bedspread. Beside them on the little, green night stand was a tightly wrapped box. Dennis' eyes went right to it. He knew that his present was inside.

Excited, Dennis picked up the box to shake it, but his father quickly intervened.

"Don't rock it, Dennis!" his father said. "Just open it."

Dennis bit his bottom lip and ripped off the white ribbon after some healthy tugging and pulling. His parents watched anxiously as a sparkle formed in Dennis' eyes. His breath got quick and his red, curly

Life One

hair nearly straightened right then and there.

"A cat! A cat!" Dennis screamed. Immediately, he picked up the scared, shivering kitty and devoured it with enough kisses to last a lifetime.

Outside two police officers could faintly be heard screaming at some old, homeless drunk, but inside, a new kitten found a home. It was a beautiful cat too. An American Tabby. He had a classic blend of black and gray stripes with one odd little marking toward his back. In a golden color was the formation of a diamond, not the kind on a fancy ring, but like a baseball field. It was above his left hind leg near his hip. Unbeknownst to Dennis, the kitten's father and brothers shared the same mark. Dennis didn't notice the diamond at first, but soon did and inspected it carefully.

"What are you going to call him, Dennis?" his mother asked.

"Perhaps something to do with that diamond?" his father suggested.

Dennis thought and thought. His eyes went to his English book, and he was reminded of his homework assignment. "Romeo," he sputtered out. "His name will be Romeo."

Mr. and Mrs. Crumb smiled and watched as the two boys became instant friends. That day, the legend of Romeo Crumb began.

Chapter Two

Over the next several weeks Romeo grew into a fine young male. He enjoyed playing with yarn and chasing ants across the kitchen floor. He even developed an interest in watching television, particularly on rainy nights. He and Dennis would curl up together on the sofa and urgently flip through the channels. Life was good.

It was not until a few weeks later when Dennis visited his grandmother that Romeo understood the meaning of being bored. He was happy with Dennis, quite happy, though he found himself longing for something more, especially when left home alone. He sat on the cold window sill in Dennis' room and stared out onto the street below hoping to spot Dennis returning home. The window was above an alley but close enough to the street corner to see all the action. It was cracked open allowing him to hear echoes of unfamiliar noises and feel the crisp evening air. Romeo had never been outside before except for the taxi cab ride from the Pound, which he hardly remembered. But as this night approached, he watched the people and the lights and the cars and buses until a growing curiosity overtook him. He wondered what life was like *down there*.

As his curious little mind started to wander more and more, something, or someone, caught his eye. Directly across the alley from Dennis' window there was another window. In it sat a cat. It belonged to a little girl named Gwen. Gwen knew of Dennis but never spoke to him. Aside from the fact that their bedroom windows faced one another, they went to different schools and led very different lives. In fact, Gwen hardly ever opened her shades out of fear of having *the boy* from across the alley look into her room.

On this particular evening the shades were up and the window was open. Romeo saw Gwen's cat but looked the other way pretending to follow a passing bird. However, his eyes quickly returned for a closer inspection.

He hadn't seen another cat since the Pound, and his memory of that was vague. He admitted to himself that this cat was rather pretty, and he could tell by its size that it was older than him. Gwen's cat seemed fixed on Romeo and stared at him through the window. This made Romeo awfully nervous. Then suddenly, the cat moved. Romeo wasn't sure but he believed it stuck out its paw signaling him in some way. Uncertain, Romeo watched again. Sure enough, the cat was motioning to him.

In complete amazement, Romeo watched as this rather ambitious feline slipped out of the window, grabbed onto a large clothesline that hung from a pole and climbed a series of vines and other such things finally reaching the barber's awning below. Once there, it slid down the striped canvas and took a courageous leap to the ground. Whoever the cat was, it had clearly done this many times before. Having disturbed barely a speck of dust, the cat stopped and looked back up at Romeo. With its tail it signaled to him again, then sat on the curb as if waiting for Romeo to do the same. Romeo was petrified, unsure what to do. Dennis never let him go outside, but now Dennis was gone for the night. Romeo figured he might as well go for it. So, with a bit more struggle than the other agile cat, Romeo plopped down to the ground below proud to have suffered only two scratches and one pulled muscle.

He carefully dusted himself off and walked over to Gwen's cat. It now sat near a street lamp at the very corner which Romeo had been admiring from his window.

"I was wondering when you were finally going to come out," it said in a girl's voice. "I've been watching you for a while." She tilted her head and gave Romeo the once over. She had shiny yellow hair and strong green eyes. Her ears and paws had a brownness to them, as did her nose. "You're new, aren't you?" she added.

Romeo didn't respond.

"That's a funny looking mark you've got there on your back," she remarked. "Is it natural or did *that boy* put it there?"

"Uh....yeah, its always been there, I guess," Romeo answered shyly.

"Oh good, you can talk. I was getting worried there for a second. Well listen, my name is Queen

Life One

Elizabeth. I know, I know what you're thinking, but Gwen, my person, has a thing for history. So, what's your name?"

Romeo paused before answering. He couldn't believe he was actually talking let alone having this conversation. "My-my name is Romeo, Romeo Crumb."

She smiled, as did he, though he wasn't sure why.

"So listen," she spoke in her scratchy voice. "Have you been out here before, or what? I get the feeling you haven't."

Romeo shook his head no and looked around in every direction. His eyes darted up to the lamp they stood under as it flickered on and off. The wind wrapped around him welcoming him to a new world of sights and sounds he never could have imagined from that window sill. The people rushed by in a hurry to get out of the chilly night. Suddenly a black spider crossed Romeo's path only inches in front of him. He watched it crawl into a sidewalk crack.

"Uh-oh," Queen Elizabeth warned. "It's always bad luck when a black spider crosses your path. That is, if you're superstitious."

"Super-what?" Romeo asked.

"Superstitious. You know, when bad things just happen," she explained. "I'm not superstitious, but my mom was. She's gone now. Where are your parents?"

Chapter Two

"Oh, my mom is dead too," Romeo offered. "They told me she died at the Pound, so did my dad. I never met them. I was told she died giving birth, whatever that is. He died later of a broken heart. My five brothers are somewhere. I'd sure like to find them. But anyway, here I am."

"That's an awfully sad story. I'm sorry to hear about your family, but I'm glad *you're* here. It's nice to meet you, Romeo Crumb."

"It's nice to meet *you* too, Queen Elizabeth."

The two cats paused a moment beneath the bustling action around them and smiled like they had known each other forever.

"Come with me, I'll show you around town," Queen Elizabeth said. "We're safe if we keep to the main streets. And don't worry about the people, they won't bother us," she added pulling Romeo into the wild world of the city.

She walked him up and down the crowded streets showing him which ones were safe, which cafes had the best scraps, and the many alleys to avoid. She introduced him to the music of the city; the sounds of the construction workers, blaring car horns, cop whistles, the cold rain, and hard wind. His new friend seemed at home on these streets and wasn't ashamed to flaunt it. Other cats greeted her as they walked by, and one tired chef threw her a stale piece of salami. It was obvious she knew the city well. Queen Elizabeth took Romeo to their final destination. A place all cats eventually came to know.

"This is it," Queen Elizabeth said as she stood and marveled at the large building in front of them.

"What is this place?" Romeo asked frightened.

He gazed up and down at the strange, tall structure that stood alone on an almost empty block. It was eight stories high made of thick stone and brick. Most all of its windows were knocked out near the top floors. The front door was boarded up with twisted pieces of wood nailed unevenly around the entrance. An old, fallen sign hung on one of its two ends and dangled in the wind. Romeo looked to the street corner and found to his surprise that they were only four blocks from his home.

"This is where all the sticks come. It's a place to feel welcome." She spoke with pride.

"Stick? What's a stick?" he asked.

"You're a stick, Romeo," she explained. "Sticks are cats that have homes. You know, domes*tic* cat, just like me. Cats with no homes are called alleys. They're left to fend for themselves. No matter what an alley may tell you, being a stick is always better."

Romeo, still confused, kept pressing. "How will I know if a cat is an alley or a stick when I meet them?"

"Oh, you'll know," she said with confidence. "Trust me. But let's go inside. I'll tell you all about the alleys later."

Romeo looked up at the dark building again.

Chapter Two

Life One

The dreary place seemed half-awful to him, yet he listened as Queen Elizabeth continued on.

"See that gray block near the back corner?" She pointed at a small cement block, the kind you see on construction sights. It sat still in the muddy ground. "That's the entrance. That's where we're going."

Romeo was afraid, yet trusting.

"Come on," she gestured. "Follow me."

Queen Elizabeth led Romeo toward the block. To get there they had to walk over a series of crackling, rotted bushes that framed the edges of the building. Romeo stepped carefully so he wouldn't hurt himself. Queen Elizabeth pointed out a safe path through some soggy leaves. She was a real pro at everything she did.

When they got to the big block, Romeo noticed two small holes in it. He was able to peek inside only to find two large, neon-yellow eyes staring back at him. Startled, he jumped.

"Who's out there?" vibrated a deep, meaty voice.

"Don't be alarmed, Romeo," Queen Elizabeth cried. "That's Waffles, the guard. As you can see, he's very good at his job."

"Waffles?" Romeo asked. "Will he let us in?"

"Of course, he will. Hey Waffles, it's me, Queen Elizabeth."

Just then, a quick thud was heard followed by what sounded like a chain being dragged. It was

Chapter Two

Waffles unlocking the door. Slowly, the block moved revealing a highly advanced security system of more chains and bolts. Security was very important.

In the entry stood a large, fat, ruffled, red cat. He seemed a little younger than Queen Elizabeth. He was almost as wide as the block and just about as heavy. With a huge grin he said, "Why didn't you tell me you were back there, Liz? Come on in."

Romeo stepped inside the building behind her. Waffle's hearty voice now had a touch of warmth to it.

"Who's your friend?" he asked.

"Waffles, this is Romeo, Romeo Crumb. He's only been around a short while."

"Well, kid," said the hefty guard, "howdy do?" He shook Romeo's paw vigorously like he was his long lost cousin. "Any friend of Liz's is a friend of mine. Welcome to the Factory." Waffles stepped aside revealing a long, narrow hallway filled with candles and paintings of all sorts of cats.

"The Factory?" Romeo inquired. "Factory for what?"

"It's a sad story, Romeo, but this building is a blessing to all sticks," Queen Elizabeth explained. "Long ago, fifty years to be exact, this was a successful umbrella factory. People came from miles around to buy a famous Stockwell umbrella. They were the best in the business and essential in a soggy city like this. Anyway, one of the younger employees lit a cigarette

 20

on his break and accidentally dropped it in a brand new umbrella. The fire was a doozy, and what you see now is all that's left of the building. After the big accident, the business went under. With no money the burned-out building remained abandoned. Mr. Stockwell, the owner of the factory, was heartbroken. Lulu, his only friend and constant feline companion, knew of his misery. Lulu also knew how tough street life was for cats, stick cats in particular who weren't born as street smart as the alleys. Lulu used the crumbling building as an opportunity to give something to the sticks. Thus, she founded the Factory which is a safe place where all sticks can come, and as you'll see, do a variety of things under the watchful eye of cats like Waffles. Mr. Stockwell and Lulu died many years ago, but their legacy lives on in every corner of the Factory. No alley cat has *ever* been allowed inside. And none ever will. A few years back an alley tried to get in. Let's just say, no alley cat has tried since."

"Why? What happened to him?" probed Romeo.

Waffles shook his head at Queen Elizabeth before she spoke. "You don't want to know, Romeo. For now, let's get on with our tour."

Romeo and Queen Elizabeth said goodbye to Waffles and continued down the corridor. Purple candles were attached to forks that jetted upwards out of the walls. They dripped dried, sticky wax that nearly reached the floor. Between the candles were beautiful paintings done on old cereal boxes, including some of Lulu. Queen Elizabeth explained the others were of great cats of long ago. Heroes to an entire nation. Legacies to live up to. Leaders of the sticks. At the end of the hall there was a small light above a wooden door. Romeo noticed a large golden B above it. He wondered what it was. Queen Elizabeth knocked on the door three times in a special, secret beat. The brass knob turned, and the door creaked open. Romeo's heart began to pound. He thought about Dennis and wondered if he'd ever find his way home through the dark streets.

When the door opened another large cat awaited them. This cat, like Waffles, was intimidating and shocking at first glance. He was very large and muscular. His deep brown coat was splattered with tiny spots of black. Oddly, he had only one whisker which twitched and shook every time he blinked.

"Romeo, meet Vittles, Waffle's brother," said Queen Elizabeth calmly. "He's stationed here most of the time. You know, as a second safety feature. We all feel very secure with him around." She gave Vittles a friendly pat on the back.

"H-hello, Mr. Vittles," murmured Romeo who by this point was completely overwhelmed.

"Drop the mister, will you son? Vittles will be fine."

Romeo smiled and was beginning to feel more comfortable. Still, for such a young cat it was hard to get used to the idea of being away from home. He wanted to go back.

Queen Elizabeth and Romeo continued down another hallway. This one, like the last, was filled with strange candles and more paintings. At the distant end of this corridor, Romeo could see an opening to some sort of room. He could hear sounds of laughter and conversation and even music. He had learned about these things watching television with Dennis.

At the end of their walk, the room opened up into a magnificent palace adorned with lovely furniture and sparkling antiques. It was called the recreation room, rec room for short, and was wide and well hidden from the dark world outside. The windows were all boarded up providing safety to those inside. Many worn velvet pillows with golden tassels lay invitingly in opened umbrellas. Small tables were set up with games and toys ready to be played with. Rich colorful rugs hid the dark soot that remained since the tragedy. The ceiling was high and still showed charred signs of the long ago fire. Flowered paper and more candles covered the walls. Many cats were there enjoying time with their friends or strumming on a homemade musical instrument. Romeo had never imagined such a place existed, and he felt sure he would come to love it.

"This is only the beginning," informed Queen Elizabeth. "Upstairs is the school house where young sticks like yourself can learn to read and become inde-

Chapter Two

pendent in the big city. We also have a cafe featuring some of the finest seafood around. Roy and Yellowtail both live above a magnificent fish market. They deliver fresh scraps everyday. There's also a library, a medicine room, an art studio, and the Thinking Room where we praise Bubastis, a guiding force for all cats. The rest of the building is off limits because it was so badly damaged in the fire. It's a great place, Romeo. Remember, without the Factory, sticks would have virtually nowhere to go outside of our homes. The alleys would surely get us on the streets."

"Tell me about the alleys," Romeo said with concern. "What's wrong with being outside? Why would they want to hurt us?" Romeo waited patiently for an explanation. He loved the Factory already, but felt spooked about these alleys everyone feared. Queen Elizabeth was well aware of his curiosity and felt an obligation to explain.

"You are young, Romeo," she spoke softly, "and need to hear the truth, but not here. Let's go up to the library. There it will be quiet and we can talk."

"Wait! Where does that door lead?" Romeo asked pointing to a small metal door near the corner of the room. A torn paper sign hung from a faded piece of tape. Scrawled across it were the words *Stay Out*.

"Don't ever go there, Romeo! That's the basement. Nobody ever goes in the basement."

"Why?" he asked, more curious than before.

"Nobody asks, nobody goes," she said sternly.

 24

Life One

"Now, let's keep moving. We've got a lot to do today."

Queen Elizabeth pointed to another door near the far corner of the room. She and Romeo walked out and stepped immediately into an old, dented soup pot big enough for the two of them, and even one more. It was attached to a hinge above by some thick wire which was tightly wound about the handles. Romeo didn't know it at first, but he was in a homemade elevator. Still thinking about that mysterious basement, he watched as Queen Elizabeth pulled and tugged at the wires. His own young paws were not yet strong enough to help. The pot rose and bounced up, up, up, sending a painful squeak through Romeo's little ears. After about a minute or so, they reached the next floor. It was darker than the first, and quieter. Queen Elizabeth hoisted herself from the pot. Next, she held out a paw and helped Romeo do the same.

"Where are we now?" Romeo asked while his eyes wandered. It was hard for him to see what was ahead because of the many fallen wooden planks. He did see two separate lights coming from two different directions. Romeo's round shadow stretched across the hard, cold floor. It met with Queen Elizabeth's forming an odd shape. The ceiling was low making it difficult to see. No candles were in this section giving the area a dark, creepy feel.

"This is the second floor," Queen Elizabeth answered. "The library is up here, like I said. Also the classroom, the art studio, and the medicine room."

"How many floors are there?"

"Only three. The building itself has eight, but we can't get up there. Starting around the fourth level the floors get very weak. They were damaged pretty badly in the fire, you see. Once, when a cat went up there looking for materials to make some furniture, the floor collapsed on top of everyone. Five cats lost lives that day. It was very sad." Her head dropped. "Since then, it is forbidden to go above the third floor. Lulu was afraid the whole building would come down. Some say it still could."

Romeo's eyes opened wide. "Really?" he asked nervously. "You mean this entire thing could come crashing down with us in it?"

"Look, kid, it's nothing you need to worry about today. Now, I believe we were headed toward the library."

They walked alongside one of the splintered planks and into a small, inviting room. The walls were covered with Asian style rugs providing warmth during the cold days and nights. There was an old fireplace, though no fire was lit. No fire was ever lit. Yet the room had enough small candles to give it the same smell that a big, cozy fire can produce. A deep red carpet blanketed the entire floor. Several small tables and benches dotted the room, carved, painted, and sanded at the Factory from smaller, unused planks. This was the library. In it many books lined the many shelves. Poetry books, history books, war books. Most of the books were people books, almost the same size as some of the cats. Some of the newer books were written and printed by the more learned sticks. They were a very skilled breed and professional about everything they did.

At the center of the quiet room stood one small, brown table and a few matching chairs. Romeo noticed a slim, gray cat with his back toward him sitting on one of the chairs. The glow of a nearby flickering candle surrounded his thick fur. He was peaceful and calm and far enough away to be mysterious. Romeo could see the wire rim of his glasses and noticed a heavy book beneath his paw. He seemed almost ghostly, and Romeo was instantly uncomfortable. Queen Elizabeth put him at ease.

"See that cat?" she whispered. "That's Mr. Sox. He's the oldest cat around."

"How old is he?" asked Romeo.

"Nobody knows for sure. But we do know that he's a niner."

"A niner?" Romeo questioned loudly. "What's that?"

"Shhhhhh," Queen Elizabeth motioned. She was about to give him a dirty look but quickly remembered how very young he was. "A niner, Romeo," she went on to explain, "is a cat that has only one more life left. In other words, he's on his ninth and last life. You see, all cats get nine lives. Once you die

Chapter Two

eight different times, you only have one life left. It's a tough time for a cat, because *that* final life is so fragile." Respectfully, she turned her eyes toward Mr. Sox.

"Well, what happens when you die the other eight times?" Romeo's tiny voice asked.

"It depends. Most times, within an hour you are fine again. I've been hit by cars, run over by kids on bikes, you know, that kind of stuff. Any major injury where your body gets completely ripped apart requires a trip to the medicine room. It's always best to be with another cat who can bring you here or get help. Be careful. Your person will think you are dead for good and do nothing about it. They don't know about the reality of the nine lives. Humans just live once."

Romeo scrunched up his nose. "Gosh. Don't all those things hurt?"

"Sure they do, but you get used to it. You just have to watch out for yourself and each other. Of course, most importantly, you must look out for the alleys as well." Her voice sunk.

"Yes," Romeo sounded. "You were supposed to tell me about them. Who are they anyway, and why are they so bad?"

"Come over here with me, kid, and meet Mr. Sox. He can explain the alleys better than anybody else around."

Romeo was hesitant about meeting old Mr.

Sox, yet drawn to him at the same time. They each took a step forward, then another, and soon another in the direction of the table at the center of the room. When they were only inches away, Queen Elizabeth opened her mouth to speak. "Mr. Sox? It's me, Queen Elizabeth."

The gray cat didn't move.

"Mr. Sox?" she called again.

Then, a skinny, yet strong paw lifted up from the book and reached toward its face. Mr. Sox took off his glasses with more poise than one would expect from such a simple task. He cleared his throat and closed his book onto a tiny bookmark made from a piece of string. When he was ready, he turned around to see who was behind him.

"Yes," he uttered with dignity. "Queen Elizabeth. How are you my child?"

"Fine, Mr. Sox. Just fine, thank you. And you?"

"Oh, I'm doing alright, I guess, for an old male," he coughed.

Romeo watched, enchanted as this grandfather-like cat talked to Queen Elizabeth. They chatted as if they'd known each other for a very long time. It was a comforting scene to see, like the ones he witnessed between Dennis and his grandmother. Mr. Sox was quite the charmer and had many noble qualities already obvious to Romeo in this short time. He was kind, polite, and gentle. His face was lined with time, evident in every silvery hair that decorated it. His eyes were sunken in, not in a sad way, but hopeful, if slightly bittersweet. He sat comfortably on a reading chair, his tail well-groomed nearly touching the floor. Romeo was immediately impressed with Mr. Sox and hoped the feeling would be mutual.

"Mr. Sox," Queen Elizabeth paused. "This is my new friend, Romeo. As you can see, he's very young. He lives across the alley from me in the *boy's* room."

Mr. Sox took a long, hard look in Romeo's direction. In fact, he put his glasses back on and checked him over so closely that Romeo was beginning to feel self-conscious.

"It's a pleasure to meet you, Romeo," Mr. Sox finally said. He squinted hard and stared at Romeo's hip. "That's an interesting mark on your back, son."

"Uh, yes, yes it is, Mr. Sox, sir," Romeo said nervously. "And I am happy to meet you too."

Mr. Sox turned his body to get a closer look at the diamond across Romeo's backside. "It almost looks familiar," he hesitated, twitching his ear. "Like something I've seen before, only I can't be sure."

Romeo looked over to Queen Elizabeth who shrugged her shoulders at the comment.

"Mr. Sox," she broke in. "I was just going to teach Romeo about the alleys. He's new in this world and needs to be made aware of the dangers right away."

"You are quite right, my child. Quite right. He

needs to know."

Queen Elizabeth smiled in Romeo's direction. "Yes, Mr. Sox, and I was hoping that perhaps you could tell him about them, you being so wise and all." She bit her lip hoping he would agree.

"Thank you, my child," Mr. Sox blushed. "You are very kind to me. I will be glad to tell Romeo everything he needs to know." He once again took off his glasses with an elegance not commonly noticed and turned all his attention toward Romeo.

"Now Romeo, sit down. There's much to tell you about...*the alleys*," he continued with an intensity in his voice.

"Yes, Mr. Sox," Romeo said almost hypnotized. "I'm ready."

Chapter Three

Mr. Sox pointed toward two empty chairs next to his. Queen Elizabeth and Romeo quickly sat down. Romeo was eager to hear Mr. Sox's explanation.

"Long ago," Mr. Sox began, "the city was far different than it is now. Imagine, if you can, these same dark, lifeless streets filled with smiling faces, perfect rainbows, and happy cats. To live in the old days was an honor. Back then, the city was new and the sounds of excitement filled every corner and alleyway. Cats from all over gathered in the park sharing stories, dreams, and a passion for life. Sure, there were hard times even in the golden days, though they were few and far between. Words such as *sticks* and *alleys* didn't exist. We were all *cats* then, just *cats*. I can remember one sunny afternoon when I was walking with Hank, my person. He was on his way to a new job. It was his first day. He couldn't have been more thrilled. Being his lifelong, faithful companion, I walked along with him all the way to the new office building on 51st Street. When Hank went inside at eight A.M. sharp, I was released into the sparkling city alone to spend my days. Sure, I was scared at first, but I soon made many feline friends. Together we would romp through the streets exploring new avenues and worlds. Occasionally, a local baker or school girl would give us a treat, just to be kind. As night fell I would return to the warmth and comfort of my home with Hank. My friends and I had many adventures in those days, each more exciting than the last. One time we even hopped on a ferry and climbed to the top of the great statue in the water. The view of the city was incredible; all the lights and skyscrapers and cars. Of course, climbing down was a bit more difficult." Mr. Sox paused and smiled as he reminisced.

"Gosh," Romeo interrupted. "That sure sounds like fun, Mr. Sox. Do you think I could go to that statue someday too?"

Mr. Sox looked up at Romeo with a grin. "Just listen carefully to the rest of my story, Romeo, and you decide."

"Okay," Romeo nodded.

"One friend in particular," Mr. Sox went on, "was named Carnival. Carnival got his name because he was born on a foggy night behind a popcorn cart at Trolley Island Carnival and Circus. Oh, it was a mag-

Chapter Three

nificent place full of wonderful neon lights, delicious smells, and the sounds of happy families. Unfortunately, since the people's war, it now lies abandoned, much like Mr. Stockwell's Umbrella Factory did until we came along. Anyway, sometimes we would go to Trolley's to meet Carnival on a pleasant summer afternoon. It was easy to just hop on a train back then, nobody seemed to mind.

From the start we knew Carnival was different from us. For one, he had no person. Many cats didn't. He was born to a sick female who lived among the carnival folk; a reckless life, rebellious and free. His mother lost a life giving birth to him, her ninth. So unfortunately he was raised by the clowns and the fat ladies, the freaks and the monkeys. His dad was around for a while but sadly lost his ninth life when the great lion escaped from his cage and went on a rampage slaying everything and everyone in sight. Carnival escaped by the skin of his teeth but was never the same cat again.

After that, it was as if a deadly curse fell upon Trolley Island, for very soon the people's war broke out. The once lively and happy carnival goers were now off fighting bloody battles and working relentlessly to save every last penny. The days grew colder, and little by little, fewer people went out to Trolley's. Until finally, one dark day the owner nailed up a sign that read: *Closed For Good*. It was sad for all the circus folk but especially for Carnival himself. Lost and alone, he moved into the big city where he felt exposed and afraid. We encouraged him to let the Pound find him and get adopted by a nice man like my Hank. He firmly refused and quickly became part of the growing population of homeless cats. Over time they simply exploded in numbers. The war did end, but the city was left under a dark cloud. Its people, tired and hungry from the war, no longer walked with big smiles and sunny outlooks. Like the days, *they* grew colder and darker. All the street animals felt its effect. The cats, mice, dogs, even bugs. Food and warm shelter were hard to come by. Cold, hungry nights became a way of life. The golden days of togetherness were gone." Mr. Sox took off his glasses and put a pained paw to his eyes. Queen Elizabeth gently stroked his back.

"Please go on, Mr. Sox," she said. "Please."

"All right," he said quietly. "Carnival was a fighter and didn't see what the harsh city was doing to him. It was destroying him. He no longer hung around me and our old gang. He was slowly turning into a cunning, calculating monster. We saw what was happening and tried to keep him grounded, but it was no use. The great Bubastis couldn't even stop Carnival. It was Carnival who began the division between cats with homes, or sticks, as he liked to call them, and alleys, what he had now become. Over time, he and his new gang of ruffians spread the word that sticks were worthless and had no right to roam the streets of the city as they once had done so freely. He thought we had it easy, therefore, we should just stay inside of our homes. Carnival became the leader of his pack and made it clear to everyone that he ran the streets. Slowly, he began using violence to send his message, and a strong line divided the two groups of cats." By now Romeo was sitting on the edge of his seat, his eyes round as saucers as Mr. Sox dramatically continued.

"The last straw happened with a sweet, but not so smart cat named Martin. He tried to befriend an alley cat. Carnival found out, and Martin was never heard from again. Some say Fidel, Carnival's grandson, still wears Martin's ID tag.

From then on a stick who went outside of his home always had to be on close watch for the alleys. Not to mention the new breed of tough dogs that now prowled the streets and alleyways. All cats, even Carnival, had to look out for them. After Carnival's nine lives were up, his sons took over his reign of terror. And now his only surviving grandson, Fidel, leads the fight of the alleys against the sticks. Each generation since Carnival has grown increasingly more cruel and heartless. Soon places like Death Alley and Vent City sprung up, dark and dangerous places to avoid."

Mr. Sox got right into Romeo's face and peered deep into his innocent eyes. "You are a stick which means you must always look over your shoulder

Life One

for Fidel and his followers. Yes, there are still some streets you will be safe on, especially during the day, and many people are kind and gentle, but beware at night. Queen Elizabeth will tell you where and what to look out for. Remember, Fidel will stop at nothing to get his way. Not even death. Here at the Factory we can come together. For some strange reason they allow us this place, and they don't bother us here. So stay off the streets as much as possible, and when you do leave your home, come directly here."

Mr. Sox leaned back in his chair and wiped the sweat from his brow. It was hard for him to remember the old days, especially the younger Carnival he once played with. He put his glasses back inside their little carrying case with his paw and picked up his book.

"All right now, Romeo," Mr. Sox said as he stood up. "I hope you learned something here today."

"Oh, I did," Romeo beamed. "Thank you, Mr. Sox. Thank you."

Mr. Sox nodded goodbye to Queen Elizabeth and Romeo. They both watched as he walked out of the library and headed toward the elevator. When he was gone, Queen Elizabeth turned to Romeo. "All right," she bubbled. "That's enough for one day."

Romeo didn't agree. He wanted to hear more. "But who's Bubastis? And where's Death Alley? What's war?"

"In time, Romeo. In time." She yanked on his

ear and pulled him out of the room. "Meet me tomorrow at the Factory at 9:30 sharp. Will that be possible?"

"Sure! Dennis is away at his grandmother's, and I heard him say something about not coming home until after dinner." Romeo said excitedly.

"You do know, Romeo," she continued, "you are going to have to establish yourself as an outdoor cat with Dennis. He must learn to trust that you can come and go as you please in safety. It may take him little while, but it's very necessary."

"I know, I know. I just don't want to worry him," Romeo added. "Dennis is so good to me."

"I understand. Anyway, we can talk about that later. You're lucky, tomorrow is registration day. We will get you enrolled in Stick School. It's right here in the Factory and something every stick must go through."

"School? Dennis hates school. Why do I have to go to school?" Romeo questioned. As much as he liked learning, he didn't want to go to school.

"Well," Queen Elizabeth began "you want to survive, don't you, kid?"

Romeo nodded his confused head.

"Then you have to go to school. You must learn how to read. Survival Class is the second hour. You'll learn about all the streets and the subways. You'll be instructed on what to avoid and how to defend yourself. My favorite class is Cat History. You'll even

 38

take a field trip. Our professors are wonderful. And besides, you'll meet lots of new cats your own age."

Romeo liked that part best. However, the thought of learning how to read and roam safely appealed to him more than he realized. Maybe he would even meet someone out on the mean streets who knew about his brothers.

Queen Elizabeth and Romeo returned to the soup pot elevator and headed back downstairs. On their way out they said goodbye to Vittles and Waffles, who were still guarding their posts.

"Come back soon, Liz," waved Waffles. "Uh, you too, kid. Anytime." His big, hearty smile left an impression on Romeo that he wouldn't forget. Romeo knew by that grin he would always feel safe at the Factory.

The two cats strolled carefully back down 17th Street. Romeo walked much more nervously than he did on the way over, constantly looking over his shoulders.

"Don't worry," Queen Elizabeth said confidently. "You're safe on this street. The alleys wouldn't dare start up on a busy street like this. The cops would call the Pound in a second if they had reason."

Romeo felt better, though still spooked, as if he was walking through a wild jungle of animals that could strike at any moment. Every little shadow creeped him out. In fact, a sudden noise startled him causing all his tiny black and gray hairs to stand straight up on end. His tail bloomed out like a feather duster, and his claws scratched against the cement. Queen Elizabeth couldn't help but laugh.

"Romeo," she teased. "It's only a mouse. Now if you're afraid of mice, then I guess we do have a problem." The tiny, white rodent scurried away before the cats had time to develop hunger pangs.

Under all his frazzled fur, Romeo blushed. "I didn't know," he said embarrassed. "All I heard was a weird noise, and I got scared. Maybe I'm just not cut out for this city stuff." He dropped his head low and kicked the ground with his back left paw.

"Oh, don't be silly. It could've happened to anybody," Queen Elizabeth lied. "You're going to be just fine."

Queen Elizabeth continued to giggle to herself as they hurried on. Feeling guilty, she apologized to Romeo again and again. She didn't tell him, but she found the whole situation cute. She reassured him of his bravery many times. Yet his paranoia had the best of him and he continued to slink with every step, his eyes darting this way and that, his ears cocked. She knew in time his confidence would grow. For now, he was just a scared, little kitty in a big, crazy world.

When they finally reached the corner of 17th and 58th Street, hardly any of the people were still out, and most places were closed. The cats did hear the hum of a saxophone somewhere in the distance and what sounded like dishes breaking.

 40

Life One

"Don't worry, Romeo," Queen Elizabeth said motherly. "It's late, but you're home now. Have a good night's rest. Tomorrow's going to be a big day." She gave him a peck on the cheek and turned to step away. Just as she did, Romeo called out,

"Uh, Queen Elizabeth?"

Slowly she turned back and faced him. He stood there looking tired and confused in the dim shadows of the evening moon. He was still quivering, possibly from the cold, possibly from fear. Queen Elizabeth noticed one of his front paws nervously twisting back and forth.

"Yes, Romeo," she answered. "What is it?"

"I-I-I was just wondering. How many lives do *you* have left?"

Queen Elizabeth smiled and stepped closer. She was flattered by his obvious concern and somehow warmed despite the chilling wind.

"Oh, never mind! It's none of my business anyway," he said.

Queen Elizabeth took her right paw and put it beneath Romeo's drooping chin.

"I've got four," she smiled. "Four more lives. Hopefully, that will last me a long time."

"Thank you," Romeo added. "I mean....for everything."

Queen Elizabeth gave him another sweet grin, this time with a wink. She stepped off the curb and began to walk toward her building. Romeo stood

Chapter Three

silently near the gutter and watched her climb. He felt grateful to have met her. Then, when Queen Elizabeth was nearly halfway up to her destination, Romeo had a sinking feeling.

"Queen Elizabeth!" he yelled loud enough for her to hear.

She looked down at him through the twisted vines and wires.

"How do I get back up?" he quivered.

Queen Elizabeth laughed to herself as she made her way back down. She quickly taught him how to climb back up to the third floor through an open vent, or by simply reversing the way he came down using a small tree to lift himself up to the awning. He did it with an ease he never expected. Romeo crawled through the open crack of Dennis' window and back into the safety of his warm room. Once inside, he looked out across the alley in Queen Elizabeth's direction. Gwen, her person, had the window shades closed, and her room was dark. Romeo jumped onto Dennis' comfy bed and quietly fell asleep. Down below in the alley between the two buildings, four alley cats lay huddled together under an empty donut box, cold and hungry.

The next morning Romeo awoke to the clanging sounds of nearby church bells. It seemed they rang and rang just for him. It was nine o'clock giving Romeo enough time for one trip to the litter box and a quick breakfast from his bowl in the kitchen. Mrs.

Life One

Crumb, Dennis' mother, always left food out, though she didn't actually bother much with Romeo at all. That was Dennis' job. And he was still at his grandmother's for the weekend.

At nine-fifteen sharp, Romeo began his short jaunt back to the Factory for registration day. He had no idea what that was but was too embarrassed to ask Queen Elizabeth anymore questions. He reached the ground after a brief struggle and paused for a moment to look out at the city. It seemed old to him, and tired. The people who were up and running didn't look like they wanted to be; all stuffed in their thick scarves and big hats. No one so much as cracked a smile. Suddenly, Romeo spied a small bug crawl up the wall to his left. Still a bit hungry, he wickedly dragged it down toward the cold concrete and into his waiting mouth. He felt a little guilty for it, but it tasted so good.

With not much time, Romeo hurried off. Along the way his eyes wandered in and out of the alleys. Though he saw no alley cats, he swore he spotted about fifty sets of glowing, yellow eyes staring at him through the darkness. He heard a low howl, almost mournful, echoing deep from behind the boxes and garbage cans. Perhaps it was just the wind. Perhaps not. A rustle here, a rustle there. It was making him more paranoid than he was the night before. Picking up his pace, he wished Queen Elizabeth was there to protect him and tell him not to worry like she had done before. But no, he was on his own now. And he knew he could do it.

Romeo quickly found his way to the Factory beyond the crackly bushes, passed the stone entry, and through Waffle's tough exterior.

"Have a good day, son," Waffles remarked pleasantly.

"Thanks, Waffles," Romeo called out as he scampered down the hall.

After a similar meeting with Vittles, Romeo entered the first floor recreation room that he had been in the previous day. He recognized the same rugs, the same tables, and some of the same cats. They were listening to the same songs and laughing in the same way. He breathed a heavy sigh of relief knowing he was safely inside. He now realized he wanted to learn everything these cats could teach him and began trembling with excitement at the thought of starting school. Surely, Dennis was wrong.

Soon Queen Elizabeth walked up with a hug in her eyes. She had been at the Factory all morning preparing Romeo's paperwork and enrollment process.

"Hey, you made it," she smiled. "And right on time too." She waved him into a smaller room where a very large black object with all sorts of buttons and knobs stood. Another cat was there lounging and looking bored as if he had been waiting for something to happen. He tapped his front paw.

"Is this him?" the bored cat asked with attitude, pointing at Romeo.

Queen Elizabeth nodded and brought Romeo over to a small metal stool.

"Sit here, Romeo," she said. "Waldo here is going to take your picture. It's for your file."

"My file?" Romeo asked.

"Yes, every cat here has a file. You know, it's got all your important information, like your name and address and stuff like that. And, of course, we have to take a picture of you as well. Not that we'll forget what you look like, or anything. It's for identification purposes." She chuckled to herself at the thought.

"Can we get on with this?" grunted Waldo, the Factory's staff photographer. Waldo was a small cat in size and character. A nice enough fellow, just not too friendly. He had long, crinkled whiskers and thin, pointy ears. His eyesight wasn't up to par, so he wore little glasses that another cat made for him from a lost pair he found in the street. Waldo got his job because he lived with an old photographer who took pictures for some magazine. Every Sunday Waldo was able to snatch a role of film from the studio and bring it back to the Factory. He didn't use the camera very often, but whenever a situation came up, he had the camera poised and ready. He even had a mini-dark room set up at the Factory for developing his film. Living with a photographer, he learned a lot.

"Yes, Waldo, just be patient," Elizabeth continued.

Chapter Three

Romeo checked his reflection briefly in a little mirror that hung crookedly on the wall. He dampened his paw to flatten out a patch of loose hairs that had blown in the wind. Dennis had a big mirror in his bathroom that Romeo liked to use. He would sit with Dennis while he cleaned the goo from his slimy teeth and would glance at his own handsome, furry reflection.

Next, Queen Elizabeth fluffed and posed Romeo into an attractive position, then...one, two, three, CLICK! Waldo took the picture. Maybe it wasn't a masterpiece, but it would do just fine.

Queen Elizabeth and Romeo took the soup pot elevator up to the classroom. It was behind the library.

"Three other students are also registering today," Queen Elizabeth added. "They're just about your age too." Romeo hoped one of them would be a long lost brother. Back at the Pound, he had only seen his siblings for a very short time, though he was certain he would recognize them. They all had the same diamond on their backs.

Romeo and Queen Elizabeth tiptoed through the quiet library where a few cats were lounging on some pillows reading to themselves. Romeo couldn't wait for the day when he could read. He wondered what was inside all those books. At the far side of the room was a door with a yellowy glow peeking out around the edges. Above it was an old, cracked

 46

sign that read: Training Room C. It was a room used during the old umbrella days. Below this sign was another which read: Stick School. Beneath the letters was a picture of an old, wise looking cat sitting on a cloud with the word, *Bubastis*. Romeo couldn't read it. Queen Elizabeth pushed open the door and led him inside.

The room housed ten wooden desks and chairs that sat beneath the blaze of a bright flashlight which could be turned on and off. The unfamiliar smell of paper and colored wax spread from corner to corner and a large chalkboard dressed the front wall. Some books were scattered around and a big flag with a print of the same cat from the door dangled above. The room looked comfortable and inviting, almost calling Romeo to come in. It was quite a contrast from the soggy world outside.

Romeo quickly caught the eye of Ms. Purrpurr. She was a tall cat, plump and round. When she walked, her large, respectable belly swished from side to side in a perfect wave motion. Her scent was of perfumed tuna and her coarse fur was brown with just a hint of white. Ms. Purrpurr's desk was hidden under a blanket of papers and big, puffy, alphabet letters. She stood up and looked confidently at the new male.

"You must be Romeo?" she called from deep in the epicenter of a heavy cloud of chalk dust.

Romeo nodded shyly. He stood framed in the doorway beside Queen Elizabeth who had placed her left paw gently on his shoulder.

Stepping in, Romeo saw that there were no other cats in the room. The ten little chairs and the ten little desks sat empty. Atop each desk was one sharpened pencil, one stack of paper, and one ball of yarn. The colors of the yarn varied from desk to desk.

"I've heard so much about you," cried Ms. Purrpurr through the chalk dust. "Queen Elizabeth spent nearly thirty minutes this morning telling me how well behaved you are. If true, you will fit in quite nicely around here." She took a step forward into the flag's shadow to get a better look at her pupil. She paced back and forth, never taking her eyes off him. She didn't smile from behind her slick whiskers, yet she gave off a warmth that was welcoming.

"Well, you're all registered. Your paperwork is in order," Ms. Purrpurr said.

"Do I start to learn now?" Romeo asked eagerly.

"There is no actual school today. Today is Sunday, just for registering. Tomorrow you are to be here at eight o'clock sharp. My name is Ms. Purrpurr, and I will be your reading teacher. Be prepared to work hard, and don't be late." She looked deeply and directly into Romeo's excited eyes. "If there's one thing I hate, it's a late student. Don't think I won't give you plenty of extra work if you disappoint me." With that, she whipped her body around and continued forcefully banging together the two erasers that she had begun to clean prior to Romeo and Queen Elizabeth's entry.

Romeo was anxious and eager to learn, yet it was obvious that Ms. Purrpurr was a strict teacher. He would always be on time and do his best to be a good student. Queen Elizabeth had already given him the confidence that he could do both, just like a loving mother would do.

Ms. Purrpurr shut the door as she waved goodbye to the two cats. In the library Queen Elizabeth whispered to Romeo, "You'll meet your other teachers tomorrow. I already gathered all the supplies you will need. They are sitting inside your desk right now. I'm sure Ms. Purrpurr will show them to you in class."

Romeo was quiet, but he said thanks with his eyes.

The two of them decided to return to their homes and relax rather than play outside. Romeo would have a big day tomorrow, and Queen Elizabeth felt he needed lots of rest.

On their way back they wove between the many feet rushing home from church. The shoes were always a little fancier on Sundays. Little things proper cats appreciated.

"Oh, I hate the rain," Queen Elizabeth complained. "Let's walk a little faster." Above, the thick sky was pouring out buckets of rain, something the city was used to. The pavement was slick and danger-

Chapter Three

ous to delicate paws. Even the fancy-shoed feet had to be careful on the wet sidewalks.

As they hurried through the drips and drops, they talked and laughed about Waldo, the photographer.

"...and one time he forgot to put film in his camera..." Queen Elizabeth was abruptly cut off by a piercing noise. It caught her completely off guard, and she jumped. It seemed to be coming from the alley ahead.

Instinctively Queen Elizabeth stepped in front of Romeo and shielded him with her paw. Slowly, she took a step and glared cautiously into the dark passageway. From behind a large trash dumpster she could see a set of neon green eyes. They penetrated her very soul. Her wet body shivered and shook.

"Let's go, Romeo," she spoke in a tone he had not heard before. "Just keep close."

Romeo did as he was told.

Just then the green eyes slinked out in front of them. "Not so fast friends, not so fast." It was a skinny cat, brown ratty fur and full of more scars and bumps than the bums who slept on the streets. His voice was high and sharp. His breath horrible, as was the glare in those green eyes. "Where are you off to in such a hurry?" The intruder circled them slowly and menacingly.

"Get away, Bait!" Queen Elizabeth ordered. "You stay away from us!"

 50

Life One

Romeo was surprised that she knew his name. It was obvious she wasn't impressed by him and not afraid to show it.

Bait stopped circling and drew very close to Queen Elizabeth's face. "Remember the ol' days, Queeny?" he said with a nasty smirk. "Hmmm?"

Queen Elizabeth started to breathe in a heavy huff. Her eyes were now in a squint, and she was trying hard not to hiss.

Bait gave her a long, hard, ominous stare and scowled, "All right, I'll let you go dis time, but Queeny, I wouldn't walk alone around here if I was you. You wouldn't want to get your pretty little self......hurt, now would ya?" His eyes still set on hers.

She snarled at Bait one last time with a growl and scurried away with Romeo.

They ran about five feet when they heard another voice from behind. "Hey, kid?"

Romeo stopped, afraid to look back.

"It's okay," Queen Elizabeth whispered. "It's just Bait again."

Romeo hesitantly turned around to look at the cat. He was now blended among the dark shadows of the alley.

"You're new around here, aren't you?" the voice from the shadows asked.

Romeo didn't budge.

"We've been watching you." He kicked a rusted can out of his way. "A little caution from an

Chapter Three

 52

Life One

alley, just don't get any......ideas, if you know what I mean." With that, he slipped into the darkness, and all they heard was the sound of a wicked laugh and a hiccup.

Romeo stood frozen with the rain pounding down on his head. He shook from fear and felt sick to his stomach.

"Don't worry about him," Queen Elizabeth mumbled in his ear. "Bait is harmless. He's just trying to scare you."

"But, what did he mean by all that?" Romeo asked. "What old days? How do you know him? *Who's* been watching me?"

"Nothing, Romeo, nothing. He's talking nonsense. Come on, let's get out of here."

The two of them continued walking home in complete silence. Queen Elizabeth held her head close to the ground. Romeo wanted to inquire more, but he let her walk as she wanted.

Bait walked into the darkest part of the alley at 56th Street with a sinister grin slapped across his face. The rain continued to come down hard. It always seemed to rain a little harder in the alleys. A roof of thunder roared above the city awakening all the buildings from their Sunday afternoon nap. Bait crept behind a big garbage pile and over to a small crack in the alley wall. He nudged open a loose brick and slipped inside.

Chapter Three

In the hollowed part of the wall was a secret place for alley cats known as Smelly's Bar. It was dank and damp and smelled of stale alcohol. The sound of an eerie drip was constant whether it was raining outside or not. Because of its location, every word said sent a howling echo through the pipes and ducts along the musty concrete walls. It was scary, even for some of the alleys. But for most it was a place to come and drink away their day.

Bait crept inside with his nose high in the air, delighted by his brief encounter with an old *friend*. Once he found his way passed the main brick entrance, he stumbled into Smelly's, his favorite dive. Smelly was a fat, round tabby who lived in an alley behind an old saloon. His fur was a mix of big orange and brown spots and smelled bad. Every night he filled a tin can with the leftover beer that sputtered from the kitchen pipes outback. He lugged it over to his bar with the help of an old roller skate he used as a wagon. Inside, an apple crate covered with red leather from an abandoned car seat served as the bar. The tight leather was torn and speckled with age. Smelly made six bar stools from flower pots and buckets he stole from some lady's back porch. A few measly tables and small chairs filled the rest of the bar, and old newspaper clippings decorated the walls. They were mostly torn-out pictures of crime scenes or cats and were nailed unevenly into the walls with not much care. Thumbs, a stubby gray cat who had

 54

Life One

an extra set of thumbs, sat in the back corner blowing on his toy saxophone which he nabbed from a whiny kid. He played sad tunes day after day, never leaving the hum of his dusty corner. Smelly put up a cracked piece of mirror behind the bar and a single red candle flickered above, keeping the room dark with only one shred of light that hit the third bar stool, and only slightly. There, at the stool, was Fidel.

Fidel always sat at the third stool. Always. He was a thin, scrawny cat, yet devilish in appearance. He was missing a chunk from his right ear. The ghastly wound was stomach-churning to look at. He had bright red eyes, often bloodshot, giving them an even more hellish gaze. His claws were sharper than needles, and his ratty brown hair was coarse and rough. Tiny spots of black dotted his face, and his crooked tail always pointed down as if suggesting something sinister. He wore a leather collar he had stolen from an unfortunate stick. On it dangled eight or so tags from some unlucky dead sticks. Perhaps the most horrible thing about Fidel was his scowl. It was as chilling as the wind itself. In the shadows behind him, his silent five sat at one of the dustier tables sucking down drink after drink. In front of him at the bar was a thimble of thick, dark beer, typical for an afternoon guzzle. However, Fidel had evidently found another tasty treat to munch on.

"Please, please," cried a desperate rat being dangled by its tail. "Please Mr. Fidel, I'll do anything,

anything!"

"Tisk, tisk," teased Fidel. He gave the rat a funny smirk and then looked up at Smelly. "What do you think, Smelly. He says he'll do *anything*."

Smelly, who was a very round, yet powerful cat, stepped into the haze of the candle. "He's a bad one, Fidel. He tried to steal some of my beer," Smelly said sarcastically.

The rat shook as much as a rat could. "No, no, Mr. Smelly!" he insisted. "I wasn't trying to steal it! Honest. I was just...just..."

"Just what?" Fidel said slowly, pulling the rat closer and closer to his evil sneer.

"Just......well......hey, you stole it too!" the trembling rat courageously blurted.

Smelly, along with his bubbling temper, slammed down a full thimble of beer as hard as he could splashing the dirty alcohol all over the rat's flailing paws and twitching body.

"I'm sorry," the rat whined. "Please let me go!"

Fidel and Smelly looked at each other like two old fashioned bank robbers on a good day. Fidel shook his head, and Smelly laughed sinisterly. Fidel raised the struggling rat high into the air with his left paw as it begged and pleaded for mercy. With evil enjoyment, Fidel slowly lowered the rat's head into his wide-open mouth. Both Fidel and Smelly heard one final scream and then, crunch, Fidel sunk his rotten fangs hard into the innocent flesh of the quivering rat. His cheeks filled as he swallowed the rat in one gulp with a smile. In the back, Thumbs continued to blow into his saxophone.

"Hey, uh, dat was a good one there, boss," said Bait with his stupid, little laugh. "That was sure funny seein' that rat squirm."

Fidel nodded and casually licked the blood from his paws.

"So tell me, *Bait*," Fidel said, emphasizing *Bait*, "what's new on the streets today? Run into any helpless, juicy mice?"

"Nope, not many of those out today. But I did bump into somebody," Bait replied.

"Who Bait? Who did you see?" Fidel took a deep gulp of his beer to wash down the hairy varmint.

"Remember Queen Elizabeth, that stick we threw into da river last year? Well, she was out prowlin' around today and..."

Fidel cut him off. "Well, well, now, how could I forget *her*. She's the one that just wouldn't give up that fish head. Feisty thing. You say she was out prowling?"

"Yep," Bait assured. "In fact, she was with a new stick. He's young and small, but he may just be one to look out for."

Fidel put down his beer and jingled the tags on his collar. "Oh? And why do you say that?"

Chapter Three

"I don't know, boss," Bait answered. "Just a hunch, I guess."

Fidel looked at Smelly and motioned for another drink. "Well, I don't think we have anything to worry about. No tiny stick could ever be a problem. And if he ever was...," Fidel smashed a passing spider. "Crunch, just like that!"

All at once Fidel, Smelly, and Bait erupted into boisterous laughter. But not Thumbs. Oblivious, he continued to play his dismal tunes.

Chapter Four

Sunday evening Romeo and Dennis finished their day in front of the television. Dennis nibbled on cold chicken, now and then letting Romeo have a lick. As he stroked Romeo's back, he told him of his weekend with Grandma Crumb. Romeo listened, but was becoming more interested with the news.

"...and it should be striking within several months," the newscaster said. "It will be a deadly storm, fierce and wild. The rain will not only last for days, perhaps weeks, but it will be heavier than our city has seen in years. Yes, El Queso is coming."

Romeo was already getting used to the constant rain, but this El Queso was going to be a doozy. Weathermen were predicting a slow build over the next six months or so before the big blow. They said it had something to do with the positioning of the planets. That part Romeo didn't understand. What's a planet?

The next morning Dennis' alarm rang at seven o'clock sharp. Both Romeo and Dennis had to get ready for a busy day at school.

Mrs. Crumb set out a warm bowl of oatmeal for her son and a healthy portion of tuna for Romeo. Both boys devoured their breakfast making sloppy sounds as they ate.

After breakfast Romeo followed Dennis to the front door.

"Where do you think you're going?" asked Dennis, looking down at Romeo.

Romeo stared Dennis in the eyes like he wanted to say something. He meowed a proud, heavy meow. Something stirred inside of Dennis as if he knew what Romeo was thinking. When he opened the front door, he allowed Romeo to run out. Romeo looked up at him with a gratifying smile.

"Just be back before dark," Dennis called out, though he felt silly for saying it to a cat. "I'm trusting you."

Romeo meowed again and walked with Dennis into the elevator. This route was much nicer and easier than climbing down those vines and awful shrubs. Not to mention the jump from the awning.

At the front of the building Dennis knelt down and gave Romeo a pat on the head. He double checked to see that Romeo's collar and ID tag were

Life One

on secure and tight.

"Have a nice day, Romeo," Dennis said as he scurried away.

"You too," Romeo muttered under his breath, though Dennis never heard.

On his way to the Factory, Romeo came across an odd sight. He was about halfway there when he noticed an older cat across the street. It sat at the base of a flickering street lamp like the one where he lived. The cat was withered and old looking, yet somehow distinguished. It had on a shiny gold collar. Its glowing purple eyes seemed to stare right through Romeo, watching his every move. Romeo looked away, hoping the mysterious cat would stop. Yet, he quickly looked back out of pure curiosity. When he did, the old cat was gone.

Romeo made it all the way to the Factory without any other weird problems. He avoided the alley where he first met Bait and soon found himself in the Factory's long hallway of paintings and candles.

Upstairs he came to the door with the words *Stick School* on the front and bashfully opened it, hoping he wasn't late.

His eyes found Ms. Purrpurr who was anticipating his arrival.

"Ahh, Romeo," she said pleased. "Do come in."

Romeo took a few timid steps into the room. He looked around and found five other cats all gawking at him. He was disappointed that none of them looked like his brothers. Still, they were sitting straight in what he assumed to be their desks, paws folded and ready to learn. He made eye contact briefly with one of the other males and smiled.

"We are just waiting for a few others and then we will begin," announced Ms. Purrpurr. "Romeo, your desk is right here."

She pointed to the desk in the second row out of three. It was the farthest desk from the door and behind one of the females. Next to him was an empty seat. While he waited in the awkward silence, he looked in his desk. There, he found paper, a pencil, two crayons, both blue, and a ball of green yarn. He was about to take out the yarn when the door opened and two other cats walked in. One of them sat in the empty seat next to Romeo.

"Very well, everyone's here," said Ms. Purrpurr. "Will you all please rise for the Pledge of Bubastis." She motioned for everybody to stand and face the flag that drooped from above their heads. "Bend your left paw and begin..."

None of the new students had a clue what to do, so they faked it as they watched the others.

"I pledge my honor," they whispered with an air of embarrassment.

"Louder!" Ms. Purrpurr rang.

"*I PLEDGE MY HONOR*," they blasted. "To the flag of Bubastis. I swear to do my best to be a worthy cat, to help a fellow cat in need, to live each of my nine

Life One

lives to its fullest, and to live with dedication under the eyes of the big, big city and Bubastis himself. May the clouds one day pass and prosperity and freedom reign."

Romeo, nor any of the others for that matter, knew what any of that meant. He decided to ask Queen Elizabeth later rather than asking the teacher now. He was afraid that somebody would laugh at him in case it turned out to be a dumb question.

"Class," Ms. Purrpurr said, "today we have three new students. Please welcome Romeo, Fluffy, and Darla." As she mentioned their names, she pointed toward each of them. "Will the rest of you please stand up and introduce yourselves. We will begin with Calvin."

Calvin was a beautiful cat full of rich soft colors and markings. He had a striking blend of white, yellow, and orange around his face and tail. The rest of his body was mostly yellow and orange. "I'm Calvin," he stated clearly and proudly. "I have been here for two weeks, and I am going to be a great actor some-day." He held his head high and didn't seem a bit bothered by the giggles. "My person, Lloyd, is going to get me into commercials."

"Very nice, Calvin," Ms. Purrpurr said. "Next."

The middle seat in the front row was occupied by Tabitha. She was a plain, simple yellow cat, but pretty in a sort of farm girl way. Her eyes sparkled, and

Chapter Four

she had the longest lashes Romeo had ever seen. "Hi," she said shyly. "I'm Tabitha and I've been here for..... three weeks. I like it. It's fun."

Ms. Purrpurr smiled in her direction and motioned for Snickers, who sat in front of Romeo. Snickers, like the teacher, was plump and round with big, chubby cheeks. Little leftover particles of jerky stuck to his red fur. "I'm Snickers, and I think that you will like it here because we do fun things and eat lots of snacks and play and eat more snacks and...."

Ms. Purrpurr cut him off before he got carried away. Immediately, Romeo could tell that he would like Snickers. As talkative as he seemed to be, he had a definite jolly quality that was contagious right from the start.

"Hey cats, I'm Twinkle Toes," said the male directly to Romeo's left. "Uh, that's all from this dude."

"All right...thank you, Twinkle Toes," Ms. Purrpurr mumbled. Twinkle Toes was all black with white paws. He seemed nice but was off in his own little beatnik world.

"Howdy, I'm Uncle Fred," the final cat said. He sat in the second row nearest the door. He was large, but not fat, with wide white stripes in his deep brown fur. Uncle Fred was a little older and abnormally bigger than most cats. He had to squirm and squish his body like a bean bag just to fit into his small chair. "I've been here for a whole year. I was supposed to graduate already, but I guess I'm still here. They just can't seem to get rid of me." He started to laugh and snort.

"Yes, Uncle Fred," Ms. Purrpurr said as she rolled her eyes. "You just have to work extra hard this time, right?"

"Sure, teach, sure."

Ms. Purrpurr, annoyed when he called her teach, politely reminded Uncle Fred how to address her. She tried not to be too tough on him knowing he was somewhat slower than the other cats.

Darla and Fluffy, the other two new students, were the only cats who sat in the back row.

"All right," Ms. Purrpurr began. "Thank you everybody." She tapped a piece of white chalk against the floor and paced. "To the new students, you will do extra work over the next few weeks in order to catch up to the others. With determination you can do it! Uh, you too Uncle Fred."

Uncle Fred closed his eyes and smiled.

"Remember, this is your reading class. In one hour I will leave and Mr. Shadow will take over. But for now, please take out your yarn and stretch it into a long piece across your desk."

The students did as she said, though Uncle Fred seemed to have a little difficulty. He accidentally unraveled the entire ball. Twinkle Toes reached over to help him before it rolled across the floor again sending Ms. Purrpurr into a fit of anger.

65

Chapter Four

Ms. Purrpurr walked around the classroom and cut the yarn into five smaller pieces with a tiny pair of sewing scissors. Snickers began to chew on one of the pieces, but stopped when Tabitha shot him a dirty look.

"Please spell out the word CAT," Ms. Purrpurr instructed the class. "New ones, watch to see what the other students do, that is, except for Uncle Fred."

Romeo, Darla, and Fluffy all watched as the others turned and twisted their strips of yarn into funny shapes. The shapes looked odd to the new students and to Uncle Fred who spelled out FAT by mistake. But by the end of the hour, and with the aid of Ms. Purrpurr's teaching skills, each student understood what the letters meant. Romeo, in particular, learned very quickly, even quicker than the older students.

"Very good, Romeo," Ms. Purrpurr said proudly. "Tomorrow you will learn more words. Class," she continued as she walked up to the front of the room, "your homework tonight is to look around your house and find five words. Tomorrow you will write them on the board. For the newer students, do the best you can."

Some of the students grumbled in their seats at the idea of the assignment, but Romeo was excited to learn more letters.

At precisely nine o'clock, reading was over. Ms. Purrpurr left the classroom with a satchel full of teacher stuff draped over her back, leaving her eight pupils alone.

"Hey, Uncle Fred," called Calvin as he turned around in his seat. "Do you think you're finally going to *pass* this time? Pretty soon you'll be older than the teachers."

Uncle Fred showed no signs of hurt, though his insides told a different story. "Whatever, Melvin."

Calvin rolled his eyes. "Uh, the name's *Calvin*, you know, with a capital *C*. Oh, I forgot, you don't know the letter *c* yet." Calvin gave Uncle Fred a bossy smirk and turned back around.

Uncle Fred began to breathe hard. He put his big head down on his desk. Romeo swore he heard a sad sniffle or two.

The rest of the cats sat tense, afraid that Calvin would bother them next.

"Uh, does anyone have any pudding?" Snickers asked stupidly as he finished a stale fig.

Just then, the door handle turned and a short and shaggy male cat walked in. Without talking he flung a big stack of papers down on the old, wooden, teacher's desk. Romeo's eyes followed a few sheets as they drifted in the air and eventually floated back down. The teacher didn't seem to notice, or to mind for that matter. He took a bunch of stuff out of his ripped pockets and scattered them around the desk. Romeo spotted a rubber band, two broken pencils, three rocks, a crumpled map of the city, and a piece of sandpaper. After the things were all arranged in whatever order he was trying to achieve, the shaggy cat finally looked up and somehow tripped on his tail.

"Good morning," he bellowed. "I see we have some new students here today. My name is Mr. Shadow, and this is Survival Class." The way he said *survival* made it all the more primal and mysterious. It was almost as if he had lived the word. The rest of him was pale gray except for the insides of his ears. They were bright pink, brighter than most. He had an old brown, leather bag that he kept crossed over his chest, though everything he used seemed to be deep in the pockets of his yellow knit sweater. At the collar the name *Shadow* was embroidered in a pretty blue thread.

"Let's start with the new students," he said directing his attention at the three cats. "I assume you've met the others, but I think *I* need to meet *you.*" When he spoke he fidgeted with his sweater and the leather bag almost to the point of being annoying.

Fluffy stood up first. He looked around the classroom before opening his mouth. "I'm Fluffy, and I live with a little girl named Casey. I-I hope I like it here. I think I will." Fluffy, who's name seemed inappropriate due to his finely combed and flattened short white fur, had an elegance to his voice and the posture of a great statue.

"Thank you, Fluffy," said Mr. Shadow, scratch-

 68

Life One

Chapter Four

ing the part of his neck that met his sweater. "Who's next?"

Romeo and Darla looked at each other. Darla gave Romeo a sweet smile and promptly stood up.

"Good morning, Mr. Shadow," Darla sparkled. She was as cute as a button and very petite. Her hair was a warm blend of browns and golds. Her gentle voice swam through the room and stuck to the walls. "I'm Darla, and I live with Mr. and Mrs. Hoffman of Hoffman's Bakery. Sometimes I get some extra scraps from the shop. Maybe I could bring them over one day. Can I go to the litteroom now?" She had a chronic bladder problem.

"What? Bakery? Did someone say bakery?" Snickers asked bolting up in his seat.

"Sit down, Snickers," Mr. Shadow answered. "Nothing you need to be concerned with right now." He looked over in Darla's direction. "Thank you, Darla, and yes, you may go. And now our last student. Would you please introduce yourself? Once again for my benefit."

Romeo slowly got up and stood tall. "Hi, I'm Romeo. I live about four blocks away with a great guy named Dennis Crumb. He's really something. Just today, in fact, he let me ride with him in the elevator and...."

Mr. Shadow cut him off suddenly. "Gosh, Romeo, that's a very interesting mark you have on your back. It looks like a diamond."

Life One

The other cats leaned over to get a better look. Uncle Fred nearly fell off of his chair. Romeo twisted around so that everybody could see.

"Cool."

"Neat."

"Oooooo," gawked the other cats.

"Yeah," said Romeo. "It's just some odd birthmark, I guess. I kinda like it." He looked proudly at his golden diamond. He had to be careful not to hurt his neck in the process. Romeo noticed that most cats he met seemed to admire his little treasure, and it made him feel special. Romeo told the class how all his brothers had the same mark and about his quest to find them. They seemed anxious to help.

Like the diamond, other cats had little spots of color here and there as well. Darla had two cute white dots above her nose, Tabitha had one black stripe down her tail, and Calvin had a splotch on his lower back which he claimed was a star, though nobody else really saw it that way.

After the introductions Mr. Shadow presented his curriculum to the new students.

"You are in here to learn how to survive on the streets," he explained, still scratching. "No, *you* don't live on the streets, but you do have to go out now and then, don't you? To come here you have to be outside. Plus, sometimes we just like going for a walk or looking for something new to eat. You are in this class for the three w's; where, when, and what. *Where* are the safest streets? *When* can I go outside? And *what* do I do in the event of an emergency, such as a confrontation with an alley cat?" Mr. Shadow took out his city map and highlighted some safe routes near the Factory.

"Avoid going out late at night," he continued. "Daylight is a stick's best friend."

Romeo felt fairly confident that he was getting used to the street system. Queen Elizabeth had also explained in detail the safest places to walk. She and Mr. Shadow both warned, however, not to be too over confident on those streets for even the safest street was connected to an alley. And they all knew what dangers lurked in alleys. "You just never know when danger will strike," Mr. Shadow warned. "Always be on alert. *Always.*"

Mr. Shadow also discussed a few more cat obstacles, ones that Queen Elizabeth had only touched on slightly.

"The Pound!" Mr. Shadow said with conviction as he paced up and down the classroom, his tail swinging behind him. "The Pound! I know the others have heard this already, but you can *never* hear it too much. *Never!* The Pound van comes around every week. Different times for different corners. If you are caught by the Pound van," his voice began to rise, "you can forget about freedom. If the Pound gets you, the city gets you! First, they throw you in a cage and lock you up! Then, they knock you out with

Life One

some pill and operate on your guts! Maybe, if you are lucky, your human, or possibly a stranger, will rescue you, but that's very rare. If you don't go home within two weeks....," Mr. Shadow made a slicing motion and a crunching sound across his neck. "It's all over for you!"

Romeo had a sinking feeling when Mr. Shadow talked about the Pound, as did all the cats. Romeo spent some time there when he was a brand new kitten but luckily went home with Dennis' father. Romeo didn't remember much about the place, just that there were other cats, including his brothers, crying and meowing all the time. And a lot of people dressed in white. Romeo wondered if the small scar he had on his stomach had something to do with this operation Mr. Shadow described. He wished his mother and father were around to explain it all to him. Romeo's face turned sad as Mr. Shadow continued.

"Who can raise their paw and tell me our number one protection against the Pound?" Mr. Shadow looked around the room before deciding who to chose. "Go ahead, Calvin. What is the answer?"

"An ID tag, sir," Calvin said with confidence. He wiggled his around to show Mr. Shadow. It was sparkly silver and had two rhinestones at the bottom.

"You are correct, Calvin. Very good. Now, everybody please hold up your ID tag for me to inspect. I want to see that all the necessary informa-

73

tion is correct."

Mr. Shadow staggered around the room checking everyone's tag. While he did, Snickers found a spider on the floor, took a chance and lunged for it.

"Snickers!" Mr. Shadow growled.

"Uh, sorry, Mr. Shadow," Snickers mumbled with four spider legs dangling from his lips. "I was just a little hungry so I thought as long as you're just walking around and stuff, I might as well..."

"Swallow that bug and show me your collar!" Mr. Shadow barked.

"Gulp."

Romeo reached down to his neck and twirled the metallic silver tag in the shape of a diamond. Engraved on it were a lot of squiggly words that Romeo couldn't read yet. He was able to at least recognize his own name, R-O-M-E-O.

"Good Romeo," said Mr. Shadow with a juicy sneeze. "Good Uncle Fred, Twinkle Toes, Calvin, Fluffy, Darla, Snickers.....uh, Tabitha?"

When Mr. Shadow reached Tabitha's desk, he found her all crouched down in her seat with her paws around her little neck. Her eyes were glossy, and she shook.

"Tabitha, let me see your collar," instructed Mr. Shadow.

She didn't budge.

"Tabitha, NOW!" Mr. Shadow insisted.

Little whimpering sounds came from Tabitha's

 74

face. She slowly removed her paws from her neck. Mr. Shadow gazed blankly at her, then stood back in horror.

"Tabitha! What happened to your collar!" he howled.

By now Tabitha was in full tears. Darla walked up to her and stroked her shaking head.

"M-M-Mr. Sh..Shadow, sir," Tabitha muttered. "My Jimmy took it off last night. He p-put it on his little sister," she wailed. "There was nothing I-I-I-I could do!!"

Mr. Shadow rolled his eyes and put his paw to his chin. "All right, Tabitha. All right. Hopefully Jimmy will put it back on you tonight. Try to find it and put it on his pillow. That usually works. If not, we will have to come up with another plan. You must have a collar. *You must!*"

Darla went back to her desk leaving Tabitha to calm down.

Mr. Shadow walked over to the chalkboard and pulled on an old piece of twine that was hanging from above. Uncle Fred leapt forward to attack and kill the twine as Mr. Shadow knocked him out of the way. The string was connected to a rolled-up poster that unraveled as Mr. Shadow tugged. It was a copy of a photograph of a rusty gray van. Some black smudges were on the doors, and two scruffy men were in the front seat.

"This, my dear students," Mr. Shadow said

Chapter Four

using his pointer, "is the Pound official van. If you ever, *ever* see this van, I don't care what else you have to do, hide, and hide fast! These men are your enemies. Remember their faces! Know their car! You will memorize the Pound collection schedule, but be forewarned, they do make surprise visits. Always, *always* be on alert!" Mr. Shadow had a habit for repeating important words twice. "Like I said, if they catch you there's no guarantee that you'll ever get back, even if you have a collar."

Romeo studied the van with an odd curiosity. He had that same sinking feeling again deep in the pit of his stomach, though he didn't know why. He almost felt like he had seen the van before, but he couldn't place when or where. Perhaps he saw it when he was walking to the Factory, however, he didn't think so. Maybe he spotted it from Dennis' window. Whatever the case, Romeo felt uneasy just looking at it. At any rate, he let it go, as did Mr. Shadow who rolled the picture back up after a few more cross warnings then went on to the next subject.

"Dogs!" Mr. Shadow shouted with dizzying eyes. "Dogs!" There was a long, empty silence.

Romeo looked at the other cats hoping he wasn't the only one who thought the teacher was going crazy.

Mr. Shadow snapped out of his gaze and went on. "Watch out for the *dogs*. They're sneaky and lurk quietly and mysteriously. One slash and they could

 76

rip your face off! One bite and you could lose all nine lives at once!" As he talked he began to crouch his body and creep around the room. He kept flexing his claws and squinting his eyes. "You never know where or when they are going to strike next. They travel in packs of about five or six. Their howls are like nothing you've ever heard. They can destroy your eardrums with one single roar. Dogs do most of their hunting during the day, hunting anything and anyone ready to rumble. Usually, very late at night they stay in their homes, but sometimes they prowl up and down the dark streets looking for trouble. About six months ago a cat, I'm not going to mention names," he continued in a very shady, spooky voice. "..a cat was chased all the way home by the dogs. They ended up cornering him in an alley and taking all his jerky. Then they viciously drooled all over him, leaving him in a gooey mess. Some alley cats were hiding nearby in an old garbage can. When the monstrous dogs finally left, the alleys laughed and teased him wickedly. In fact, some still laugh at him when he walks by today." Mr. Shadow paused and stared off into space with a vile, wretched look.

"Mr. Shadow?" called Tabitha. "Mr. Shadow?"

"Yes, what is it?" he answered, going back to tugging at his sweater.

"How do you know all this?" she asked.

He gave her a hard look and said, "Anyway, especially be on the lookout for Bull, their leader. He may be the smallest dog, but he is the fiercest. He's what people call a Bulldog which means he's got a squashed in face like somebody punched him, only nobody would *dare* punch Bull. His legs are very short, and he's beige in color with bits of black. Some say he's even worse than Fidel, and you know the stories about him!"

The students nodded their heads.

"There is one good thing about the dogs though. They hate the alleys as much as they hate the sticks. If they were on the alleys' side, imagine how much harder our lives would be. But, as it stands, the alleys are just as scared of the dogs as we are. Even Fidel!"

"Who are the *dogs* afraid of?" Snickers asked out of turn.

Calvin rolled his eyes and huffed in his direction.

Mr. Shadow walked up to Snicker's desk. He flicked the last little spider leg that was stuck to Snicker's fur. "The Pound," he blurted. "They are in just as much danger from the Pound as any of us around here. An advantage we have over dogs is our ability to climb. Though a dog can run very fast," he said with that same look of disgust, "a dog cannot suddenly dart up a tree or climb over a tall fence. Cats can. And your climbing skills will get even better and stronger as you grow older."

Romeo sat back in his chair and allowed the warnings to soak in. Between Queen Elizabeth, Mr.

 78

Life One

Sox, and now Mr. Shadow, he was beginning to wonder why any cat would bother leaving his own home at all. Was it actually worth the risks? How could there be so many dangers waiting for such a good little cat? None of it made a bit of sense to Romeo. Yet there was nothing he could do about it. Nothing he was aware of at least.

"All right," Mr. Shadow concluded. "That's all the time we have today. Soon we will talk about Death Alley and the subway system." With that, he picked up all his scattered belongings and stuffed them back into his crumpled leather bag. Romeo and the others still wondered what the rubber band, rock, and sandpaper were for. They politely said goodbye to Mr. Shadow as the second hour of school came to a close.

All eight cats stood up for a quick stretch before the third and final class. Their bodies were getting hungry for a little exercise. With one wee hour left, they sat back down and awaited their next teacher. Tired, nobody said a word. Even Calvin was too beat to tease anyone.

From his seat Romeo could hear some heavy footsteps approaching the door. After a few rustling noises and a cough, the door opened. To everyone's surprise, it was Waffles. He stood, practically bigger than the whole room, picking something from between his long, yellow teeth. Being Romeo's first day, he assumed that Waffles must be the teacher, though he

Chapter Four

didn't seem to be the history teacher type.

"Where's Miss Cleo?" Tabitha asked concerned. "Will she be absent today?"

Waffles looked at each of the eight young cats. "Uh," he began, "Miss Cleo will not be your teacher anymore."

A sudden gasp was heard throughout the room. The older cats had quite a fondness for Miss Cleo's kindness and patience. Tears began to well up in Tabitha's eyes. "Why not?" she asked.

"It seems that Audrey, her person, had a fight with her boyfriend, or something silly like that, and decided to head out west for a new life. I know you guys will all miss her." He smiled in Romeo's direction knowing he hadn't the foggiest notion who this Cleo cat was.

"Wow, Miss Cleo out west," thought Snickers outloud.

"Yeah," added Uncle Fred. "Lucky her."

Nobody actually knew what *out west* really meant. Rumor had it that the farther west one got, the prettier the place. Supposedly there were no rain clouds or muggy, stormy nights. They had heard that the sun always shone, and the people were always kind to cats and other animals. They'd heard there were separate sidewalks just for cats lined with cat food, and some for dogs too. Though many *dreamed* of going west, few actually did.

"No, I'm not your teacher," Waffles said, real-

80

izing why they were looking at him so weirdly. "I'm just waiting here until the real teacher shows up."

"Who's it gonna be?" Snickers asked. "Is it going to be somebody nice, because Miss Cleo was really nice and I think that we should, I mean, we deserve...."

Just then Waffles turned his head as someone approached through the library. "Mr. Sox!" Romeo jumped.

The fourteen other eyes widened as Mr. Sox walked in on his tired, old legs. Everyone was quiet, and Romeo was more than pleased about Mr. Sox being their teacher.

Mr. Sox thanked Waffles for staying, then kindly asked him to leave. He closed the door after him and faced the class.

"Yes, I will be your new cat history teacher. I regret that Miss Cleo is gone, though I do believe she is off to far bigger and better things." Mr. Sox paused for a moment and smiled. He began to walk casually up and down the aisles as he talked. "I said I would never teach again, that was three years ago. But when I heard the news of Miss Cleo, and considering how important this class is, I couldn't say no. So without further ado, let's begin." He turned around to write something on the chalkboard.

Just then Romeo saw a piece of paper sail over-head and land on Twinkle Toes' desk. Twinkle Toes grabbed the crumpled note and immediately tore it

Chapter Four

open. It seemed to have come from Calvin's direction.

"I believe that I know all of you already," Mr. Sox began. "So I don't think we need any...." He stopped. The sound of the noisy paper caught his attention. Calmly, without hesitation, he walked over to Twinkle Toes who didn't even notice what was going on until a large paw stretched under his face.

"Give me the note, Mr. Toes," Mr. Sox said with disappointment.

Startled, Twinkle Toes timidly gave him the note. He shook and shuddered in his chair as Mr. Sox opened it.

Mr. Sox inspected the secret letter and put on a very dissatisfied face. "So, Calvin," he said turning to the right. "You think I'm a funny looking old man, do you?"

Calvin sat in horror. Apparently he drew an unflattering picture of the distinguished cat before tossing it to his friend. "No, Mr. Sox, I'm sorry, I....."

"After class you will spend one full hour with me in the library, and I will personally teach you how to be a respectful and proper young cat. Am I understood?" Mr. Sox put his two front paws on Calvin's desk and leaned in close to his face. Romeo and the others watched through the thick tension.

"Yes, Mr. Sox, I'll be there," Calvin whined.

Mr. Sox gave him one final stare and continued. He acted unaffected by the whole thing, though Romeo caught a glimpse of Mr. Sox's face when he turned back around. It was a sad face. Soon enough, Mr. Sox was deeply involved in his lecture. The students sat at the edge of their seats as they listened to exciting stories about Carnival and the golden days. Though Romeo had heard the story before, there was something enchanting about listening to the wisdom of Mr. Sox.

Chapter Five

After class Romeo and the others headed down to the recreation room, except for Calvin who had to stay behind with Mr. Sox. Snickers politely asked Romeo if he'd like to join him for a snack.

"I hear Roy and Yellowtail got some really good stuff today," Snickers said licking his lips. "I think I smell crab cakes!"

"Okay, sure," Romeo said delighted. He noticed Fluffy a few feet away staring at them with that helpless puppy dog look. "Fluffy?" he asked in his direction. "Would you like to come with us for some fish?"

Excited, Fluffy answered, "Oh yes, yes. Thank you both."

In class Fluffy usually kept to himself, not talking or participating much. Perhaps he was shy,

 84

but under those sweet eyes a genius was waiting to bloom. Romeo was drawn to the unique and exceptional and recognized something special about Fluffy right away. He was happy Fluffy was joining them for an afternoon snack.

"Come on, guys," Snickers whined, pulling Romeo's ear. "It's over this way...."

Suddenly, out of nowhere a loud thunder of footsteps was heard coming down the hall. Romeo and Fluffy paused, though Snickers kept tugging.

The big door flew open. There stood Vittles breathing hard and sweating from his brow. He clutched one paw up to his chest and braced his large body in the doorway with the other paw. All the cats from the rec room, twenty or so, waited anxiously for him to speak.

"...It's Queen Elizabeth!" He finally huffed. "Th-there's been an accident! Come quick! Get Mr. Sox!"

Without hesitation Romeo charged for the door. Snickers finally gave up on Romeo's ear but not on the crab cakes. He loved food more than anything, and nothing interfered with snack time.

Romeo ran down the long hallway of candles and paintings, Vittles and many others following frantically. When they reached the front entrance, a few cats were already huddled near the door buzzing about the situation.

"Let me through! Let me through!" Romeo

roared desperately trying to get past the barricade of cats. "Let me out there!"

Vittles bumped him in the shoulders and blocked his path. "No Romeo, you're too young! You're too young for this!"

"Tell us what happened!" cried MayBelle, a cat from the back.

"Okay, okay! Everyone calm down!" Vittles looked at the young cats in front of him. "Queen Elizabeth was hit by a bus. Waffles is with her, but he needs some of you to help him."

A wall of cats lunged forward waving their paws in the air.

"Wait!" Vittles called. "We need to do this quickly, but orderly."

Romeo threw his paws over his eyes in disbelief.

"How did it happen?" Fluffy asked fighting back the tears.

"She was trying to go downtown to see a friend when she got run over. The bus driver got out and dragged her to the side of the road. Luckily Waffles spotted her lying in the gutter when he was on his break. She's bleeding pretty bad and, and...."

Nobody moved. Vittles held his head low.

"Tell us, Vittles," Romeo pleaded.

"She's....she's....she's pretty twisted up. If we don't do something, she'll *keep* dying. She's already lost one life. We've got to help her or else she'll....."

 86

Life One

"Okay," Mr. Sox burst in. "Here's what we're going to do. Vittles, you go out and help your brother carry her in here. MayBell, you grab a large cloth from the art room. Roy, Yellowtail, you help prepare the cats in the medicine room. I'll stay here and guard the door. And Soot, get the soup pot ready to lift Queen Elizabeth. Make sure it is lowered all the way to the bottom. It won't be easy getting her in there. As for the rest of you, pray that Bubastis will come."

"Bubastis?" Fluffy asked. "Who's he anyway?"

"Later, Fluffy," Mr. Sox explained. "Later."

"What can I do, Mr. Sox?" Romeo whined.

Mr. Sox quickly pulled him aside. "Look Romeo, I know you want to help, but I need you to sit down and wait. That's all you can do."

"No!" Romeo yelled as he headed out the front entrance.

"Romeo!!" Mr. Sox hollered. "You get back here right now! You'll just get in the way! Now, sit down if you care what happens to your friend!"

Romeo sank to his butt and started to weep. He felt helpless and scared. Surely there was something he could do. He owed it to Queen Elizabeth. After all, without her he would still be staring at the walls of Dennis' room, never going outside, never learning how to read, never meeting new friends, never looking for his brothers, never knowing *her*.

Chapter Five

He lay there on the floor as other cats rushed about panicking from the situation. Fluffy had retreated back to the library with Snickers who was still hungry. Through all the chaos Romeo felt a gentle tap on his shoulder. It was Tabitha.

"Romeo," she whispered. "Come with me over to the couch. Please, Romeo."

Though he didn't want to, he did. It was no use talking to Mr. Sox anymore. Romeo knew he would just be in the way. Tabitha was kind and sensed his anguish. They plopped down on the large red pillow that had been restuffed and formed into a small sofa. There, Romeo could see all the action in the hallway. He watched as Vittles and Waffles carried Queen Elizabeth carefully through the rec room toward the soup pot. Vittles was right. She was blood soaked from head to toe and covered with dirt from the puddle of mud she had been lying in. Romeo shivered at the horrifying sight and felt sick at the thought of some overworked bus driver leaving her quivering body in the gutter while a bunch of people just sat and stared from their comfortable bus seats. It was all too much for Romeo to bear. He wanted to learn about cat life, but not like this. Why did it have to be her?

When they rushed Queen Elizabeth to the elevator pot, small drops of blood dripped from her body and splashed onto the floor. Romeo stared at one of them, unable to actually look at Queen Elizabeth's frail, lifeless body. When he did look up, he unfortu-

 88

nately caught a glimpse of her bloody face. Romeo couldn't take his eyes away. Her tongue was hanging out of her mouth, and her eyes were opened but rolled back inside of her head. Her sweet paws dangled and swayed like limp rags. Her insides looked mangled. Romeo desperately wanted to run to her but he followed orders. Grim, he waited impatiently with Tabitha and the others.

After two painful hours Mr. Sox emerged from the soup pot. His legs were covered in blood, and his face told a sad story. Romeo sat on the edge of the couch as Tabitha held his paw. Mr. Sox took off his foggy glasses and spoke.

"She's sleeping now. She'll be all right." He took a deep breath and let it out slowly. "It's been a tough day, and I think we should all go home." He began to walk away.

"Wait, Mr. Sox," Romeo beckoned. "Did she..."

Mr. Sox looked up with his woeful eyes. "Because of the severity of the accident," he took a long pause before continuing, "and the time it took us to stop the bleeding, she lost two lives. If we had gotten to her sooner, she would have only lost one."

Romeo remembered what Queen Elizabeth had taught him about the nine lives of a cat. She said that in most cases a cat had one hour to be restored before it would come to life again. The wounds would heal themselves, and sicknesses would disappear as the next life slowly crept back in. But, in a more serious situation like this, where the body had been severely mangled and ripped apart, every hour that passed was another life lost. Without any medical treatment a cat could die completely. Luckily Mr. Sox and a few other medically trained cats were able to help.

"Two lives!" somebody shouted out.

"How many does she have left?" asked another.

Romeo sat up straight. "She's got two, just two."

The others dropped their heads low.

"Wow," Roy said, handing out some leftover shrimp. "She's almost a niner."

The mood in the room was upsetting, yet hopeful. Yes, she would be all right, but losing two lives from one accident was a disturbing thing.

Romeo was finally allowed upstairs to the medicine room. Apparently Queen Elizabeth was resting comfortably. Romeo, having seen her lifeless body only hours ago, had to see her revived for himself.

"Come with me to the elevator," Mr. Sox said to Romeo.

Romeo thanked Tabitha for her kindness and followed Mr. Sox to the soup pot without making a sound. Once at the third floor, they got off and headed toward a room that Romeo had not been in yet.

Life One

"She's in here," Mr. Sox said as he pushed open the door.

Inside the cramped room were several small tables cluttered with all kinds of tiny bottles and strange looking metal clamps and needles. The foggy bottles were marked with all types of those little squiggly lines Romeo was learning in Ms. Purrpurr's reading class. The room itself was terribly cold, cold enough to see your own breath in front of your face.

Like the classroom there was a small silver flashlight giving the room necessary light. In the center was a large table that was made from what seemed to be two old metal lunch boxes. The handles, still attached, made it easy for the cats to move the boxes around when needed. The lids were liftable making them fine places to store linens and other medical equipment. On one, a large gray cloth hid the faded painting of a cowboy on his horse and a large piece of yellow tape with the name *Billy* written across it. Watching over Queen Elizabeth was another cat Romeo had never seen. He had on some sort of a doctor's coat, but not like the ones Romeo saw on Dennis' TV. His paws were stained with blood, and he looked tired.

Romeo took one step toward Queen Elizabeth before Mr. Sox blocked him from going any farther with his paw. "Just a minute, Romeo. Let me go first."

Mr. Sox approached Queen Elizabeth. She

91

slept quietly on the table. Her head rested on a soft pillow, and her body was kept warm by a heavy blanket. Mr. Sox gently stroked her forehead which was now cleaned of the blood and muddy rain water with the help of the cats who worked in the medicine room. Most of them lived with the people doctors who worked at City Hospital.

Queen Elizabeth looked peaceful. Romeo was thrilled to see her furry chest moving up and down. And he could hear wheezing through her tiny pink nose.

Mr. Sox's expression was a combination of relief, sadness, and worry. Though he was in the same room during the entire operation, he still seemed shocked by the situation. While cats commonly lose lives everyday, it was never easy to see a close friend lose one, let alone two.

Romeo looked around the room as he waited for Queen Elizabeth to wake up. He noticed that this room was the smallest he had seen and showed the most visible damage from the great fire. The walls were covered in heavy black soot, and the ceiling was ripped with holes. With every step the doctor cat took, the floor seemed to creak a little bit louder. Romeo spotted some long claw marks along one of the walls and wondered how they got there.

"Where are the others?" Mr. Sox said to Frederick, the cat behind the table.

"They went home, Mr. Sox. They were tired.

Bubastis left as well. At least, we *think* he was here. I said I'd stay behind and watch her," Frederick added.

Bubastis. There was that name again.

"Thank you, Frederick," said Mr. Sox. "When will she be ready to go home? Her family will be worried."

Frederick thought, "In about an hour or so. As you can see the wounds are healed, and she's back with us. She's just exhausted now, that's all. When she awakens from this nap, the whole ordeal will be over. Then she can go home."

Frederick stood back allowing Mr. Sox to get another close look at Queen Elizabeth for himself.

"Good work, Frederick," Mr. Sox said looking at the patient. "Tell the others I said so. By the way, will she be all right walking home alone?"

Romeo leapt forward. He had wanted to help Queen Elizabeth in the worst way, and this was possibly his best chance.

"Mr. Sox?" Romeo asked. "I could walk her home. She lives across the alley from me. Can I Mr. Sox? Can I please walk her home?"

Mr. Sox looked down at Romeo's innocent, little eyes which had seen so much pain that day and softly said, "Yes, Romeo, She would like that."

Romeo stood proud and smiled.

Chapter Six

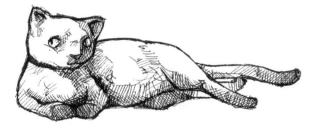

About an hour later Queen Elizabeth awoke from her sleep just like Frederick had predicted. Both Mr. Sox and Romeo watched anxiously as she moaned and twisted her head. Her two shiny blue eyes slowly opened, and she saw the hazy forms before her.

"Mr. Sox? Is that you?" she asked in a weak, scratchy voice, squinting.

"Put your head down, Queen Elizabeth," Mr. Sox urged. "Don't get up so fast"

She let her head drift back down to the pillow and closed her eyes again. They thought she was going back to sleep, but she uttered a few faint words instead.

"Romeo?" she called. "Please come over here, would you?" She reached out her left paw from

 94

Life One

under the blanket and waited for Romeo to take it. "Were you scared?" she asked with concern. Romeo looked at Mr. Sox before answering.

"I-I guess so. I mean, yes, I was scared," he whispered in a quivering voice. "I'm sorry you had to see all this, Romeo. But, it's okay now. I'm fine," she reassured him. "Cats are lucky. We get to live on. Don't ever take that for granted though. Make every life count. *Don't* forget that, Romeo."

At that moment Romeo didn't understand everything she said, though he would never forget holding her paw as she lay there that day in the medicine room or the feeling of knowing he had found a true friend. Her words would echo in his head for a lifetime, nine to be exact.

Soon Queen Elizabeth felt strong enough to walk home. Mr. Sox said goodbye and told the two cats to be careful on their journey. He expected Romeo to be very cautious and never let Queen Elizabeth out of his sight. Romeo understood and promised with everything he had to keep a watchful eye out for her. Before leaving Mr. Sox said something to Queen Elizabeth in private. Romeo didn't know what it was but watched as they touched goodbye. Queen Elizabeth mouthed the words, "Thank you," before stepping away.

On the walk home Romeo shielded Queen Elizabeth as much as he could from the nasty weather.

Chapter Six

The awnings above only blocked some of the down-pour, and Romeo made sure Queen Elizabeth walked beneath them. At times it was hard for Romeo to see her because it was so foggy out that night. The sky was black and most of the street lamps were doing their typical on and off dance.

Queen Elizabeth held her head low to the ground and didn't say a word. She seemed subdued and forlorn. She didn't know it, but Romeo saw her shudder every time a bus drove by. Romeo braced her back with his tail to let her know he was there.

Luckily the alleys didn't give them too much trouble that night, except for one small occurrence when they passed the alleyway at 57th Street. Deep in the darkness they heard a high-pitched laugh. Romeo instinctively huddled closer to Queen Elizabeth like a bodyguard would do. Then they heard a creepy whisper somewhere in the depths of the shadows calling, "Watch where you're going next time. Those buses can sneak up on you." It was followed by more of that eerie laugh. Queen Elizabeth didn't react. Rather, she kept her head low to the ground not making a peep.

Eventually Romeo needed to break the silence. It was making him very uncomfortable. He thought hard for a question. One that would not necessarily be about the accident.

"Queen Elizabeth," he said hesitantly. "Who's Bubastis?"

Life One

She lifted her weary head and looked Romeo straight in the eyes. "Bubastis? Why do you want to talk about Bubastis?"

Romeo wondered if he had asked the wrong question. She seemed a bit put off by it. "Uh," he muttered, "I heard his name mentioned a few times today and I was just wondering...."

"Later Romeo. I'll tell you all about him later. Tonight I'm just too tired, so tired. I always get tired when I lose a life, but tonight I seem even *more* tired than before."

Something struck Romeo about what she had just said. Something wasn't right. As they walked home under the hidden stars and dripping rain, it dawned on Romeo that Queen Elizabeth didn't know *exactly* what had happened to her. Could she actually be thinking she had only lost one life? Is it possible that nobody told her the truth? Or did she just say that because she didn't want to worry him? He had to know, and he had to know then.

"Queen Elizabeth?" Romeo quivered.

She looked up at him without a word.

"What did Mr. Sox tell you about tonight. I mean, well, what did he say?"

Queen Elizabeth looked at him with confused eyes. "What do you mean, Romeo?"

His heart was pounding. "Oh, I was just curious, that's all."

"He told me about the bus and how everyone

Chapter Six

came to my aid. Why?" she questioned again.

Romeo exhaled a very heavy sigh and wondered if he even dare mention it. Certainly she knew. But if she didn't know, it wasn't fair to let her walk around believing she had more lives than she actually did. What kind of a friend would he be if he didn't tell her the truth?

He stopped walking, breathed in some exhaust from a passing taxi cab and gathered up all the strength he could muster.

"Oh no, Queen Elizabeth," he blurted. "You....you....lost *two* lives tonight! Two!"

He looked into her tired, but wise eyes, and for the first time they looked like those of a scared little kitten. She stared at Romeo, then turned away into the rain. It seemed like forever before she turned back again to face him.

"Let's keep going, Romeo. Let's go home." She started walking faster and held her head even lower than before. Romeo wanted to say something more, but he didn't know what. It was a long walk home that night. Queen Elizabeth sniffled to herself the rest of the way.

Once Romeo knew Queen Elizabeth was safely inside Gwen's room, he climbed back up to his home. He and Dennis laid on the couch and watched the evening news under a blanket of potato chips.

".....and tomorrow more of the same. Heavy rain with a chance of lightning," the weatherman said. "More cold temperatures. The fog will be very low so be careful out there. Keep those cats and dogs on a leash, you wouldn't want to lose them."

Dennis gave Romeo a pat on the back.

".....Remember, El Queso is quickly approaching. We are feeling the early stages of its dangerous rampage. For now, hang on to those umbrellas and stay dry."

Over the next few weeks Romeo became one of the most popular cats in his class with the other students, and the teachers as well. Because of all their hard work, Romeo and the other new cats were almost caught up to the older ones. Not only was Romeo very bright and a quick learner, but he really enjoyed going to school. Whereas other cats like Calvin detested it. He continually made snide comments and bragged about his future acting career. Queen Elizabeth was getting back to her old self and adjusting to the idea that she had lost two lives. Initially she was angry with Mr. Sox for not telling her, but after talking to him, she understood his concern. Apparently, he wanted to wait a day until she had regained some of her strength.

After school Romeo, Snickers, and Fluffy enjoyed spending the afternoons together. They would prowl the old, abandoned hallways of the Factory looking for a tasty mouse to gnaw on or go up to Roy and Yellowtail's fish stand for a sumptuous bite. On occasion Tabitha or one of the others would join

Chapter Six

them. They were all quickly becoming good friends. Before the sun set they would usually go home to their people and wind down in front of the TV.

One Friday during class Mr. Shadow went into more detail on a subject which he had only mentioned briefly. He had everyone's rapt attention except Twinkle Toes who was nodding off.

".....It's called Death Alley. You must *never*," emphasis on never, "never go near it! Not even for a second. Do you understand?"

Mr. Shadow looked around the room in the same yellow sweater he wore everyday and stared each cat in the eye until he was sure that his message was heard. Romeo knocked Twinkle Toes in the shoulder because he had fallen asleep and was about to start snoring for the second time that week. Mr. Shadow turned around and pulled out a large paper from his leather bag, unraveling it. He was always bumping into things and dropping stuff on the ground. He had a hard time. He kept jabbing himself in the face with the corner of the paper, plus it kept rerolling back up like a new poster. The students struggled hard not to laugh, though Uncle Fred wasn't so successful. After a moment or so of biting his tongue, he erupted into an annoying guffaw filled with snorts and hiccups. Mr. Shadow ordered him to stop. After two more giggles, he did.

Finally Mr. Shadow got the paper unraveled. He held it backwards so the cats could not see the picture. "What you are about to see is not pretty. Just remember, this could happen to you." He took one bothered look at the paper, then turned it around so that everybody could see. A loud gasp echoed throughout the classroom. Each student stared in horror and disgust at the image. Mr. Shadow walked around the room holding the picture close to each cat for better viewing.

"This photograph," Mr. Shadow explained, "was taken by Waldo last year, but as you can see, it was too late. Notice Skid's eyes..." Mr. Shadow went on to describe in detail what happened to the unfortunate cat in the enlarged photo. Apparently Skid, a Siamese mix, decided to visit Death Alley to prove just how brave he was. Nobody knew exactly what happened to him in there, but when his brothers went looking for him, they found a heap of Skid's bloody hairballs gathered near the entrance. His brothers couldn't see a thing, but heard clanging and some sort of odd howling coming from the fog. They didn't dare go closer, though they could smell the scent of death. Sadly, they found Skid in a nearby trash can in front of the Thai restaurant. His body was viciously turned inside out and had large teeth marks all around it, possibly from some sort of mutant cat. Skid's paws were broken and his jaw was split in two. Waldo was called immediately to photograph the body for study, though nobody ever found out the actual events of the crime. They only knew that Skid went to Death Alley and didn't come out alive. Because of his injuries he lost his last three lives, one hour at a time.

Darla clutched her paw over her mouth and ran for the door. From inside the classroom they could hear her pounding paw steps dash through the library and into the girls' litteroom. The morbid photo of Skid was too much for her little stomach to take. Tabitha ran after her to see if she was all right. The others started to gawk and point at the photo.

"Yuck!" cried Uncle Fred. "That's gross, Mr. Shadow. Didn't you show us that last year too?"

"You would know, old man," Calvin sneered while he filed his claws.

"That is the most disgusting thing I've ever seen, Mr. Shadow," said Snickers. "It reminds me of the time when I was hiding in this old movie house, and this movie named *Monster Murder* came on, and we all were there in the popcorn and..."

Snickers was once again cut off short. Mr. Shadow shot him a nasty look. Snickers sank back into his chair and curled his tail, insulted.

Mr. Shadow walked over to Romeo's desk. Unlike the others, Romeo hadn't said a word about the disturbing photograph. Rather, he just sat there staring at it as though it were someone he knew. His eyes squinted and tightened, never blinking. Something was clicking inside of his little head. Mr. Shadow's years of teaching experience could sense it. He waved his paw in front of Romeo's face to break his stare.

Life One

"Mr. Shadow," Romeo said startled. "W-what's the matter?"

Mr. Shadow looked at him surprised. "What's the matter with *me*? What's the matter with you?"

"What do you mean?"

"Well," Mr. Shadow said as he began to pace around the room, bumping into desks along the way. "You're practically comatose." He sat at his chair and put his paw on the desk. "Tell me, Romeo, how do you feel when you see a picture like this?"

Romeo fussed about in his chair and had that look like he had something important to say. The others waited as Uncle Fred sloppily cleaned his paws with his gritty tongue.

"Stop that, Uncle Fred," Mr. Shadow snapped. "You know better than to do that in class."

"Sorry," Uncle Fred said clueless. He had a mess of fur stuck to his tongue.

"Now tell me, Romeo," Mr. Shadow asked again. "How do you *really* feel? What do you think?"

Romeo stood up from his chair and walked closer to the picture. Tabitha watched him closely as he studied the photo. "Well, Mr. Shadow," he finally began. "This picture makes me sick, not just because it's gross like the others said, but...well, this isn't right, you know?"

Mr. Shadow grinned and said, "Yes, Romeo, I know what you mean, but that's life on the streets. It can be exciting and adventurous, but it can and will often be heartless and cruel. That's just the way it is."

"But what can we do about it?" Romeo asked as he looked out at the other cats.

"Good question, and there's only one answer for that. The only thing we can do is protect ourselves. Educate yourselves about city safety and learn how to look out for one another. This class is merely the first step."

The students sat in silence.

"It's just not fair," Romeo continued. "Isn't there something else we can do?"

Calvin and Twinkle Toes both shook their heads. Darla and Tabitha slowly crept back into the classroom but quickly dashed back out when they saw the photo again.

"Remember, Romeo, *we* are the lucky ones here," Mr. Shadow reminded him. "Lucky in two ways. For one, we cats, unlike the other animals of the world, get nine lives. Everyone else gets only one. Think of Queen Elizabeth and what happened to her the other day."

Romeo dropped his head.

"If she had been anything other than a cat, she would be dead forever now."

"What's the other thing, Mr. Shadow?" Snickers asked.

"Yes, Snickers." Mr. Shadow paused to scratch

under his yellow sweater where the seams touched his fur. "We are lucky because we have homes. Think of the alleys. Why do you think they have become such cold and menacing cats? They *stay* on the streets while we go to warm homes and food." Mr. Shadow began to roll up the ghastly picture.

"But that's not good enough," Romeo whined. "I mean...."

Just then the clock struck ten, and it was time for Mr. Shadow to leave. He grabbed his satchel of odds and ends that he never seemed to use and hurried out the door. He tripped over his tail as he went, but miraculously only dropped his glasses once.

"See you Monday. Oh, and will somebody please remind Tabitha to get her collar back on?" he said as he stumbled through the library.

While the class waited for Mr. Sox to arrive, Uncle Fred went back to licking his paws, Tabitha re-entered and stared in Romeo's direction. Romeo's eyes wandered to the far corners of the room as his mind went somewhere else. What Romeo didn't see up in those corners was a tiny, hidden crack along the part of the wall that met the ceiling, and just beyond it were two glowing green eyes and one very large pair of healthy ears. This cat was no stick, it was an alley. And he was where he didn't belong.

Chapter Seven

The green eyes were attached to Bait, who snuck in from the roof. He had found a small area that was strong enough to support his lanky body and allowed him to climb down the shafts to the second floor. A tall, twisted nearby tree provided him the height he needed to make the leap. Only a skilled jumping cat could survive such a distance. Bait was just that cat. Waffles didn't see him.

Feeling satisfied with his earful, Bait slithered back up the pipes and beams and slipped out of a fourth floor window making sure no one was watching. Then, he snuck out of sight.

In ten minutes he made it all the way to Smelly's Bar at 56th and 11th. There he found Fidel waiting patiently for his arrival.

Fidel sat at the third stool, always the third

stool, and chugged his stale beer. His pack of followers, the silent five, sat slouched in their seats at a far-off table. Smelly rubbed his own thick stomach and burped loud enough to scatter a large family of roaches hiding under the bar. In the dingy back corner Thumbs played circus tunes that nobody bothered to notice.

Bait had a stupid grin on his face like a snotty little girl who just stole the neighbor's doll. He crawled up to Fidel and put his paw on the bar for Smelly to see.

"Hey, Smelly," Bait said to his fat friend. "Gimme a beer!" Bait kept his eyes on Fidel who pounded a beer in one dangerous gulp.

Smelly poured Bait a heaping serving of foam and slapped it on the bar, causing it to splash in Bait's face. Smelly didn't care. Neither did Bait. He would enjoy licking it off later.

Fidel, who didn't appear to be in a particularly good mood, turned to face him. As he did, the red leather of his bar stool made funny, farting noises. Bait laughed.

"Shut up!" snapped Fidel.

Bait shut his mouth faster than a mouse trap. His eyes grew wide, and he seemed to shrink in his seat.

Fidel slid his beer mug away with his grubby right paw and fixed his eyes on Bait. He got close enough to be smelled and asked with a low voice,

Chapter Seven

Life One

"So, Bait, tell me, what's going on out *there* today? Any interesting...news to report?" He drummed his jagged nails on his stolen ID tags.

Bait took a small sip of his brew and answered. "Not really, just little things. I saw two birds die today 'cause some kid ran over 'em *on purpose* with his bike. It was really cool." He started laughing in a very high pitch. Fidel slapped his paw against the bar and Bait continued. "Okay, uh...I found a new mouse hole for you to invade. And I got into da Factory again." He took another sip of his drink using both paws and stared at the bubbles.

Fidel choked. "What? You went to the *Factory*? Without telling *me*? Are you crazy?" He reached over the bar knocking off both mugs and grabbed Bait tightly by the skin of his neck. Smelly stepped back, and Thumbs started playing faster.

"D-d-d-don't worry, boss," Bait quivered. "Nobody s-saw me. Honest, they didn't."

Fidel tightened his grip and then let go. He sat back and calmly flattened the hairs on his head. "Are you sure?" he added as his angry eyes began to follow a passing fly.

"Yes, yes, boss. I went in through the roof, like last time. Nobody saw a thing. *Stu*pid sticks."

"Fine, fine," Fidel said annoyed. "Just tell me what you saw, and make it quick. I got *stuff* to do."

Bait looked over at Smelly who was licking the spilled beer off the bar. As unclean as he himself was, he found the whole idea a tad disturbing to watch. "Anyway," Bait continued, staring at the slobbering tongue, "there was nothing strange going on there, just a bunch of idiots sittin' around readin', you know. Oh, but, there was this *one* cat..." He paused.

Fidel nudged, "Well? What about this *cat*?"

"Oh, yeah. Anyway, he was sitting in that dumb school room, and they was all lookin' at pictures of Skid. You remember Skid?" He looked over at Smelly, and they both started to laugh. Fidel sat waiting with an agitated look in his eye. "Okay, so there was this one cat and he seemed, you know, anxious."

"Anxious for what?" Fidel said as he plucked broken wings off of the screaming fly.

"Anxious to...I don't know, maybe he was just weird or somethin'," Bait added. "Dat must be it."

Fidel bit off the fly's head. "Will he be a problem for us?"

"I don't think so. Naw, he's harmless. He's just some stupid kid. His name is Romeo. I've seen him once before with Queen Elizabeth."

An evil grin slapped across Fidel's face. "Oh yes," he nodded. "Of course, I remember her." Fidel rubbed his greasy paws together.

Just then another cat entered the bar. It was dark near the entrance. In fact, the entire place was very dark. As the door opened, a slight hint of neon light from a nearby shoe shop illuminated the curvaceous shape of a cat that Fidel had been expecting. He put down his beer mug and slinked up to the door. "Raven," Fidel said with deep penetrating eyes. "Right on time."

Raven looked up at Fidel with the same probing look. She stood perfectly framed in the doorway. She was a black cat, head to toe, and walked with the kind of strut that turned heads. Her big yellow eyes were hypnotizing, like the swirly things at the fun house. Her neck was draped in stolen pearls, and she had a piece of stark white fur wrapped around her shoulders. Her claws were stained a deep red, and they were sharp like needles. "Hello, Fidel," she sighed.

"Are you ready?" Fidel asked, catching a whiff of her intoxicating scent.

She nodded with a nasty wink. Fidel stood next to her like a magnet. He put his tail on her back and the two headed out the door. Raven never took either of her bewitching eyes off of her male. They were almost out of sight when Fidel turned around.

"Oh, Bait," Fidel said. "Keep an eye out for that new kid, will ya?"

Bait raised his mug and shook his head yes. Fidel and Raven were out the door.

Back at Stick School, Mr. Sox had just finished a long lecture on the history of war. He focused primarily on the people's war that had occurred during Carnival's time. Most of the cats seemed mildly interested, except for a few snoozers like Uncle Fred and Calvin. Snickers was busy eating the pastries Darla brought from the bakery. And Darla spent the morning peeing in the litteroom.

As for Calvin, his mind was busy thinking about the coming afternoon. It promised to be a glorious one for him, one that he had dreamed of for weeks. His first audition. Yes, Calvin finally had an audition. All that grooming really did pay off. The audition was for a commercial for a new brand of whiskey. Calvin, of course, was auditioning for the part of the cat. He would race home after school and wait for Lloyd.

But now, Calvin sat at his desk in the Factory and dreamed of being a star. He would be worshipped. Roy and Yellowtail would give him the best fish scraps. Old Mr. Sox wouldn't bother him with homework. Even the alleys would bow graciously as he walked by, shielding him from the rain with large golden umbrellas. Glitter would magically sprout from his head and everybody would shout, "Hey, wasn't that Calvin, the famous star, that just passed by?" Oh, how he dreamed himself silly. In fact, he didn't even notice that school had ended because he was so busy gazing out into space. Snickers smacked him on his head and back to reality.

Calvin raced downstairs, flew passed Vittles' and Waffles' heavily chained doors and headed straight for Lloyd's apartment. It was a long twenty blocks away down 54th Street. He knew he could make it quickly, but not by walking. He would have to hurry and catch the Number 477 bus. Its 11:05 stop was at the corner only three blocks from the Factory.

Calvin ran and ran tossing mud and street rubbish as he went. He dodged his way between baby strollers and rickety, old wheelchairs. He ran so fast he actually slid on a bruised banana peel and skidded down the 54th Street sidewalk. Up ahead an elderly woman was coming the other way. In her arms were two stuffed grocery bags blocking her view. Calvin turned and twisted his body, but it was no use. As he continued to slide on the rotten fruit, he braced himself for what would surely be a disaster. He threw his future-star paws up over his eyes as he plowed butt-first into the woman. She let out a howling scream as she went flying into the air. Even higher went her carton of milk and orthopedic shoes. Calvin dashed on never looking back, though he heard all sorts of angry sounds coming from underneath the mound of groceries. He huffed and puffed his way through the lunch crowd finally nearing the corner of 54th and 10th.

"What's with that cat?" he heard someone call from across the street.

Calvin was only feet away from the bus, and he could already see its enormous wheels beginning to turn away from the curb. The exhaust pipe spit out buckets of its noxious fumes as the driver slowly began to pull away. Calvin, desperate to get to that bus, sprung from his back paws toward it and grabbed onto whatever he came in contact with.

Calvin could feel that his body was on the bus, though he didn't know where. The wind was rushing and slapping through every little hair on his body. It seemed as though the bus was flying faster than an airplane. Once he realized that his paws were secure, he slowly opened his eyes afraid of what he might see. To his dismay, he found himself in a much different place than he imagined. He hoped to be near the bottom of the bus, at least that is what he aimed for. That's where all the cats go when they take the bus. However, his paws were clutched tightly to the bottom edge of one of the windows. They were beginning to slip from the slick grease that clung to the sides of the bus. Yet, there he dangled only inches away from the cold glass. Behind it, face to face, was a very fat, confused woman with far too much make-up and crusty chocolate stains on her lips. Calvin couldn't hear, but he could tell she was screaming. Her mouth was as wide as the window.

On they went down the street, Calvin hanging on for dear life. He could see his stop approaching by the time the bus driver noticed what was going on. With all his might, Calvin flung himself off the bus as it began to slow down. The people inside continued to scream and point. But Calvin was safe as he sped off toward his building. His front legs were awfully tired and cramped, yet he wasn't going to stop now.

After a few more steps, he made it. He was facing Lloyd's apartment. Lloyd lived high up on the sixth floor in apartment 6Z. It would take him some energy to get up there. He followed his usual route up the vines and shrubs and fire escape ladders until he finally reached the balcony of the sixth floor. The bathroom window was open. It was always open allowing Calvin to come and go, though Lloyd had no idea where he went all day.

Calvin crawled inside with a few minutes to spare. He helped himself to a slurp of foggy water from the rusted tin can on the floor under the kitchen counter. Unfortunately, there was no food in his bowl or his stomach. He couldn't go to an audition hungry. How would he concentrate? Luckily, as he was wandering about his apartment wondering how to fix his fur attractively, he heard a scurrying sound from around the corner. He looked, and yes, he was right, a meaty roach was making its way over to a divine looking bread crumb on the floor. Calvin dashed out with the little ounce of energy he had left from the bus ride and got the roach in one whack. One by one he pealed its legs off before taking a big chunk out of his crunchy exoskeleton. When finished, he licked his own sticky paws and ate the bread crumb for dessert.

By the time Lloyd got home Calvin had given

Chapter Seven

himself a clean bath and even found time to take a short nap.

"Hey there, sport," Lloyd greeted. "Today's the big day."

"Meow," Calvin replied.

In his dusty overalls, Lloyd knelt down to Calvin and said, "You have no idea what I'm talking about, do you, *Calvinator*?"

Calvin, of course, couldn't let on that he did, so he did what every cat does, he gave him a blank, stupid look. Lloyd smiled and petted him on the head.

Lloyd was an actor as well, at least he tried to be. The city was loaded with theaters, mostly old, but some new. The older ones were dark and haunting and filled with memories of the bygone days. Actors like himself dreamed of making it on the big stage under the blazing lights. However, the theater didn't romanticize about Lloyd the way he romanticized about it. The only theater job he ever got was removing coffee smudges and ink blots from scripts. He got fired for tap dancing on stage when nobody else seemed to be around. His curtain hadn't opened yet, though he had all the hope in the world that someday it would.

Quite frankly, Lloyd was not even that talented, not many actors were, and some said he was too old. At forty-five and scraggly looking with a silly, little moustache, Lloyd still tried and tried, taking acting

Life One

classes and workshops after his shift at the subway station. After he got fired from the theater, he took a job cleaning the stuff off the tracks. As he crouched down day after day at the dirty station, he dreamed of the time he'd at least have a famous cat. Everyone would want to know who its owner was. If Lloyd couldn't make it, Calvin would be his ticket to stardom.

Lloyd took a sip, or rather a bite, from his tar-thick coffee and put Calvin in his dreaded cat carrier. The carrier completely insulted Calvin's pride and dignity, yet under the circumstances he went in without much of a fight. With barely a smidge of room to move around, he gnawed on the torn towel Lloyd had thrown inside. He only hoped that he wouldn't see any other cats he knew.

Moments later they were in a cab being driven by a half-balding, older, foreign, taxi driver who was covered in more muck than the exhaust pipe on bus 477. Lloyd put Calvin above the back seat allowing him to look out the window at the afternoon city. There, Calvin could see a pack of dogs walking by. They looked tough and mean. The small one in front had a stiff scowl. He wondered if those were the dogs Mr. Sox had warned him about.

Soon they reached their destination. Lloyd paid the cab fare leaving the driver a very stingy tip. They entered the building on 8th Street through the two large front doors, aided by a huge gust of wind that kicked them inside.

The deranged security guard with half a mouthful of teeth directed them up the elevator and down a long hallway. Calvin noticed some hanging spider webs through the bars of his carrier and some zapping light bulbs. At the end of the hall, Lloyd carried Calvin into a big, mildewy room. The furniture looked very old, almost antique, but hardly valuable. One large desk was in the center, and behind it sat a skinny, pale-faced woman about thirty years of age. Lloyd exchanged a few words with her and was given a small stack of white papers and a pen. Then, he and Calvin sat in one of the mustier chairs. Lloyd wrote all kinds of things on the papers as Calvin looked out from the metal bars at his competition. Like Calvin, they all sat scrunched in their cages. It was a meager crowd of hopefuls, about ten or so. One of them looked far too young, another too scrawny, but most of them just looked big and dumb. Certainly, not a one seemed to be a match for Calvin.

He's a fat one, Calvin thought to himself while looking at one of the felines. He noticed some of the others looking at him. He was sure they felt threatened by his good looks, but didn't care. In fact, the longer Calvin studied these cats, the higher his confidence grew. It was certain that no one else had star quality like he did.

Feeling calm and relaxed, Calvin sat back in his carrier and imagined himself smoking a fine cigar,

Life One

allowing the sweet aroma to fill his cage.

"This one's in the bag," he whispered to himself full of vanity.

Just as the audition process got started, the front entrance door opened. Calvin sat up straight to get a glimpse of who was coming in. Probably another loser. Calvin couldn't see the cat very clearly because the new guy's carrier was turned sideways. Unlike Calvin's, it was lined with diamonds and painted gold. On the box was also stuck a piece of perfect tape. There was writing on it. Calvin knew the letters. They were, *T-H-E-O-D-O-R-E, J-R. #3*. It was being carried by a pretty woman, short and young. She sat on the opposite side of the room. The carrier turned, and Calvin took a long hard look. He felt his heart drop to the floor. Inside sat the most dapper and suave cat you ever did see. He sat even taller than Calvin and brighter than a bowl of fresh cherries. His neon white fur glistened, as did his eyes which didn't even bother to look around the room. Immediately, a light bulb went on in Calvin's squashed head. He recognized this cat. He was the cat from the Kitty Fresh Pee Remover Kits that were so hot in the city. He was the cat in the commercial who was always filmed relieving himself in odd places.

Why don't you go home and give somebody else a chance? Calvin thought in his head. His cocky grin turned to a grimace. He could feel his stomach tighten and his tail curl up. Yet, being the professional actor that he was, he kept his composure and showed no outward signs of jealously towards this infamous cat.

Calvin slowly moved to the back of his cage and laid down with a long sigh. Every time he looked at that cat, he rolled his eyes.

Suddenly, the thin, pale woman from behind the desk stood up and spoke. "Theo, Jr.?" she announced. Her eyes wandered about the room until *you know who* got up. She led the little prodigy and his person beyond yet another door where they didn't come out for ten whole minutes. Why did *he* get to go first?

After ten more cats did the same thing, Calvin and Lloyd, now alone in the cramped waiting room, were finally called.

"Right this way, please," said the woman.

She led Calvin and Lloyd through the second door with hardly a smile. Through that door was yet another room, smaller than the first. It was somebody's office, and it was filled with deep brown furniture and a terrible, purple, leather couch. Near the back of the room was a large desk beneath a heap of papers and pens. The pictures of all the other cats sat on this desk, Calvin's being on the top. Calvin noticed that off to the far right the Pee Remover cat's picture sat alone. Behind the desk was not one, but two rather large, heavy set men. They looked alike, perhaps twins. They both had thick, rough beards, wirey mustaches, and different patterns of moles around their faces. They shook sweaty hands with Lloyd and all sat down.

"Take him out of there, please," one of them said to Lloyd with a deep sounding voice.

Calvin was turned upside down and dumped out of his cage. He sat on the desk among all the pictures and papers. He could see strands of the other cats' fur sprinkled about. Calvin figured they must have shed from nervousness, perhaps even the famous guy.

Calvin wasn't nervous, not one bit. He just lay there and allowed the men to pick and probe at him. They held him like an old rag doll, flopping him this way and that. They inspected every inch of his body, not something Calvin was a fan of. He began to feel like he was at the vet. Calvin's instincts were telling him to hiss, but he dared not if he wanted that job.

"Can he sit still for long periods of time?" one of them asked.

What a silly question.

"Of course he can," Lloyd said proudly. "He can do just about anything you ask him to do."

"All right," said the other man. He put his big hands on his hips and whispered something to his partner. They looked back at Lloyd, then at Calvin. "Thank you, that will be all."

After that was said the men didn't look up at Lloyd again. Lloyd put on a phony smile and stretched out his hand to shake, but they didn't notice. They were too busy mumbling something to each other. Lloyd saw them mix Calvin's picture in the pile with the other cats and pick up the one of Theodore. Lloyd dropped his head and quickly put Calvin back in the carrier. He walked slowly to the door and looked back as if to say something. But when he saw them engrossed in a conversation over Theodore's picture, he turned away and left.

The taxi cab ride home was a somber one. Lloyd didn't say a word, except to tell the driver where to go. He seemed real sad, like he knew that this audition was a failure, just like all of his. This time he tipped the driver even less. He and Calvin climbed upstairs to their dreary apartment and went to bed.

The next day at Stick School, Calvin didn't talk much. The others took notice, but rather than question him, they simply enjoyed it.

Everyone noticed that Tabitha was late that morning, except for Darla who was held up in the litteroom. Tabitha finally crept in having missed Ms. Purrpurr's entire hour. She looked haggard and dirty. Tiny crunchy leaves were stuck to her pretty yellow fur and she smelled horrid. Mr. Shadow gave her a funny look as she snuck in. She shyly sat down at her seat never once taking her eyes from her peering teacher.

Mr. Shadow interrupted his lecture on mouse

catching to speak to Tabitha. He walked over to her, still in his yellow knit sweater, and scolded, "Tabitha, why are you late?"

She looked up from her desk with tears in her eyes.

"Tabitha?" he said again. All the other cats waited in the thick, tense atmosphere for Tabitha's response.

She finally wiped her watery eyes and spoke softly. "I was walking here and....I thought I saw *Them*, so I..."

"Them?" Mr. Shadow said as he stumbled over a piece of chalk. "Who is Them?"

Tabitha took a deep breath and continued. "The Pound, sir. I thought I saw the Pound."

Mr. Shadow had a disappointed look in his eyes. He sat down on his back paws and took off his glasses.

Tabitha went on. "I got scared, so I hid in an alley. Only that was even scarier. I didn't know what to do. Then, I heard noises." Looking frightened and shaken, she glanced around the classroom at the other cats, "I jumped into a garbage can, but it was filled with rats, so many rats. I climbed out, and when I looked, the gray van was gone. That's when I ran here." She looked immediately at Romeo. He gave her a smile and a nod.

"Tabitha, do you realize what could have happened to you?" Mr. Shadow asked. "You obviously forgot everything you've been taught."

She nodded her head humiliated.

Mr. Shadow took his front left paw and lifted up her chin. "Just as I thought, young lady," he scowled again. "No collar. You may as well stand in the street and hold up a sign that says, '*TAKE ME TO THE POUND.*' Is that what you want? Huh? Do you? *Do you?*"

He kept probing and probing her until she finally burst into a million tears. She dashed out of the room and flew onto a couch in the library. Romeo remembered how she had helped him during the Queen Elizabeth ordeal and ran after her. He found her sobbing on top of a copy of *Hamlet*. He managed to calm her down.

"He's just looking out for you, Tabitha. We all want you to be safe."

"I know, I know," she whimpered.

The two cats returned to class and managed to carry on the rest of the day. The fact of the matter was, Mr. Shadow had every right to be angry at her. If she didn't get a collar, she surely would get picked up by the Pound. It was only a matter of time.

Chapter Eight

Romeo and Fluffy met up with Queen Elizabeth after school. The plan was to find a tasty lunch and walk around the city. Although he had seen a lot of the city already, there were still many places that Romeo had yet to go.

Patiently they waited for Queen Elizabeth down in the recreation room. Some other cats were there chatting and listening to loud music to mask the sound of thunder coming from outside. Calvin was sitting alone in the corner strumming on a toy ukelele, though it had only one string.

"Hey Calvin," said Romeo, "what's wrong?" Romeo walked over to him and sat down. Fluffy didn't bother. He waited by the door.

Calvin had a sad look on his face, one Romeo was not used to seeing. Calvin looked up from his ukelele and sighed, "Oh, it's nothing."

"Are you sure?" Romeo asked.

"Yes, you wouldn't understand. Artists like myself have our ups and downs. Today just happens to be a down. Please go away."

"Yeah, sure, whatever," Romeo said as he walked away.

Queen Elizabeth, Romeo, and Fluffy all set out for an afternoon journey. After leaving the Factory they headed south to some prime mouse catching locations.

Along the way, the streets were filled with people and their stomping feet who rushed down the slick sidewalks holding umbrellas high above their heads. The speedy winds pushed them along whistling an eerie tune. As for the cats, Queen Elizabeth carefully took the lead.

"Look out for the buses," she warned with a shudder. "Sometimes they speed up."

She led them down the crowded sidewalk to a place with a large blue sign out front. It was a little farther than some of the other places, but well worth the walk. Romeo could almost read it thanks to his work in Ms. Purrpurr's class. It said: *Mo's Eats.* Mo's was a greasy diner and according to Queen Elizabeth, attracted many plump mice. They came for the leftover ham that the chefs tossed out the back door.

"I've had some great times here," Queen Elizabeth smiled looking up at the big blue sign. "Come on, I'll show you the way."

She led them around the side of the cafe. It was on the corner of the block, but not at an alley. Romeo inspected the building from the sidewalk. They had to be careful not to bother the people inside. They wouldn't want the boss calling the Pound on them.

The cafe had big windows on all sides, though some were cracked or taped up. It was a small place, for people that is. There were about twenty or so orange vinyl booths with little bits of stuffing poking out of the tears. Fluffy climbed on top of a garbage can that had double its size in garbage. From there he could see the hot grill and its sweaty cook flipping and tossing meat the same color as the sign outside. Romeo's nose quickly found the delicious trail of smells that poured from the diner door. As good as mice were, and they were quite tasty, there was something to be said for *cooked* food.

Romeo and Fluffy were getting hungrier and hungrier. Their tongues hung low and they started to drool over the wet concrete. While Queen Elizabeth searched for the mouse hole she once dined at, Fluffy and Romeo continued to stare in the windows at all the people. They were eating huge portions of stuff they didn't recognize, though it looked yummy just the same. The waiters were hustling around here and there and flopping heaping plates down in front of the customers. Fluffy warned Romeo not to get too close to the window, but he didn't listen. Rather, he lifted himself up on a cinder block and with the help of his front paws pressed his nose right up against the glass. A big, angry man with ketchup all over his mouth hit the glass hard with his fist.

"Get away, cat!" he said through the window. "Scram!"

Romeo hissed and leapt down. He hid behind Queen Elizabeth and shook nervously.

"Romeo," she said disappointed, "if you're going to get all scared over something like that, then you have no business being out here on the streets. You may as well sit inside all day with Dennis. Is that what you want?"

Romeo lowered his head and frowned. He stepped away from Queen Elizabeth embarrassed. "No, I guess I just got a little nervous, that's all."

"Come on, Romeo," Fluffy said pulling his ear. "Let's wait over here."

The two students moved away from the windows and waited again for Queen Elizabeth. Romeo sat patiently. His eyes followed a gray cloud as it sunk lower and lower into the city.

"Here it is," Queen Elizabeth said with her head stuck behind a potato crate. "They're in here."

Romeo could hear his own stomach growl. He wondered if anybody else could. Fluffy didn't. He was concentrating on something else. He had heard a frightful rattle coming from behind him. He thought he heard footsteps and chains too. Alarmed, Fluffy stood frozen and waited for the sound to go away. It didn't. Romeo was too busy watching Queen Elizabeth shoving her front paws into the wall to notice. Fluffy heard the noise again, only this time it was louder and more disturbing. He was afraid to turn around and face the awful noise, though he knew he should. With every moment that passed, the rumble grew closer and closer. He tried to call out to Queen Elizabeth but his mouth wouldn't allow it.

"Q-Q-Q-Q-ueeeeeeen...," he stumbled. "Queeeee..."

He struggled to get Romeo's attention, but Romeo had now moved closer to Queen Elizabeth. Fluffy started throwing things their way. That didn't do any good either.

"What are you doing?" Romeo asked throwing back the rock which Fluffy threw at him.

With only seconds to spare, Fluffy took a deep breath and screamed with all his might, "Queen Elizabeth!!!"

Startled, she whipped around. She removed her right paw from the mouse hole. Romeo saw a long tail go scurrying back in. Queen Elizabeth stared right at Fluffy.

"What is it?" she barked annoyed. "You just made me lose a perfectly good....." Her voice trailed off and so did her eyes. She stepped away from the potato crate and gazed in shock at what she saw in the distance. It was a rolling thunder cloud of dust a few

Chapter Eight

doors down. At the center was one of the most horrifying, gruesome sights a cat could ever see. "Dogs!" she screamed. "Run! Let's go!!!"

In a flash, the three cats dashed away from the diner along with their hopes of catching mice. Fluffy didn't look back, neither did Romeo. Queen Elizabeth led the race in perfect stride. She sped off like a winning horse on a track, fast and with purpose. She panted and panted so hard that her chest began to hurt. When she looked back, she saw them. Five or six big, heavy dogs. The leader seemed to be the small one with a scrunched up face. Queen Elizabeth figured he was Bull, the mad bulldog. The dogs zoomed after the cats down the sidewalks, weaving through the scurrying feet. They were on a mission.

With a giant leapt, Queen Elizabeth called back as loud as she could, "Whatever you do, don't go into the alleys!" Fluffy heard her, though Romeo did not.

Romeo was the slowest runner, leaving him the closest to the dogs. His little paws tried with all their might, but they were no match for the big, burly hounds who were quickly approaching.

Queen Elizabeth shouted again but it was no use. Romeo couldn't hear her because of the distance between them and the fact that all the people in their path were screaming and shouting at the action below their knees.

The faster the cats ran, the closer the dogs got. Romeo was trailing far behind and becoming

 130

more and more scared. His little heart was pounding louder and louder. With the dogs now only feet away, he quickly darted off to the right hoping to trick them. However, when he did so, he ran right into a dark alley. Queen Elizabeth turned around and saw what had happened. Fluffy continued to run forward.

"Nooo!" cried Queen Elizabeth, watching in horror as Romeo disappeared into the darkness. Instantly she dashed toward to him, forgetting all about Fluffy.

Bull and his pack ran forward, then suddenly stopped. They turned and headed for Romeo. Six angry dogs against one small cat was just what they wanted. Especially in the confines of a narrow alley.

Romeo had not even a single second to decide what to do next. He stopped briefly and found himself in the darkest place he had ever seen. Even his keen feline vision couldn't penetrate through the thick haze that filled the corridor.

He could hear the dogs nearing the alley entrance. Standing in the blackness, he quickly thought of a plan. It was like being blind. He could only hear what was around him, and he didn't like it. Squeaky noises, like big rats echoed through the walls. He heard the jolting crash of a garbage can being knocked over. Then more scratching and clawing sounds. Whoever or *what*ever it was scurried around like a disease. Romeo's body was twisting

131

this way and that as he grew more and more paranoid. To make matters worse, the alley smelled awful. Suddenly, a bolt of lightening shot across the sky illuminating the fog for a brief moment. What Romeo saw, he'll never forget. Aside from all the garbage and empty boxes, he swore he saw three cats, all dead, laying with their eyes staring wide open. The pupils were neon green and beginning to rot into the skulls that housed them. He immediately felt queasy and nauseous. Instinctively, he pulled himself together. He had to hide, and he had to do it fast. The barking was only feet away. He could almost feel the breath of the dogs against his neck. They were now in the alley using their keen sense of smell to find their prey.

When the lightening flashed, Romeo caught a quick glimpse of the corner of the alley. There was a small opening in the bricks. It was his only chance. He raced over to it trying not to think of the bodies that lay around him, though the horrible stench reminded him anyway.

In the darkness Romeo felt the hole with his paws, and though filled with fright, he climbed inside.

"Romeo!" Queen Elizabeth yelled "Romeo! Romeo!!"

Her voice was too far away. Romeo knew she wouldn't find him. Besides, he didn't want her to risk losing a life at the rage of the dogs. She had already been through enough.

 132

Life One

Romeo nestled himself in the tiny opening of the wall. It was a small, musty space with huge wooden beams. Long strands of dangling spider webs hit his face and got in his mouth. He couldn't bring himself to look around, scared of what he might find. He heard an eerie dripping, probably the rain, and the howls and growls of the advancing angry pack.

Then, silence. No more howls. No more growls. Romeo didn't hear a thing. He thought for a moment about what to do. He hoped and believed that perhaps the dogs gave up and left. He did it! He really outsmarted the dogs!

Romeo waited a few more long seconds before making his way back out into the creepy alley. In his head he tried to imagine where he saw those decaying cats. He didn't want to step near them.

Up above, the thunder continued to roll and the hazy afternoon sun was quickly covered by a blanket of clouds. Romeo sniffed his way around in the hole and stuck his left paw far out of the entry. He felt the ground in front of him. It was cold and slick. Slowly, he began to inch his way out. All around him were soggy boxes and other big, empty, rusted containers of beans and stuff like that.

After his paw, Romeo stuck out his nose until he had his entire head out of the hole. He still was unable to see anything because of the ghostly fog. As startling as it was, he was hoping for another explosion of lightning to brighten his way. He only hoped that Queen Elizabeth was all right and still waiting for him. Fluffy too.

In one final heave, Romeo completely stepped out of the chamber he was in. Suddenly he heard a noise. It was different and unexpected and almost sounded like breathing, heavy breathing. Romeo stood frozen and confused. He listened again. The breathing grew deeper.

"What is that?" he thought.

Just then, another neon bolt of lightning flashed over the city illuminating the entire alley. For one fraction of a second he saw what was before him. A virtual wall of dogs surrounded him on all sides. They were different sizes and colors and kinds, but all monsters just the same. Some of them had bloody knees or spiked collars. All had the same scowls. Their teeth were dirty and sharp, and they drooled violently. Their eyes were like piercing red beams. They crouched down in attack mode as they waited for Romeo's next move. Beyond petrified, Romeo barely had enough time to think. Instinctively, he began to back away into the hole he had just come out of. As he did, the breathing and wheezing only moved closer.

"This is it!" Romeo thought. "Life one over!"

Bull was the ugliest and the smallest, not much bigger than a fat cat, but he was the cruelest. He had a reputation for committing unspeakable, ghastly crimes against all cats and birds.

 134

Life One

Chapter Eight

Romeo's whole body shook like mad, and he wanted to scream and cry. Though he couldn't see them, he clearly could sense the enormity of the pack around him. For the first time he felt like an insignificant nothing in this huge, strange city. Yet, he picked up the pace and struggled to get back into the hole. At first he couldn't find it. The dogs watched with evil delight as Romeo shoved his butt into one of the bean cans. Finally, his back paws found the opening in the wall just as Bull lunged forward with a nasty growl. He landed on his two front paws right in front of the hole. Romeo scurried back trying to get as far in as he could. He stuffed his body through the jagged bricks and sticky spider webs. Once in, he quickly came to a dead end, a big wooden plank blocking his way. He was only inches passed the opening, surely not far enough away to be safe.

From outside he could hear the angry grunts of the dogs. He now could smell their breath coming into the hole. It sent a shiver through Romeo's body. Those dogs were too big to crawl inside, but smart enough to know Romeo had to come out sometime.

Romeo sat there shivering, wishing he was back with Dennis. He prayed for Bubastis to come to his rescue. Then, a frightful thing happened. Romeo felt a strong, fierce paw reaching for him in the hole. One of the dogs was trying to pull him out. With nowhere to move, Romeo whined and cried, curling himself up in the smallest ball he could. His fur

 136

was standing straight up on end giving him a cold, tingling feeling. The sharp paw was getting closer and closer. It swatted a few times, grazing Romeo's young flesh. Though he couldn't see it, he could feel his own blood spouting out from his neck. It stung like fire.

Outside the dogs were getting more and more excited. They started jumping back and forth as they waited impatiently. Then the dog's paw stopped flailing around and clenched onto Romeo's back. It held on tight, digging deeper and deeper, strangling his skin. Romeo let out a yelp, though it was no use. The powerful dog pulled with all his might. He pulled Romeo completely out of the hole. Romeo's little body was putting up a valiant fight, but the dog was far too strong for him.

The dog held Romeo high in the air for the longest second of Romeo's life. Another bolt of lightning struck, and Romeo saw his destiny. In that flash, from above the dogs he saw that his captor was the little one, Bull. All of the other dogs were howling and laughing, their mouths revealing sets of the most painful looking jaws and teeth. The look in the little one's eyes was like looking directly into hell. The lightning stopped and Romeo felt himself being lowered. He continued to whimper and whine though it was no use.

"We've got you now, pretty boy," Bull growled. "Did you think you could get away from us?"

Chapter Eight

"Please, please!" Romeo begged. "Let me go!" He squirmed and fought like the mouse that Fidel tortured at Smelly's.

The other dogs laughed with a sinister enjoyment.

"What are we going to do first, Bull?" one of the others called out.

"Can we skin him, huh? Can we?" another muttered in the dark.

Romeo stuck out his claws and hissed until his little throat hurt.

"Good work, Bull," one of the larger ones yelled as the rain poured over his head. "As always, you got'm."

Bull lowered Romeo to the hungry, waiting dogs. They cheered and howled as Romeo's pathetic, helpless paws drew closer to them. Romeo gave up on his hissing. It was only making them laugh more and more. Bull, however, never laughed. He looked determined and serious. Just as Romeo was inches away from being tossed into the center of all the dogs, his body gave up. His eyes rolled back into his head, and he fainted. His lifeless body hung in the fearsome clutches of Bull. This only made the dogs more pleased. Now the fun could really begin.

First, they tossed him around like a rag doll, back and forth to one another. Then, Bull put him on the ground and began to drag him around the alley to the cheers of the others.

 138

Life One

"What to do now?" Bull said sarcastically. "Stick-on-a-stick anyone?"

"Yeah!" the dogs roared with evil delight.

They all moved in closer and huddled around Bull, watching in admiration as he held Romeo down. Bull raised his right paw and extended his claws as much as possible. His face had a monstrous grin. Just as his paw was about to come slicing down, a loud, sinister sound was heard from above. Bull kept his killing paw high in the air as he turned his scrunched face to see what it was. The other dogs looked up as well. The lightning flashed. Bull could not believe what he saw. It was Fluffy. He was standing high atop the building with a nasty look on his face. His eye's were glowing yellow and filled with rage. Bull roared with warning, still holding Romeo to the cold ground.

"What are you going to do, *cat*?" shouted one of the bigger dogs.

Fluffy looked down at the mob from that third story roof and hollered, "Take this you *vile* creatures!!"

Fluffy reached over and pushed container after container of thick, sticky tar over the edge. Apparently some roofers had left it there. The tar came crashing down in a violent mess covering the dogs completely. They started yelping and gasping from the fumes. As they did, the tar seeped into their mouths and blinded their eyes. Fluffy continued to pour gallon after gallon. His rage fueled the strength within him that he needed to turn over the heavy tubs. After a few moments, he looked down.

Through the haze and gloom he saw the dogs dripping in tar and disoriented. They no longer seemed fierce and angry. Their gooey bodies looked skinny and frail. In fact, they looked pathetic. One at a time the dogs scurried out of the alley and down the long street. People jumped out of their way scared of getting dirty or bitten.

Once all the dogs had cleared away, one lone body still lay on the alley floor. It was Romeo, and he was hit the hardest from the tar. Because he had fainted, he lay unaware of what had just happened. Fluffy couldn't tell from the roof if he was alive or dead. He turned around and was startled to find Queen Elizabeth standing behind him. She looked shaken, but moved.

"That was a brave thing you just did, Fluffy," she whispered. "They would have surely killed him, possibly several times."

Hesitantly, she stepped up to Fluffy and nestled him in her fur. She let out a few tears and purred. Fluffy gave her a gentle lick on the top of her head.

Then Fluffy blurted, "Come on! We must get Romeo before they come back."

Queen Elizabeth nodded in agreement.

Quickly they crept down the side of the building to the alley floor. The dead cats Romeo had seen earlier were buried under inches of heavy tar, except one. At the last minute he was taken as a souvenir by one of the more morbid dogs.

Fluffy and Queen Elizabeth hurriedly found Romeo. He was near the back wall.

Carefully Queen Elizabeth approached him. She was afraid that he had lost a life. At his young age it would surely be a tragedy. From what she could see through the fog, he was beaten up pretty badly. She felt awfully sorry for him and mad at herself for taking him so far from the Factory.

On close inspection Romeo was a most ghostly sight. His sad, little body was bloodied and shivering. His beautiful fur was a mess, and some of it had been torn off. A tear ran down Queen Elizabeth's face. Gently she scooped some of the tar away from Romeo's eyes and nose. She put her paw to his chest to see if he was breathing. Fluffy waited nervously a few feet back.

"He's alive!" she said relieved. "Oh, Romeo, you're alive!"

Together Fluffy and Queen Elizabeth cleaned off Romeo as best they could. The tar could not be licked off because the fumes were so toxic. Fluffy found an old t-shirt behind a box and used it to wipe away some of the black goo. They made sure to get his eyes clean, as well as his nose and mouth. The rest would have to be done later.

"Those damn dogs!" she whimpered. "Why

Chapter Eight

don't they leave us alone?"

She knelt down next to Romeo, who still lay unconscious, and wept. Fluffy pulled her away. They had to get Romeo out of there, no matter what they saw, including the dead cats. The rancid smell oozing from their rotting carcasses mixed with the tar nearly made Fluffy sick.

With her teeth, Queen Elizabeth was able to drag Romeo near the entrance of the alley. They would be safe there for a while. It was brighter and people were around. Some of them stopped at the ghastly sight of a cat covered in tar. Queen Elizabeth got some of it in her mouth, but it was nothing compared to what Romeo had. The dogs wouldn't come back, not yet at least.

"Look at the poor kitty, momma," whined one little passing girl. "Can we take him home?"

"No!" her mother said forcefully, pulling the girl away by her ponytail.

"Let's wait here for him to wake up. It shouldn't be long," Queen Elizabeth said. "With these wounds though, I wonder if we should take him to the medicine room." She examined Romeo's body and found several open cuts that were under the layer of tar.

"Won't they heal like yours did from the bus?" asked Fluffy.

Queen Elizabeth looked up at Fluffy as she rubbed Romeo's back. "No, Fluffy," she explained. "My wounds healed because I died. Everything heals as you come back to life. Thank goodness Romeo's not dead. He's just asleep. His wounds are real and here to stay. If he doesn't wake up soon, we're going to have to carry him ourselves."

Fluffy thought about that for a moment. "Won't that look odd to all the people walking by?"

"Sure it will, but what else can we do? We can't leave him here. Let's just see if he wakes up before we make any rash decisions."

Fluffy agreed. He lay next to Romeo who was cradled up against Queen Elizabeth. They sat silenty waiting for Romeo to come to. On the sidewalk they could see patterns of smudged tar prints leading away from the alley. They trailed off somewhere around the corner, but the rain had washed most of them away. The people rushing by continued to point and stare at the strange sight like the little girl had done. Luckily, no one bothered them.

After about twenty minutes, Romeo did wake up. Lucky too, because soon the dogs would be cleaned up and back for revenge.

Romeo first wiggled making little moaning sounds. Then, he slowly lifted his head off the ground.

"Romeo?" Queen Elizabeth quietly called. "Romeo, are you all right?"

His young eyes slowly opened. Romeo looked around. His vision was blurred. Fluffy stuck his head out in front of Romeo's face.

Chapter Eight

"Hey, you're back," Fluffy said joyfully, smiling as much as a cat can.

Romeo bobbed his head around. He made a scrunched face as soon as the tar fumes reached his nose.

"You were in a fight with the dogs. Do you remember?" Queen Elizabeth asked.

Romeo bolted up from the ground. "Where are they?" he asked as if the fight hadn't ended. As soon as he sat up, his body began to hurt from all the wounds and bruises. He painfully put his head back down on the cold cement.

"The dogs are gone, Romeo," Fluffy said. "Do you remember what happened?"

Queen Elizabeth looked at Fluffy and shook her head. "Don't worry about it now, Romeo. We can talk about that later. We've got to get you home."

She decided that the best thing for Romeo was to go directly home. He couldn't very well show up with bandages from the medicine room. What would Dennis think? Queen Elizabeth knew Dennis was a concerned guy and would take good care of Romeo. He'd clean him up and give him what he needed. Maybe even take him to.....The Vet.

As they walked away, something bright caught Queen Elizabeth's attention. She looked back toward the alley corridor and saw two glowing purple eyes in the shadows. She looked at Fluffy, then looked back. They were gone.

 144

Life One

It was a long walk to Romeo's home. People stared at them as they trudged by, but luckily that was all they did. Fluffy lived on a different street than Romeo and Queen Elizabeth. He said his goodbyes sooner.

"See you in school tomorrow," Fluffy said to Romeo. Before he turned away, he looked in Queen Elizabeth's direction.

"Thank you again," she mouthed.

Fluffy felt warmed and proud by what he had done even if Romeo didn't remember.

Romeo and Queen Elizabeth continued walking slowly. Romeo was in a lot of pain and was still bleeding a bit from the scratches on his neck and back. The tar made his fur gooey and sticky. He felt sick and tired and had a pounding headache. A passing roach barely turned Romeo's head. Queen Elizabeth quickly nabbed it when Romeo wasn't looking. She swallowed it in one juicy gulp.

Finally, they made it all the way to the two buildings where they both lived. However, Romeo was unable to climb up his side. Queen Elizabeth suggested that Romeo wait near the front entrance of the apartment building. When Dennis came home he would see him there and take him inside. Romeo wished that he could go to his warm, comfy bed right away but knew he couldn't make the climb. He immediately found a dry spot to lay down and wait. Queen Elizabeth would stay nearby under a mailbox

Chapter Eight

until Romeo was safe and inside. Unfortunately, the rain started to come down once again. Though it was only a drizzle, it was enough to chill Romeo's already aching body.

After about an hour, Queen Elizabeth spotted Dennis walking up the street. He had a worried look on his face, probably from something that happened at school. Romeo said Dennis was always getting into trouble with his teachers. Like the time he pulled down Mary Beth's skirt. He had no recess for a week after that prank.

Dennis carried his school books in one hand and a long stick in the other, strumming against everything he saw, even the mailbox Queen Elizabeth was hiding under. The noise vibrated through the box and straight into her ears.

Dennis' hand reached in his pocket and stayed there until he found his key. He walked up to his building and waved at the gargoyles out front. He was about to go in when something caught his eye. Off to the right was his tiny, striped kitten, shivering.

Dennis raced over to him. He knelt down and mournfully said, "Oh, Romeo! What happened?"

He cradled Romeo in his arms. Queen Elizabeth watched as Dennis picked him up and carried him inside. Once they were out of sight, she crawled from under the mailbox and climbed up to her own home.

Life One

An hour passed. From her window Queen Elizabeth could see Dennis rocking Romeo in a chair. He had him all wrapped up in a towel as he held little Romeo against his chest. It made Queen Elizabeth happy to know that her friend was now safe, though she wished she could have done more herself.

Chapter Nine

The next day at school Romeo was absent.

"Yesterday we had a little problem with the dogs," Queen Elizabeth explained to the class. "But Romeo's going to be just fine. He's resting at home. I saw him in the window today."

"Did...did he lose a life?" Tabitha asked nervously.

"No, honey," Queen Elizabeth said. "Luckily no. Your classmate Fluffy is responsible for saving Romeo." Everyone looked over at Fluffy. Oddly, he was wearing a large, pink bow around his neck. Cassie, his person, put it there. He was beyond humiliated.

Snickers gave him a funny stare.

"What about the dogs?" asked Twinkle Toes as he tugged his own whiskers.

 148

Life One

Queen Elizabeth walked over to him. "Just like always, be on the look out. If you see them coming, just get out of their way fast. But don't do what Romeo did and run into an alley. That's exactly what they want you to do. I'm sure you will be fine as long as you're observant and careful."

The little cats liked Queen Elizabeth and looked up to her. She had known all of them since they came to the Factory and felt almost maternal towards them. But none as much as Romeo.

Ms. Purrpurr thanked Queen Elizabeth for coming and talking to the class, as did all the students. Queen Elizabeth had to hurry because she was meeting Mr. Sox for breakfast in the rec room. She didn't like to keep him waiting.

In the classroom Ms. Purrpurr was getting back to business. Fluffy tugged at his new satin bow which was tied tightly to his collar. Uncle Fred laughed at him all morning.

"Quit it, Uncle Fred!" Fluffy whined. "It's not funny."

"Whatever you say, *cutie pie*," Uncle Fred said with a giggle.

Despite the interruptions, Ms. Purrpurr maintained control of her class. Something she was very good at. "All right, everybody," she said with her nose high in the air. "Take out your yarn pieces, and I want you to spell out the word *street*." When she talked her voice sounded snobby and rich, especially when the class was acting up. She usually didn't smile the whole day.

Everyone did as they were told, except for Snickers. He stopped licking his paws, but his eyes wandered to a lost bug. It was a spider scurrying around in the corner. Its eight juicy legs and body could make any cat's mouth water. Snickers hadn't eaten since he was fed almost an entire hour ago. To a glutton like him, it seemed an eternity. He wanted that bug, and he wanted it bad.

Snickers' stomach began to growl louder and louder. Swishy, echoey noises filled the room.

He tried to think of a plan. If he just lunged for the bug, Ms. Purrpurr would get mad and give him extra homework. Perhaps he could distract her and then reach for it. He looked around the room for such a distraction. Then it came to him.

"Ms. Purrpurr?" Snickers asked shifty-eyed as he raised his paw high in the air and waved it around wildly.

"Yes, Snickers. What do you want?" the teacher asked.

"Uh, I think someone's at the door. Yeah, that's it," he said keeping one eye on the spider. "You'd better get it."

"Nobody's at the door," Ms. Purrpurr yapped. "Did anybody else hear a knock?"

All the cats shook their heads no and stared at Snickers. It was obvious he was up to something.

Life One

Snickers wasn't a very smart cat. He sat there, almost sweating, never quite sure about what to do next. Every eye was on him. He could feel their stares. Ms. Purrpurr tapped her chalk on the floor and glared at him. Meanwhile, the spider he so desired was heading toward a small crack in the wall. Snickers panicked and took a flying leap at the floor. He aimed right for the spider which he could see moving quickly for the crack in the room. The others watched him crash, as if in slow motion into the corner of the wall bumping his round head. Their jaws dropped. Snickers fell with a plop right where the spider had been hovering earlier. By now it was gone, back in its home. The disappointed and drooling cat paused a moment, then hesitantly looked up. All his peers were staring at him with pity. Suddenly, Calvin started to laugh. Then, they all began to laugh. Angrily, Ms. Purrpurr rattled off some added homework, though Snickers didn't hear a word of it. Because of his crashing into the wall, his ears were ringing like church bells, and his vision was blurred. In fact, he saw three of each cat in the room.

Snickers opened his mouth to say something, but just as he did, he collapsed back down with a thud and fainted.

While Ms. Purrpurr and the others revived him with some water and smelling salts, the spider named Octavian, breathed a sigh of relief. *Man*, he said to himself, *that fat cat almost got me this time.* He scurried away deeper into the wall, unable to shake the image of blubbery Snickers falling on him. He felt lucky to be alive. He walked down the inside of the Factory wall on all eight legs to find his siblings. They were deep in the wood behind a pipe near the classroom, all 165 of them.

If the Factory was at all dismal, the inner walls were worse, at least as far as the cats were concerned. Yet, for a spider, it was great. The Factory was a spider's playground. Something new around every turn. They spent hours preparing the fields of cobwebs over the endless places to climb and play. But best of all, it was a virtual candy store, enough to eat for a lifetime. Sometimes juicy flies would wander into the larger rooms on the higher floors through the broken windows. The spiders took great pleasure in capturing and devouring every last one.

When Octavian found his brothers and sisters, they were all eating, or rather sucking, blood. Some had ants, others small worms, one even had a bee in his web. Octavian's multi-eyes focused on a plump termite. Lucky for the cats there were plenty of hungry spiders to take care of the wood eaters.

With his keen soldier-like instincts, Octavian crept up behind the termite as it happily sat eating wood chips. When the moment was right, he enclosed it in his eight legs. The bug never stood a chance. Octavian quickly wrapped it up with his spinners and dragged him over to his family to share his conquest before hunting for another. A spider's life could be very exciting.

Down below in the rec room, Queen Elizabeth sat with Mr. Sox. "Romeo is a fine student," Mr. Sox said. "I'd say he's one to watch."

"That's great," Queen Elizabeth responded pleased. "I'm so glad. I just knew he would be a good kid."

Mr. Sox took a heavy puff of his pipe. It was carved from a small ear of corn. "Fluffy is a fine cat too," he added. "It does not surprise me that he saved Romeo from the dogs."

"I agree, Mr. Sox," Queen Elizabeth said. "I just wish we could help Romeo find his brothers, poor thing. They could be anywhere. They could even be alleys!"

"Yes, that is always a possibility," Mr. Sox warned exhaling the pipe smoke. "That's why we must be particularly careful."

Queen Elizabeth nodded and took the last bite of her tuna ball. It was very good. Roy made them from the leftover tuna at the restaurant. Yellowtail wasn't much of a cook himself, rather, he was in charge of carrying the fish to the Factory and unfortunately cleaning the bowls.

Later that day some of the other cats spent the afternoon in the Thinking Room. They often went there after a busy morning or whenever they

Chapter Nine

just wanted to think about important things. It was a small, quiet place on the third floor near the medicine room, comfortable enough for about twenty cats.

The Thinking Room was the most beautiful room at the Factory. The cats would sit in a long, carpeted area. A large statue of Bubastis, with his painted deep purple eyes, stood tall and proud at the front of the room. It was a gift from Mr. Sox when the real Bubastis died. He paid some cats from the art district plenty of tuna to build it. Made from a large stone found near the Factory, it had become a chiseled shrine. Cats would weep at Bubastis' feet and pray for their dead friends or for another life.

The walls were decorated by Skid, a cat long dead who used to live near a department store. Late at night he and a few of his friends brought over some leftover paint from the store's hardware section. They almost got caught by store security several times. Undaunted, Skid and the others painted the Thinking Room with golden colors of yellow. It was by far the brightest room in the building. Like the first floor, many great paintings covered the walls. Various cats made them right in the Factory art room. Bubastis himself would show up now and then, or so everyone believed.

Once again, Bait was lurking about in the rafters unbeknownst to anyone. He heard the conversation between Queen Elizabeth and Mr. Sox and felt

 154

that Fidel should know about it. He carefully slipped out of the Factory without being seen, taking his usual route down a tree on the opposite side of the guards.

Bait roamed the streets looking for Fidel. Naturally, he tried Smelly's first. Fidel was almost always there. Smelly said he had already left with his pack and didn't know where they were going.

Bait prowled around town looking in the usual spots. While he did, he enjoyed hissing and growling at the little children walking by with their parents. His usual routine began with a deadly stare from down the street, preferably in an especially foggy spot for dramatic effect. Once eye contact was made, the children would clutch onto their parent's hand and hide behind their legs. Bait would continue to stare as they got closer and closer to him. The parents never knew. Once the child was only feet away, Bait would crouch down and let out a roaring hiss, showing all his needle-sharp teeth sometimes still bloody from lunch. The kids always screamed, and one even fainted. The parents would grumble a few swear words as Bait walked away with a nasty laugh. If he had time, he would do it all over again. It didn't take much to amuse him.

Bait searched through the cold and windy streets. He went to a small, cramped alley near 57th and 6th. It was where Fidel usually lived. He was the only cat in that alley, except when Raven or one of his *others* were invited. The ground was littered with half-eaten skeletons of mice and rats and birds. Fidel had a collection of weapons stored under a trash bin, rocks, sling shots *(stolen from kids)*, even a set of matches which he always threatened to use. He had them sealed in a used Tupperware container to keep them from getting soggy. Fidel slept on top of a big stained blanket which his loyal five found for him. He kept it in a broken toy chest which had been left in the alley. Near his blanket was a torn picture of Carnival. He looked at it every night for strength and power.

Along the way, as Bait was scaring the little children, he scared the wrong one. This kid was with her father, a large, fierce-looking man. When Bait did his hissing thing, the man picked up Bait, dragged him in the alley, and bopped him in the head with a rock from the ground. The little girl screamed. Her dad spit on Bait as he lay dead on the alley floor. About twenty minutes later, Bait came to, with one less life. Only four more to go.

Bait finally found Fidel as he staggered through the city. He was with a bunch of younger cats under a small bridge at City Park. City Park was a few blocks uptown from the Factory near 60th Street. It was a huge area filled with many things that people do for recreation. There were playgrounds, riding trails, picnic areas, and small ponds, all mostly rundown. Occasionally in the past, the city hosted concerts or other such fun events. But because of the damp weather and its poor condition, the park was hardly used for what it was intended. Rather, it became known as a scary, crime infested place. The city's lowlifes would do their *business* at the park, and young, repressed teenagers would go there to escape the confines of their parents' rules. City Park was also popular with the animals. Fidel often held his meetings or other outings there. The place was filled with birds, which always made nice snacks for hungry cats. Unfortunately, the dogs took an equal fancy to City Park. They usually stuck to the northern side, while the cats hung out on the southern side. Of course, it was always rare for a stick to go to the park alone. Especially at night.

"Bait," Fidel cracked. "Where have you been? And what happened to your head?"

Bait stood back and felt the huge swelling bump that was protruding between his ratty ears. "I uh..forgot where you were. I was out lookin' around." He bit his lip, a known habit when he lied.

Fidel walked over to him, expressionless. His own half-bitten ear was twisted back, and the other stood up straight and pointed. Fidel lifted his left paw and smacked it hard against the bump atop Bait's head. Bait let out a howl that was louder than gunfire. He pushed Fidel out of the way and backed off. Rubbing his poor little head, Bait fought the tears that teetered on the edge of his lids.

"What happened to your head, Bait?" Fidel

said with a snap. "Tell me the truth or I'll do it again." He raised his paw threateningly.

"All right, all right," Bait said shaking. "I scared some brat, and her owner knocked me in the head. And yes, I lost a life." Bait said it with such a low mumble that Fidel insisted he say it again. "I LOST A LIFE!"

Smoke shot from Fidel's ears. "Bait, do you realize how important it is for you to be careful? You are my messenger!" Fidel walked in circles around him. "What would happen to me if....!" He paused and calmed himself before he lost control. "Look, just be careful out there. *Don't* let this happen again!"

Bait nodded his head obediently.

"Now," Fidel went on, "let me finish my business here, then you can tell me what you found out today."

Fidel turned and faced the four other cats he was with, all very young, no older than a few months. Three boys and one pretty girl and all terribly nervous. They were new kittens born from a female that lived in an alley near Smelly's. Fidel liked that, they were very impressionable and vulnerable to the harsh ways of alley life. He was training them on the art of being an alley, and they were awed by his presence, even though being cold and hungry all the time wasn't very appealing. When they did eat, Fidel took all the good mice leaving them the skinny ones and leftover bug parts. At least they could have some milk when they were with their mothers, but for all its displeasure, Fidel offered them a life of excitement.

Fidel's silent pack of oddball alleys were stationed on a steamy sewer top. The willowy fog poured from the manhole covering them like a dirty blanket. The loyal bunch watched Fidel work his magic as they cleaned and sharpened their claws.

"Now, as I was saying," Fidel announced to his four students, "the park is where you can find many birds. Give the bird a fight. Never win easy. Pride is the *first* word in an alley's language. To begin with, *first*, when you see a bird, hunt it with your eyes....." Fidel went onto describe the proper stages of trapping and killing birds. It involved ripping off feathers and twisting beaks. He told them to avoid crows, because if they got away, they would tell the dogs. The crows were friends with the dogs.

The four little cats listened intently. Steak, the smallest, watched and drooled as his black tail swung high in the air. The more Fidel talked, the more his hunger for hunting grew. Big, the fattest one, wasn't only interested in meat. He loved to eat the soggy grass and maybe a sock or two. Fish always smelled like fish. He had short, white fur and sharp, pointy ears and stood at attention hoping to impress Fidel. Candle was the shy, pretty girl who shivered and quivered at the sight of Fidel. Her slick, golden body was crowned by a tuft of bright red fur. She listened with wariness and concern. She relished a tasty bird,

Chapter Nine

but felt uneasy by the pleasure Fidel took in torturing them. Yet, she wanted to be a good alley and paid attention just the same.

Finally, Fidel made Bait demonstrate the actual act of bird killing. Spotting an innocent pigeon getting a sip from the nearby pond, he instructed Bait to fetch lunch. Bait, still a little groggy from his recent death, did as he was told.

All the cats watched as Bait stalked his prey. Slowly, he crept up behind the bird not making a sound. The stocky pigeon continued to drink unknowingly. Bait drew closer and closer, his heart pounding hard, his fur standing straight up. With his back arched, he was ready to pounce. In an instant he leapt forward, landing on the clueless prey sending other birds fluttering into the sky.

The pigeon flapped his wings and kicked savagely, trying anyway possible to free himself from the clutches of the deranged cat. Bait hissed and wailed as he dug his front claws deeper into the bird's flesh. The other alley wannabes watched with anticipation and excitement. Candle, however, had to turn away.

The ravaged pigeon continued to put up a fight, but gradually his flailing and kicking slowed down. He was losing his final battle. One mournful moan echoed from the dying bird as he realized his fate.

"Good work, Bait!" Fidel said with a maniacal look in his swirling eyes. "Everyone, come closer."

The bird was still alive, though barely. His chest

heaved up and down as his eyes sunk in. Bait continued to hold him with his claws just as he took his final breath. Fidel huddled everybody around, encircling the humiliated bird.

"All right, who wants to go first?" Fidel asked. "Who's ready to get the next bird?"

Steak stepped forward offering himself. He was still drooling, especially now at the sight of the dead body.

Steak did the deed well, just as Fidel instructed. Big and Fish were to go next. They had a little trouble at first, but quickly caught on, each standing proudly next to his own bird.

Fidel watched and laughed devilishly. He was succeeding in training the young alleys to be ruthless hunters. Candle was called next. She hesitantly walked up to the gruesome sight, shivering as she went.

"Candle," Fidel said deeply. "It's your turn. I know you can do it." He stepped aside and waited for his next fix of violence. His need was demonic and pleasurable all the way through to his ratty bones.

Candle stared blankly at the birds gathering nearby. While most of them had flown away after the first bird had been killed, some of the dumber birds stuck around.

Full of anxiety, Candle crept up just like Bait had done. The others continued to watch anxiously. Just as she was about to carry out her assignment, something inside of her snapped. She screamed, "I can't do it! I can't do it!"

Candle turned around sobbing. Fidel tapped his paw hard on a nearby rock and exploded, "Do it Candle! Do it now!"

"Nooooo!" she wailed. "It's too cruel! I just can't!" She threw herself down in the mud and cried under her little front paws. Fidel was outraged, though he kept his cool.

"Kill the bird! You're a cat, ain't ya?" Bait howled.

Fidel walked up to Candle who was still crying in the mud. By now, the bird had flown away. Fidel had to handle this one firmly, yet properly.

"Candle," he said with phony concern. "Listen, I know how you feel. I felt they same way when I killed my first bird." He rubbed the top of her head, then twiddled the tags on his collar.

"Y-y-you did?" she asked between sobs.

"Of course, we all did. But, you are an alley, and you have to learn to do these things for yourself. I know you think it's too cruel, right?"

Candle nodded her head yes.

"Well, in the whole scheme of things, it's important. We as alleys have an obligation, a destiny to establish ourselves as the leaders of this city," he boasted with the lure of a great dictator. "Let's say other birds saw what happened here today. They'll tell their friends, and eventually it will get back to the dogs. We have to let them know *we* rule this town, no matter how we have to do it. There can be no weak links or we'll be vulnerable. Understand?"

Though Candle did not, she simply nodded her head and got up. She and Fidel joined the others for a nibble of fat pigeon meat. When no one was looking, she spit her helping out. Her stomach was in too much turmoil to eat.

Chapter Ten

Bait was happily chewing on his pigeon leg, tugging at the muscles and tendons, when Fidel pulled him over to a tree. "So, what happened on your route today?" Fidel asked inquisitively.

"Well," Bait said with a mouthful, "I did over-hear something dat I think you might find interesting." He wrapped his lips around the bone and took a sip of the marrow.

Fidel smacked him in the shoulder. "Yeah?"

"Well," Bait continued, "I went to the Factory, you know, and boy, do they have some nice lookin' mice in that joint."

Fidel gave him a scornful look.

"Anyway, so I was up there overlooking one of their pathetic little rooms, and I was listening to that old guy, what's his name, Mr. Rocks."

 164

Life One

"Mr. *Sox*," Fidel said rolling his sinister green eyes.

"Yeah, that's it. So, Sox was talkin' with that broad, Queeny. And they're talkin' about that dog fight we heard about. Well, it turns out two of the real new sticks was the guys who stopped it. One was that Romeo kid I mentioned before, only he kinda got thrashed." Bait stopped to laugh. "But, the other guy, Friffy or Fluffy, I think, did something real big, and the dogs left, even Bull. Anyway, I thought you'd like to know."

Bait went back to his pigeon leg as Fidel paced back and forth, shaking his head to and fro. Finally he looked up and said, "We've gotta get these guys before they start thinking they run this city. If anyone's going to outsmart the dogs, it's going to be *me*! Not some stupid stick!" Angry, Fidel pounded his paw into the ground. Something was building inside of him. Something pure evil.

Later that week, Romeo and his class set out on their first field trip. Perfect timing, for Romeo had completely recovered from his fight with the dogs. Mr. Shadow arranged the outing, having Queen Elizabeth tag along as the only chaperone. Everyone was excited, including Ms. Purrpurr and Mr. Sox who didn't have to teach that day on account of the trip.

The class would take a journey on the subway. Mr. Shadow had already explained to them how the

Chapter Ten

subway system worked and why it was a good source of transportation when going longer distances. The class was to meet at 8:00 A.M. sharp. They would be gone for two hours. When they returned to the Factory, they would review what they saw and did, and discuss the dangers of the subway. Then, Roy and Yellowtail would serve them a special lunch as a reward for their full day of hard work.

At 7:30 A.M. Romeo awoke to the screeching sounds of Dennis' alarm. Dennis was still grounded, leaving him in a grumpy mood. He was instructed to come directly home after school. As he put on his faded jeans, Romeo watched a commercial for the Kitty Fresh Pee Removal Kit. *That must be Theodore*, he said to himself. He knew of Theodore from listening to Calvin.

After breakfast the two pals entered the elevator together, then journeyed outside. They said their goodbyes by the lamp post with the flickering light. Waving good-bye, Dennis went one way and Romeo the other.

By 8:00 A.M. Romeo was in his seat, ready and eager. The other cats were there as well. Even Tabitha was on time, however, still with no collar. She had it the day before, but for whatever reason, Jimmy, her person, took it off again.

"This time he put it on Sally's doll," Tabitha explained. "What was I to do?"

Mr. Shadow thought for a moment. "All right,

 166

we will just have to keep an extra eye on you," he said. "But, it just makes me so mad."

Once Queen Elizabeth arrived they all left the classroom. Everyone was in good spirits, except for Twinkle Toes who was awfully tired. He dragged his little white paws sluggishly along with the others.

"Now class," Mr. Shadow went on. "Remember the rules. Stay with your partners and your group leader. Don't wander off! And if you see trouble, hiss twice."

Each cat was given a partner and an adult leader. This was arranged for organizational purposes, but above all, safety. Mr. Shadow didn't want anybody wandering around alone. His group consisted of the partnered Tabitha and Darla, and Snickers and Uncle Fred. Calvin and Twinkle Toes and Romeo and Fluffy were in Queen Elizabeth's group. Of course, *all* the cats were to be eye and ear shot from each other for the entire trip.

The ten cats left the old umbrella factory single file and walked straight down 54th Street. Thankfully it wasn't raining, though it was awfully chilly for the cats, even under their fur coats.

Mr. Shadow led the way, bumping into two mailboxes and one street lamp. The plan was to go to the subway station at 54th. They would hop a train and get off on 37th Street for a short visit to another part of the city. At the corner of 54th and 8th, Romeo looked around the busy sidewalks, and an odd sen-

Chapter Ten

sation came over him. He somehow felt like he had been there before.

"All right, we are here," Mr. Shadow announced. All the cats stood at the corner of the building away from the people. "When I give the meow signal, we'll go down these stairs. Then, we'll run as fast as we can along the wall to the left. Keep going until you get all the way to the end. Nobody will bother us at the end."

Romeo looked over the top of the stone staircase. There were about ten steep, cracked steps leading down under the city floor. He could see a big, opened, metal, cage-like door. The entryway was small and narrow. Inside it seemed dark, but no more so than an alley. People were rushing in and out making Romeo nervous. Would they wonder why ten cats were walking into a subway station two-by-two? Romeo was old enough to question such oddities.

Above the stairs was a big sign that read: 54th Street Station. Romeo was proud of himself for being able to read it.

"Now, another thing," Mr. Shadow said. "We are going to get onto the last car of the train. You should always, *always*, get onto the last car. The people never go there."

"Why, Mr. Shadow?" asked Darla.

Mr. Shadow looked at Queen Elizabeth. "I may as well tell them," he whispered to her. He

 168

shuffled all the cats around the corner out of sight. "You see, kids, a long time ago there was a terrible tragedy right here on the subway."

A sudden gasp was heard from the cats.

"Was it a cat? Did the dogs kill it?" asked Calvin with grotesque images floating in his head.

"No," Mr. Shadow continued. "In fact, it was people. See, there were two very wealthy people, a young man and his new bride. They lived back in the days when life was good. Has Mr. Sox talked about the old days with you?"

The cats all nodded their little heads.

Mr. Shadow rolled up his itchy, yellow-knit sleeves. "Anyway, the ritzy couple was heading home from the theater. Rumor had it their car broke down, so they were forced to take the subway. To make a long, gruesome story short, they were savagely murdered in the last subway car by a starving jewelry thief. An old lady found their bloody bodies. Sadly, the thief was never captured."

"Is he still out there?" Romeo asked nervously.

Mr. Shadow smiled. "No, Romeo. He's long gone. But the people of the city felt that ever since the incident, the last subway car was haunted by the angry spirits of the young couple. Supposedly, they are still there, stop after stop, trying to get home. The people claim to have heard all sorts of odd, unexplained noises in the last car of each train.

Chapter Ten

They say they can even feel the chill of death. Over time, the rumors have panicked them so that nobody ever goes in the last car, which is good for us."

"Whoa," Tabitha said, "is all that really true? 'Cause if it is, I don't want to go into a haunted subway."

"Me too," Darla shook.

"Actually, we cats believe a different story. We believe all the creaks and noises are not the ghosts of those two humans, but Bubastis patrolling the city."

"Who is *he* already?" Romeo asked anxiously.

Mr. Shadow swallowed deeply and cleared his throat. He took a step forward and said, "Little is known about Bubastis. From the old stories that have been passed along, some claim to remember him as a mysterious cat passing briefly through the city during Carnival's evil downfall. They say this lone, mystical cat spoke of hope and love and prosperity. Those who supposedly heard him speak, knew of his incredible wisdom far beyond that of a normal cat. He wanted peace between all animals, strength and fraternity. There are those who even say he magically saved many animals from death and sickness with only his purple stare."

Romeo thought to himself, *Could that be the old cat I saw with the purple eyes?*

"History writes that Bubastis was to be a great leader," Mr. Shadow continued, "that his presence alone evoked power and security. Though one day, he curiously vanished, gone from sight. Some say he was killed by Carnival who felt threatened by his powers, others say he never existed to begin with. That he was only a figment of imagination in the desperate minds of the miserable cats looking for a force to believe in. We don't know the whole story, though we do know *today* Bubastis represents everything that is good in all cats. He symbolizes that common bond between us and all animals. That is why we like to believe that Bubastis' spirit roams the lonely subways, helping when he can."

"Really? Why the subways?" Fluffy asked dazed.

"I think he likes the freedom of the empty cars, the solitude and darkness. He ventures out when danger strikes, or so we think. It's nice to believe that Bubastis is somewhere watching over us. Some cats say they've seen his purple eyes reflected in windows or in rain puddles." Mr. Shadow's voice turned sour. "You know, the alleys pray to *him* as well. Not for the same reasons, but they pray that his strength will continue to enrich the alleys and empower them as it indirectly did for Carnival. They feel that Bubastis was intent on creating a supreme cat race, powerful and force-ful leaders of the city. Alleys feel that they are that race. It's not so. I feel that Fidel, most of all, has twisted Bubastis' peaceful vision to somehow revolve around him. Another great tragedy for all cats alike." Mr. Shadow looked out at the crowd and felt a sadness for them. He wanted something better for this generation, though he knew it was not possible.

Romeo had listened very closely to Mr. Shadow's story and felt a rush through his body. He looked up and for a quick moment swore he saw that same cat from the street the other morning sitting in a far window. When he looked again, he realized it was only the reflection of a plant on the sill.

"All right, let's get going," Queen Elizabeth finally said.

All ten cats readied themselves at the top of the downward staircase. When there was a break in the flow of people, Mr. Shadow gave his meow signal.

Like a small herd, they raced down the stairs and through the entryway. The station was drab and dismal. The walls, which showed scattered signs of once being glossy white, were now gray like the clouds outside. The cracked, tiled floor looked as though it had been mopped with a muddy rag. People were rushing around, pushing others out of the way as they ran for the next train to somewhere. There were long unfriendly lines for the over-priced tokens given out by an angry looking woman who sat inside a small cage. In the distance, the pounding of massive subway trains bounced off the high ceilings and trembling walls. It was like another world.

Life One

The cats ran under the turnstile and alongside the left wall like Mr. Shadow had instructed. They were moving so fast Romeo hardly had a chance to look around, not that there was much to see.

As they bolted through the station toward the train, they hit a bump, a large bump in the form of a man sitting in his own urine looking dirtier than any person they had ever seen. The poor guy was skinny and sad faced, with torn brown clothes and a long, scraggly beard. On the platform in front of him was a flat, funny hat. In it were three pennies and one nickel. The man was mumbling something unrecognizable as the people zoomed by hardly giving him a second glance. Beside him was a half eaten can of beans with an expiration date long ago reached. Looking back at the other cats, Mr. Shadow ran head first into the homeless man. The cat stood paralyzed. Suddenly, he felt a cold, bony hand reach around his middle as the bum picked him up. Mr. Shadow froze and stared blankly at the other sticks. They stood for a moment not knowing what to do. The toothless man inspected Mr. Shadow, noticing the blue monogrammed letters on his little sweater.

"Sh-Sh-Shadow," the man struggled. "Well, Shadow, looks like I have a new friend."

The strange man held Mr. Shadow tightly against his filthy body. Mr. Shadow turned his nose away as far as he could, the man's foul stench far too strong for him to endure.

Chapter Ten

Mr. Shadow was being firmly hugged, and although terrified, he could feel that this sad man hadn't held anyone in a very long time. Through all that muck, he could feel a forgotten tenderness oozing out of his pores.

Mr. Shadow struggled to get away. He tried to motion the cats to keep going, but they just stood there shocked. Uncle Fred started licking between his own toes.

Then suddenly, Queen Elizabeth leapt forward and bit down hard on the man's skinny arm. She sunk her teeth so deep, she hit bone. The man let out a yell and pulled his arm back, freeing Mr. Shadow. Relieved, the cat dashed away. The others followed, as did Queen Elizabeth who spit bits of dried skin from her mouth, completely losing her growing appetite.

Finally, they reached the far end of the subway train platform. At this point all ten cats had a chance to get a good look at the busy dirty station. They stood far back from the train and the people.

"Now, when we hear the train coming, that's our cue to get ready," Mr. Shadow explained. "I will give the same meow signal as before. Remember, stay with your partner! And if your partner doesn't get on, *you* don't get on! Whatever you do, I don't, *don't*, want you to be alone! Understood? *Understood?*"

Everyone nodded. They understood.

Within minutes, a train could be heard rumbling down the tracks. The excitement and anticipation grew in the kittens. Some of the people passengers were inching their way to the edge of the platform. The tracks were about three feet below and strewn with tons of trash.

"Mommy, mommy," a little boy tugged. "Look! Look at all the rats!"

Down below, along the walls near the tracks, scurried several big hungry rats. They traveled in and out of holes in the concrete grabbing anything they could find before the next train sent them away again. Snickers heard what the little boy said and yelled, "Rats? Where? I'm starved." He licked his lips and dashed forward toward the edge. The little boy saw him coming and flinched. Uncle Fred ran after his partner.

"No, Snickers! No!" Queen Elizabeth cried. "Come back!"

Just then, the next subway train came roaring into the station. It was louder and windier than the cats imagined. Frazzled, Mr. Shadow gave the meow signal, though half the cats were already rushing after Snickers.

Calvin nudged Twinkle Toes who had fallen asleep on the dirty ground. "Come on, Twinkle Toes," Calvin cried as he pulled his partner.

Twinkle Toes groggily came to. His heavy eyes slowly opened. He could see the blurry image of all the other cats boarding the subway car, even Snickers. They were yelling for him to jump. The automatic doors would be closing quickly.

"Hurry!" Romeo yelled to them both.

Calvin bit Twinkle Toes' ear and tugged. He managed to move Twinkle only inches from the train car when a large buzzer sounded warning all to step away from the doors. They were closing. The cats inside continued to jump and howl at their friends still on the platform.

Calvin, being the selfish type, gave up and leapt forward into the car leaving Twinkle Toes still standing on the platform as the doors were slowly shutting. Instinctively, Romeo shoved Snickers and Uncle Fred aside and reached out of the train car as far as he could. He grabbed tightly to the back of Twinkle Toes' neck and lifted him off the ground with all his might. The train was now moving. The doors, nearly closed, bounced back and forth against Romeo's paw. Twinkle Toes dangled from the subway car which was quickly approaching a very narrow tunnel. If he didn't get in the car fast, he would surely be crushed between the train and the wall. Fluffy and Uncle Fred panicked and with all their strength pried open the subway doors.

"Hurry! Hurry!" Tabitha yelled.

Only inches from the passageway, Romeo, Fluffy, and Uncle Fred yanked Twinkle Toes inside. The force of their pull caused them all to fly against the opposite side of the subway car and smash into the doors like bowling pins. Gathering themselves together, Fluffy approached Calvin. "What were you thinking?" he snapped.

Calvin stood there looking guilty. Darla and Tabitha rushed over to Romeo and Twinkle Toes to make sure they were all right.

"Huh?" Fluffy barked again shoving Calvin in the shoulder, pushing him toward the back of the train car.

Just then, Mr. Shadow and Queen Elizabeth stepped in, Mr. Shadow clumsily tripping over a soda can on the floor. He spoke first. "Now, Fluffy," he said. "Stop this! Stop this right now!"

Fluffy looked into Calvin's eyes with a deep, hostile stare. Calvin continued to back away.

"Mr. Shadow's right," Queen Elizabeth said next. "This isn't going to get us anywhere."

Fluffy turned and looked at both of them. "But Calvin broke the rule. He left his partner alone. Twinkle Toes could have been killed. How do we know we can count on him out there?"

For the first time Calvin broke down and cried. Very uncharacteristic of him. He sobbed and sobbed, which pleasured Fluffy.

"I'm sorry, okay?" Calvin muttered. "I just panicked. I swear, it'll never happen again. Please, Fluffy, you have to believe me!"

Mr. Shadow pulled Fluffy to the other side of the car and talked the anger out of him. Fluffy understood, though it took some tough coaxing.

Chapter Ten

Queen Elizabeth sat with Calvin who was filled with remorse. He even found a moment to apologize to Twinkle Toes. The others gazed out the windows as the subway train roared forward into the darkness, leaving the old bum and the platform far behind.

Chapter Eleven

The cats felt like they were flying, especially when the train emerged from the tunnel and came above ground. It was a rush they never knew existed. Everyone watched out the windows as the city blew by, passed the blurry buildings and cars. After a few blocks, the train went back underground again. People got on and off at different stops while the cats marveled from their cool, mobile classroom.

Once everything was settled, Mr. Shadow spoke. "Okay, class," he said, "what do you think so far?"

"This is great!" blurted Darla pinning her knees together. She could feel her bladder jolting every time the train came to a stop.

"Yeah, really cool!" Tabitha yelled in Romeo's direction.

Chapter Eleven

"This is even better than last time," added Uncle Fred who had gone on this same adventure with last year's class. He snorted and scratched his ears violently. Snickers, on the other hand, was busy trying to kill a string that was hanging above the seats.

The underground tunnel was dark and loud as the pulsing train rumbled over the tracks.

"Who can tell me when you should use the subway?" Mr. Shadow asked from one of the gum-splattered seats.

Fluffy raised his paw. "When you have too far to walk, Mr. Shadow," he answered quickly. "Oh, and only during the daytime."

"Excellent, Fluffy, and you must be very careful. Now, who can tell me when you shouldn't use the subway?"

Uncle Fred answered. "You shouldn't use the subway if you just ate. You don't want to get a stomach ache." He looked up with a proud grin showing off his yellow teeth.

"Uh, no..not really," Mr. Shadow said with a tinge of sharpness. "That really has nothing to do with it. Who else would like to try?"

Nobody raised a paw, so Mr. Shadow pointed to Darla. She answered shyly. "Um, you shouldn't use the subway at night or if alleys are around."

"Very good, Darla." Mr. Shadow smiled as he paced throughout the car slamming into the sides from the jolting and jerking. Sliding on the slick floor, he caught his sweater on one of the seats. He tugged it back down, though it kept rising above his belly. Either he had gained weight or his person had shrunk it.

"And don't forget," Queen Elizabeth interrupted, "we are getting off at 37th Street. When the big doors open, jump out and run to the same spot we were in at the other station, near the end of the platform. All the stations are designed the same. And, of course, stay with your partners!" She shot Calvin a warning look. Calvin smiled and looked down to the ground.

Romeo pulled Queen Elizabeth aside to ask her a question in private. "Queen Elizabeth," he whispered. "I could come here everyday and get off on different stops and look for my brothers." His face glowed like fire when he spoke of his siblings. "They're out here somewhere, and somebody has got to know them. I could ask all the cats I meet. This could be the perfect thing for me. What do you think?" He waited anxiously for her approval.

While Queen Elizabeth understood Romeo's need to find his family, she hardly thought that his plan was the best solution. It was risky and dangerous.

"Look, Romeo," she began. She put her right paw on his and looked deep into his young eyes. "I want to help you, kid, any way possible. Believe me,

Chapter Eleven

I do. But hey, I don't think it's worth possibly losing your lives."

Romeo gave her a funny look. He didn't like what she was saying one bit.

She continued. "Romeo, getting on the subway is always a risk. It should be used only when necessary, like going very long distances. Wandering around isn't going to get you anything but killed. You know *our* part of the city, but most other neighborhoods you know nothing about. I know nothing about. They are all run by Fidel, and well, I don't want to see you getting yourself hurt. Besides, there are thousands, maybe millions, of cats out there. This plan is just going to take you in circles. I know there's got to be another way. Trust me, I'll help you find it and your brothers. We'll do it together."

Romeo looked up at her with disappointed eyes. He thought his plan was brilliant, pure and simple. He felt like getting mad and telling her she didn't know what she was talking about. After all, he was a male. He could handle a few lousy streets and subways. But deep down he knew she was right. He would just have to think a little harder for that perfect plan.

Romeo was quiet the rest of the morning. Though he had been a part of the Factory for several weeks now, the field trip awakened his need to find his brothers. Learning and socializing were only half of his battle. While everyone piled out of the subway

 182

Life One

onto 37th Street, Romeo continued thinking of family and reunion.

The class roamed around the 30's and up 9th Avenue. For the most part, the 30's looked the same as the 50's. They were just as cold and just as gloomy. The only difference was the street numbers. Uncle Fred kept wandering away from his partner and group leader. He loved to sniff the old men's ankles. A nasty habit nobody understood. Mr. Shadow finally threatened to take him home.

"No, Mr. Shadow!" Uncle Fred begged. "I promise, I'll be good." He shook his big head up and down.

"We'll see," grumbled Mr. Shadow.

Darla had to stop three times to relieve herself because of her overactive bladder. She almost made it home after that, but had to go one more time. She hid under a mailbox to do her business. The others turned away pretending not to look, except for Twinkle Toes. He watched as a little yellow stream came from under the blue metal box.

Calvin couldn't help but notice the many ads for the Kitty Fresh Pee Removal Kit on buses, billboards, even in store windows. They were all decorated with enormous pictures of Theodore, even some he hadn't seen before. Theo was in all sorts of dorky and embarrassing poses. They had him sitting on a litter box, walking through a garden, peeing on a sailboat. Calvin laughed, almost convincing himself he felt bad for the guy. Still, he sneered at each picture and poster wishing it was his face plastered on them. His stomach was in jealous knots by the time the morning was over.

Near the subway station Mr. Shadow pulled everybody aside to a quiet part of the street. It wasn't an alley, but rather a tight alcove set back from the sidewalk and the feet.

"Before we get back on the subway to go home, I want to explain something to you. When we go to the far end of the platform like we did before, take notice of a small vent across the track to the right."

Queen Elizabeth quickly reminded them with her paws which was left and which was right.

"When you see this vent," Mr. Shadow continued, "I want you to remember never, *never*, go near it. You should never be playing in the station anyway, so it should not be a problem."

"Why, Mr. Shadow?" Darla asked. "Where does it lead?"

"Good question, Darla. Now, every station, and there are many in the city, has that same vent against the far wall." Mr. Shadow motioned for everybody to come closer to him. He looked around before he continued, making sure no unsuspecting critters were listening. "Those vents," he whispered as low as he could. "Those vents lead to the most terrible place, more terrible than over there," he pointed.

 184

Life One

Chapter Eleven

"Death Alley..."

Mr. Shadow's voice trailed through Snicker's ears. Snickers turned around and saw what clearly was Death Alley. He saw its signature haze of smoke hovering overhead swirling like a black hole. There was a silence about it making it ghoulish and taboo. Snickers turned away from Death Alley and immediately thought of the forbidden vents Mr. Shadow spoke of. They were intriguing and curious. Before he would hear anymore of Mr. Shadow's thrilling explanation, Snickers slithered away from the group and crept back down into the subway station when nobody was looking.

He ditched and dodged his way through the zombie-like crowd and shuffled over to the track's edge. As Snickers stood there staring, he wondered what was beyond that small, metal vent which so enticingly seemed to stare back.

The actual vent was across the tracks, a dangerous threshold to cross. Snickers stepped back several feet and planned his jump. In the distance he could hear the roar of a coming subway car only seconds away. With no time to spare, he sucked in a hearty breath, and when nobody was looking began his running leap toward the tracks. He charged forward and flung himself off the concrete plank in perfect form, soaring above the rails, belly swishing about. As he landed, his tail braised over one track zapping him like a lightning bolt. He quickly dusted himself off, made sure nobody was watching, and slipped behind the bars of the small, dusty, forbidden vent.

Once inside, he could feel the rumble of the subway car. It raced by him like a loud, forceful wind. Once the car had passed, Snickers turned his head for a look around. It was dark, very dark, and smelled a rancid, foul stench. Such smells he had never imagined. Though he couldn't see a thing, Snickers sensed the enormity of the place. He could hear a single drip off somewhere far, far below. It creeped him out, and he wondered how he could catch up with the others, a thought that had never entered his mind when he left the group.

Snickers took a few steps in the direction of a faint, far away light. He stepped on things that crunched and wiggled beneath his paws. He heard a moan behind him and immediately felt a tinge of nausea. As he inched closer to the dim light, he grew more and more terrified of who or what he would find. Perhaps he should have listened to Mr. Shadow before stepping into the vent.

Near the strange, glowing light came odd and eerie noises. Low noises, mournful noises like from a nightmare. He soon came upon some sort of a make-shift wall. It was sloppily built and crackling throughout. There was a small hole, behind it, light emanated. Carefully, Snickers pressed his eye up to the opening and peered inside. What he saw there,

Chapter Eleven

he would never forget. On the other side of the wall was an endless city, dangling three stories below ground, and stretching forever. It was gloomy and foggy, drippy and drab. The musty air formed swirls of the darkest blue imaginable, with slick shreds of light peeking out at random corners and spots. There were a few crumbling structures made of boxes and mountains of spit balls, which seemed to form some sort of building, or housing. But for what or for whom? From way up top, Snickers could barely make out the ground. It was scattered with bizarre objects of twisted shapes and mangled images.

On second glance Snickers found those very things to be creatures. The underground city was plagued by grotesque, mutated creatures infested with disease. The snarled, crippled things were like the living dead. Snickers stood in horror at their ravenous conditions and hellish existence. No normal animal could survive down there, not in that wretched place. Through the tiny hole Snickers could see what shockingly seemed to be a cat turned inside out, and a half dog/ half iguana with six ears and a tongue that reached nearly three feet. It limped around groaning and gagging with others that looked the same. Haunting, screechy voices and shrilling sounds echoed through Snicker's ears. He knew he had found hell right there under his city. Snickers took quick, sharp glances at each and every disgusting sight when suddenly a gritty, bloody eye appeared in the hole. Some-

 188

one was watching him. Snickers exploded back as the mystery creature stared him down. He could hear its claws begin to scratch and chisel at the wooden wall. It was coming after him.

"Eeek!" Snicker shrieked. He leapt off with a roar and ran and ran his little heart out. From behind him he heard the gurgling growls of his predator and its thunderous footsteps. Running faster, he saw another light up ahead. Afraid of where it led, but desperate to get out, Snickers dashed toward the glow and jumped right through the bars surrounding it. He closed his eyes and ducked as his body flew through the air. He landed with a thud on the subway tracks just as a muddy subway car came zooming forward.

"Ahhhhh!" Snickers hollered, dashing out of the way in the nick of time. Without realizing it, he had jumped through the vent of another subway stop. He looked up and surprisingly saw the faces of Mr. Shadow and his class in the train windows. The subway stopped to pick up a handful of people. As it did, Snickers crunched his body under the train, curled around, and swung himself into the last car just as the doors were closing. From the force of his mad entry, his body flew across the car smashing into one of the vinyl seats. He lay there for a moment panting and shivering. When he finally caught his breath and opened his eyes, he found a very angry Mr. Shadow glaring at his face. Steam poured from his teacher's ears. Queen Elizabeth had the same fierce look, as did

Chapter Eleven

the others. Snickers knew he was in huge trouble, still he peeked out of the window and searched for the tiny vent. He saw it immediately. From behind the vent door, two rather large, greenish paws wriggled back into the darkness.

Just then, Mr. Shadow grabbed hold of Snickers' back and yanked him away from the glass. He was livid. "Where have you been?" he rumbled. "What have you been doing?"

"Uh...uh," Snickers struggled. Sweat poured over his face and a strange, slimy muck covered his paws. "I guess I got lost?"

Mr. Shadow and Queen Elizabeth spent the rest of the ride howling and screaming at Snickers. They both yelled so loud and so fast and with such a racket that nobody could understand a word they said. Snickers cried under a seat the entire time. He was told he would never be allowed on another field trip ever again.

Everybody cheered as they approached the 54th Street Station, that is, everyone except Snickers. Still, all were exhausted and hungry. They dreamed and drooled of the special meal Roy and Yellowtail had promised them.

The ten cats hustled back through the last few blocks to the Factory, two-by-two, with Mr. Shadow in the lead and Queen Elizabeth bringing up the rear. It was almost eleven o'clock, and the forgotten sun showed no indication of waking up. Thick storm clouds were closing in for their afternoon hover over the city. It seemed the clouds never took a day off.

The closer everyone got to the Factory, the more and more obvious it became that something wasn't right. A small crowd of cats were gathered outside of the burned out building. An odd sight for such a discrete group. There seemed to be some sort of commotion out front. From a block away, nobody could tell what it was. Mr. Shadow took a deep, concentrated look in the direction, but lost his balance, tripped and fell on Twinkle Toes' tail, sending him into a frenzy.

"Whoooo!" Twinkled Toes wailed. He grabbed his tail between his legs and cradled it, rocking back and forth as he screamed right there on the street corner. Some of the people stopped to look at what seemed like a deranged cat, but that's all they did.

"Twinkle Toes," Mr. Shadow said. "Gosh, I'm awful sorry. Are you all right? Do you need help?" He held out a paw to assist him up.

All the cats looked down at Twinkle Toes in a huddle as he clutched his throbbing tail. After a moment he looked up. "No, it's cool, man," he said calmly, though forcibly. "Really, I'm fine. Just a bruise, nothing to worry about. Thanks, brother, for the concern."

Twinkle Toes stood up and appeared to be all right. He wobbled for a moment before he started walking again. Everyone focused their attention back on the commotion at the Factory. Snickers frantically licked the remaining goo from his paws.

Outside the building Vittles and Waffles were arguing with Mr. Sox. Some of the other regulars like MayBelle and Soot were there too. Nobody could hear what they were saying, but the way their tails swung and their paws flailed, it was obvious they were all upset.

Just then, Uncle Fred looked up to follow a lost balloon. That's when he saw *it*. He was the first one to actually see it in a far off window near the corner of the building. It was a paw-written sign on pale yellow paper in some sort of red ink.

While Mr. Shadow and the others walked faster, Uncle Fred stopped to read the mysterious message. He stuck his nose high in the air and squinted his eyes real tight. He thought hard about Ms. Purrpurr's lessons on words and letters and sounds.

"Come on, Uncle Fred," barked Queen Elizabeth as she passed him.

He didn't listen. He wasn't going to move until he read all the words. He concentrated very hard, almost hurting his head. Then, a light bulb clicked. He immediately started to shake.

"Uh...uh....Mr. Sh..Shadow?" he struggled to say. "Mr. Shadow! *Mr. SHADOW!!*"

Mr. Shadow tugged at his sweater and turned around annoyed. Uncle Fred was standing in the middle of the street with his mouth wide open. "What is it Uncle Fred? Can't you see there's something going on over there?" He gave Uncle Fred a cruel look and stuck out his bottom jaw like a teenager would do.

Uncle Fred pointed at the window. Mr. Shadow looked up. So did the others.

"What is it, Mr. Shadow?" Darla asked.

Romeo began to read the words aloud. The others listened.

stickz, Don't forget Allyz roole!
4ined,
Fidel
leedr ov thv allyz

Nobody moved.

"Man, those cats sure can't spell," blurted Twinkle Toes.

"What does it mean?" Tabitha asked nervously.

"Nothing children," Queen Elizabeth said. "Nothing. I've seen this kind of thing before, but not

Chapter Eleven

since....Look, Fidel's just trying to scare us. He does that now and then. Really, there's nothing to worry about." She almost sounded convincing as she nuzzled up to a few of the more scared cats and comforted them. Her eyes met with Mr. Shadow's. They stared at each other with a familiar worry.

Mr. Shadow left the group and ran up to the Factory to join Mr. Sox and the others. The closer he got to the yellow and red sign hanging in the window, the more disturbing it became.

It was obvious now what the other cats were talking about. Mr. Shadow stayed back a moment, then inched his way up to Mr. Sox.

"What's this all about?" Mr. Shadow asked. As he did, a tiny rain drop fell on his nose as if to say, *here we come.*

Mr. Sox turned away from Vittles and Waffles to talk to his colleague. "Did you see what they did?" he asked in his shaky, old voice. Mr. Sox turned his whole head toward the upper windows.

"Yes. Yes I did," Mr. Shadow said. "When did it happen? Did anyone see who put it there?"

"No. Nobody saw who or when it happened. The reality is, it wouldn't matter anyway. An alley got in here somehow, and we know Fidel was behind it. He always is." Mr. Sox sat down on his hind legs and took off his glasses. "Those kids over there," he motioned to Romeo and the others, "have they seen the sign? Did they read it?"

 194

Life One

"Yes, Mr. Sox. In fact, Romeo read it to everybody."

"I'm not surprised," Mr. Sox smiled with pride. "Take them inside to the rec room right away. Assure them they are safe now. Whoever did this is gone. I'll be in soon."

Mr. Shadow agreed and returned to the others. He and Queen Elizabeth brought everyone into the Factory. Tabitha and Darla were the most scared. Darla was so shaken that she had to go to the litteroom more than usual. She insisted Tabitha go with her. Tabitha understood.

Inside, everyone waited for Mr. Sox. By now it was beginning to drizzle, slow but steady. All the cats were confused and concerned. Even Octavian the spider listened with his many brothers and sisters from deep inside the wall while they watched the action below. Romeo's curious mind raced through many different scenarios, all scary. Twinkle Toes had fallen asleep on one of the pillows, and Calvin insisted on going home. Mr. Shadow and Queen Elizabeth continued to console the younger, quivering cats. Though the teachers tried, they weren't able to calm everyone down.

"This is the end of the world! I feel it!" cried MayBell from under a chair.

"It's just a matter of time!" Snickers whined stuffing a meaty cockroach between his teeth. "Fidel could attack at any moment!"

Chapter Eleven

"You're both crazy. Nothing's going to happen," insisted Roy.

"Yeah, well...." MayBell scolded back.

All the cats began to argue louder and louder. Romeo and his friends watched the ranting and raving. The scared ones were even more frightened than before.

"Everybody calm down!" Mr. Sox said, surprising them as he walked into the room. Behind him were Waffles and Vittles, standing strong and confident like two brick walls. Fluffy and Romeo sat up straight anxious to hear exactly what Mr. Sox had to say. "Now relax, just relax." Mr. Sox continued firmly. He quickly looked everyone in the eye. He didn't like it when sticks fought with sticks. It was against their nature and exactly what the alleys wanted. Divide, then conquer.

"What are we going to do, Mr. Sox? What will happen to us now?" Darla cried out. "Are we going to die?"

Mr. Sox walked over to Darla who had begun to cry. He sat beside her and stroked her pretty fur. "No! Of course, we are not going to die," he told her. "In fact, nothing is going to happen at all." He circled the room with confidence. "Every now and then Fidel sends us a little reminder that he is still out there. It's just a trick. Don't worry, he has never done anything more, unless it was a *personal* issue." Mr. Sox paused, then added, "What worries me more is that an alley obviously got in here! But how? It wasn't through

the front entrance, we have fine guardsmen there."
He shot a proud look over to Waffles and Vittles.
"I suspect they may have come in through an open
window, or perhaps another entrance that we are not
aware of. As for now Vittles and Waffles have checked
the entire building and no alleys are here. But, we are
going to have to be a little more careful. Watch what
you say, and by all means, if you see something odd,
tell me right away." His little gray whiskers drooped
when he finished talking.

Snickers opened his mouth, something he had
been dying to do for a while. "But Mr. Sox," he began,
"what if the alleys come back? What if they are walking in here right now and have big rocks or something
like that. What will we do? Huh, Mr. Sox? Huh?"

Mr. Sox walked over to Snickers. "Look son,"
he said. "Right now, and for as long as necessary, we
will have guards stationed at every point of this building. In fact, we are taking volunteers for these posi-
tions to work in four hour shifts. Please see me after
this meeting if you are interested."

Romeo and Fluffy looked at each other with
the same light bulb illuminating over their heads.

The meeting ended and everyone sat in silence.
Scared to speak. Scared that the alleys were listening.
Even though Mr. Sox said everything was all right,
they couldn't help but be paranoid.

After a few moments, Fluffy and Romeo
jumped up and ran over to Mr. Sox. They were sud-

Chapter Eleven

denly so excited about something, an opposite emotion from the deadly mood that surrounded the rest of the cats. They practically trampled the old teacher, almost knocking him down as they eagerly jumped in circles around him.

"What is this?" Mr. Sox asked confused. "What are you boys doing?"

"We want to help! We want to help!" laughed Fluffy.

"Yes, Mr. Sox," Romeo added. "We want to be security guards. What do ya say?" Romeo and Fluffy posed like Waffles and Vittles did when they were in their serious, tough guy modes. They made mean faces and growled as deeply as they could.

"Look, boys," Mr. Sox began, "I know you want to help, and trust me, you will get your chance, but I can't use you as guards. You're still kittens. You've only been here a short time, and besides, you don't even know your way around the entire building. What if something did happen? What would you do? No offense, but you're not strong enough to fight anybody off."

"But, Mr. Sox," Fluffy pleaded, "you said yourself that nothing's going to happen anyway."

"Yes, but we still have to be as properly prepared as we can. I don't *think* anything will happen, but with Fidel you can never be completely sure. Like I said, he has done this sort of thing before, and luckily, nothing came of it. But who's to say this time won't be

 198

different? I'm sorry, but I'm just not going to put you two in that position. It's for your own good."

"But," Romeo whined. "Mr. Sox....."

"Hush Romeo. In time," Mr. Sox whispered. "Trust me, in time you will have your day."

Romeo and Fluffy walked off dragging their tails on the floor. Their day. When would *that* be?

Chapter Twelve

Deep in the alley Fidel and Bait laughed at their little adventure. They gnawed on a juicy mouse they had just captured and torn apart. Bait got the legs, while Fidel took the middle. His paws were bloody and speckled with mouse guts, though most of the red liquid was washed away by the rain. Sinisterly, the wind blew Fidel's ID tags like an eerie wind chime around his neck.

"You're sure nobody saw you at that Factory, right?" Fidel asked.

"Yeah, boss. Those loser sticks didn't see a thing," Bait said proudly.

"Good! Good work, Bait." Fidel picked his teeth with a mouse bone splinter as Raven watched from under the flaps of a broken umbrella. Her fur was soaked, and her red painted claws bled onto the

 200

alley floor.

Fidel's posse kept close, but as always, sat in complete silence. Fidel never allowed them to speak. They practiced gritting their teeth and planned great chases in their heads.

"You should have seen 'em, Fidel," Bait laughed. "The old guy was running around screaming. The girls were cryin'. And they all just looked like idiots."

Fidel's eyes glowed and a slick grin slapped across his face. He tightened his left paw and crushed the remaining mouse bones into dozens of tiny pieces. He threw them onto the pavement with a nasty laugh then leaned in closer to Bait who still sported the same devilish grin. "What about that new kid? Was he there?"

Bait thought for a second, then answered. "Oh yeah, he was there with Queeny. By the time I left the old shack, he was all happy about somethin'. I didn't catch what it was." Bait crunched down hard on the mouse's severed left leg.

Fidel slapped his paw hard against the concrete splashing a wall of rain water onto Bait's battered face.

"He was happy, not *scared*?" Fidel howled. "He better get scared! Scared to death! That's the whole darn point! If we don't get to young sticks like him, there's no telling what they'll grow up to do." Fidel was getting louder and more fierce. Raven sunk deeper behind the umbrella, and the posse took a careful step back. "You go back to that *shack*, and I don't care what you have to do, but you get those losers scared stiff. Kill one if you have to. Just do it! And do it right this time!"

Fidel leapt forward and knocked over several boxes and garbage cans with his angry paw. Bait flew back startled as his hair bloomed out like a duster. Fidel grabbed Raven's tail with his teeth and pulled her as he walked away. She clawed on the ground until she gained her balance and was able to stand up. Fidel stalked off in a terrible huff giving Bait a look of pure evil. It was like his eyes swirled around in a freakish frenzy. Fidel's gang followed their leader the usual ten feet behind. After they turned the corner, Bait was left standing alone in the cold downpour, his blood raging like fire.

Over the next few days, it was business as usual at the Factory. Mr. Sox had placed more guards around the building to ensure the safety of those inside. Romeo and Fluffy were not part of that team, unfortunately. Uncle Fred, being a year older than the others, was chosen to guard the northwest corner. He got to stand behind a broken plank and peek out into the street. He was not Mr. Sox's first choice, but he was one of the few willing to help out. Most of the others were too scared. Like Romeo and Fluffy, Queen Elizabeth wanted to be a guard, but Mr. Sox wouldn't allow it. Not because she was a female, but because of her bus accident. He didn't want to see her possibly lose another life. Always a team player, she did her best to keep up the morale of the cats inside. She had a natural talent for this, which Mr. Sox had recognized in her for a long time.

Over the weekend Romeo didn't go to the Factory at all. He had to spend it with Dennis at his grandmother's house. Dennis brought him there for a visit once in a while but had never taken him for the whole weekend.

Grandma Crumb lived only a short distance away, yet far enough out of Romeo's neighborhood for him to feel lost. She lived alone with her pet mouse Rich, who Romeo eyed and drooled over the entire weekend. Romeo seriously thought about eating him. He was so plump and would be such an easy catch. The mouse was sitting in a little cage on the bureau just waiting to be devoured. But when Romeo saw Grandma Crumb playing with the delicious rodent, he quickly realized the critter would be sorely missed. What a waste of a perfectly good mouse.

Romeo enjoyed Grandma Crumb's house. It was very similar to Dennis' home, even down to the same family photos on the walls. She had a beautiful piano that she played, though not very well. But Romeo still liked the sound. Most of all, Romeo was fed like a guest. Rather than canned cat food, he was given poached salmon. Snickers would have been in absolute heaven. His water, in a fancy porcelain bowl,

Chapter Twelve

was cold and changed often. Grandma Crumb treated all animals well, even her stupid mouse.

During the day Dennis and his Grandmother ventured out into the big city leaving Romeo alone. He had no way out of the apartment, thus was forced to watch the world from the window like so many other indoor cats.

As soon as Dennis left, Romeo planted himself on the peeling window sill, pressing his little nose against the cold glass. Outside it was windy. Not only could Romeo see it, but he could hear it as well. It growled like an angry ghost. The people below clutched tightly to their hats and their children so they would not blow away.

Later in the afternoon, after Romeo ate some leftover tuna, he looked down at the sidewalk. There, he spotted Bull and the dogs. His body tightened as he watched the hounds scaring everyone in their path. The tar stains on their fur were clearly gone, though Romeo wondered if the memory still lingered. Probably. Maybe they were looking for *him*. As the beasts walked past Grandma Crumb's building, Romeo stepped out of sight from the seventh floor window, just in case.

Feeling safe again, Romeo could see directly into a nearby alley from his high perch. With the help of some flickering street lamps, he watched some cats hide when the dogs strolled by. Though they were alley cats, Romeo felt a tinge of relief that the vicious dogs didn't find them.

As he watched the alley cats a little longer, he became intrigued with their behavior and began to study them with new eyes. They were playing games, catching bugs, hiding from the dogs, and just having a good time. Hours went by before Romeo realized how mesmerized he had become. Though he wouldn't admit it to the others at the Factory, the alleys seemed to be doing a lot of the same things the sticks did. He almost wanted to join them. That is... until a stick walked by. Romeo learned quickly how to spot a stick from an alley. A stick was usually cleaner, often groomed, but most importantly had a collar and ID tag. Of course, some alleys like Fidel had stolen collars. This cat that Romeo saw fit the description of a typical stick, nice hairdo and sporting a cute plaid collar. For a second Romeo thought he looked familiar. Maybe not. From the window sill, Romeo could see that the alleys had spotted the stick coming up the street also. They quickly huddled, planning something. Panicked, Romeo wanted to shout down to the unsuspecting cat. He couldn't.

Suddenly, one of the alleys jumped on top of a garbage can, back arched high. A second stood behind a big piece of metal pipe. Some of the others crouched near the entrance to the alley. As the dapper cat approached, Romeo chewed his claws nervously and turned away, afraid to look.

Crash! Romeo heard a deafening noise and

swore he felt a rumble beneath him. He looked out the window and suctioned himself to the glass horrified. With all his strength, the alley cat hiding behind the pipe rolled the big, steel cylinder right into the passing stick. It struck him like a sudden bolt of lightning, throwing him into a state of shock. The stick hissed and squirmed disoriented as the alleys laughed viciously.

Romeo clawed at the window, though it was no use. Next, the alley on the trash can sent the bin tumbling over. It landed on top of the innocent cat. He was covered in rotten banana peels, sharp beer cans, used tissues, and other garbage. The high-pitched cackling from the hiding alleys sounded like a coven of witches. The poor thing lay there alone in all the muck, embarrassed and confused, as the people walked by disgusted and disinterested. The bad cats moved deeper into the alley. Romeo could see them praising each other with menacing high-fives. Once again, he saw them as the monsters they were and felt ashamed for even thinking he could relate to them only moments ago.

Just then, a little girl passing by stopped to look at the mangled cat that blocked her way. Seeing his quivering body, she let out a screeching scream. The black balloon she clenched bobbed and shook savagely in the wind. Her father pulled her away, but her eyes stayed on the cat. However, the balloon escaped her cold hand. It rose high into the air, all

Life One

the way up to the seventh floor. Oddly, it hovered for a brief moment directly in front of Romeo's window before continuing on its long journey. Romeo watched as it quietly drifted off into the clouds and disappeared forever.

Chapter Thirteen

Monday morning Romeo and Queen Elizabeth walked to the Factory together. He spotted her through Dennis' window, and motioned to wait for him outside.

They met below at the broken street lamp at a few minutes to eight. Dennis tromped off to school, dropping his homework in the mud. He didn't notice and probably didn't care.

On their way Queen Elizabeth told Romeo things had calmed down at the Factory, and Mr. Sox didn't feel it necessary to have so many guards patrolling anymore.

"Fidel hasn't sent another warning," she explained. "And I don't think he will. Nobody thinks they will try to sneak in again now that we're onto them."

Life One

Romeo walked quickly to keep up. "I hope you're right, Queen Elizabeth. A lot of the other kids are really scared. I don't like seeing them like that. They're good cats, you know."

Queen Elizabeth nodded. She was charmed by his honest concern for the others rather than for himself. She smiled in his direction.

Suddenly, Romeo heard a strange noise behind him. Clanging and banging and loud shriekish laughs. They were getting closer, and he was afraid to turn around.

"What the heck is that?" he asked, his lower lip trembling.

Queen Elizabeth heard the same disturbing sounds and turned around to look. She put one paw up to Romeo and said, "Stand back, Romeo. Get out of his way."

"Who? Who is it?"

Just then, a cat, an odd, skinny cat with ratty fur and dazed eyes, came bumbling by. He was banging into everything he saw like a drunken bum. He walked right up to Romeo and Queen Elizabeth, then stopped, though not still. He swayed from right to left making Romeo a little dizzy. Queen Elizabeth held Romeo back, protecting him from this oddball. By his frazzled look, Romeo assumed he was an alley. And after the savagery he saw happen near Grandma Crumb's home, he didn't want to get too close.

The strange cat squinted his beady eyes and

Chapter Thirteen

tried to focus on Queen Elizabeth. His mouth was wide open and his tongue hung out. "Hey thar, Queeeeeen Bethbeth," he mumbled. Just as he said that, he fell on the ground and started laughing uncontrollably, kicking himself repeatedly in the head with his back paw.

Romeo stood farther back behind Queen Elizabeth. He noticed she didn't seem scared, but rather totally annoyed.

"Come on, Romeo," she said rolling her eyes. "Let's keep going." Then she shouted, "Spaz, you go home!"

They continued on their way as Romeo looked back at the cat. He was now up and walking zigzagged through the busy street as taxis and cars honked him out of their way.

"Who was that?" Romeo asked. "*What* was that?"

"That was Spaz," Queen Elizabeth sighed. She leaned into Romeo and whispered, "He's on *the nip*. He's a stick, believe it or not. Once he was even a handsome, smart fellow. Not anymore though. He was kicked out of the Factory because... *the nip*." She shook her head in disappointment and kept walking.

Romeo thought for a second about this new word. "What's nip? Is it some sort of cat food?"

"No, kiddo, it's bad, real bad. You need to stay away from it unless you want to end up like Spaz," she scolded motherly.

Romeo looked back and could still see Spaz

 210

weaving in and out between the cars practically getting flattened several times.

At the Factory Queen Elizabeth went off to chat with some of her friends while Romeo proceeded directly to the art room for Ms. Purrpurr's class. They would be meeting there all week. Romeo hadn't been to the art room yet and was excited to play around with paints and colors. Whenever he saw another cat coming from the art room, it was always dotted with specs of blue or purple and globs of gooey clay. Romeo and the others were thrilled. The art room was open, and Romeo didn't hesitate to go inside. He was the first to arrive.

On the dusty shelves, which were once home to umbrella equipment, rested old soup and vegetable cans. Pieces of their original labels were still stuck on the tin, all for things Romeo didn't like, for example, waxed green beans and beets. The cans were now rusted and dented, yet cleaned out to hold pretty colors, blues, reds, and yellows. Much of them were left behind after the fire. The rest were carefully carried over by Skid.

Beside the cans of paint, were big, bushy brushes, dirty rags, and a small bucket of water which was a deep, murky purple. The paint smell was strong and even made Romeo feel a little lightheaded. The old desk tops served as work stations. A few of them had big balls of clay placed there by someone, perhaps Ms. Purrpurr.

Chapter Thirteen

The room itself was strangely dark and very dusty. There was a ton of soot sprinkled about the floor and a large hole in the ceiling that led to the fourth floor. The walls were covered with paintings done by students. Many were decorated with paw prints and stuff like that. One painting that hung near the door was of a devilish-looking creature with horns on its head and long sharp fangs. Romeo wondered who painted that one, and why.

Soon, some of the other students arrived. Snickers and Uncle Fred walked in with fish bones hanging out of their mouths, followed by Twinkle Toes. His front right paw was completely wrapped in a tight bandage, and he walked with a slight limp.

"What happened to your leg, Twinkle Toes?" asked Uncle Fred.

"Oh that," Twinkle Toes said calmly. "Oh yeah, bro, that's nothin'. I, uh, had a little accident, that's all. It's nothing to worry about. My guy put this on just as a precaution. Thanks anyway."

Uncle Fred and Romeo glanced at each other with tight eyes and wondered if Twinkle Toes was telling the truth. They watched him as he lay across one of the desks and closed his eyes.

Ms. Purrpurr entered next along with most of the others. Then came Fluffy. He stuck his head in the door, but didn't come all the way in. The look on his face was strange, almost like he was going to cry.

Ms. Purrpurr saw him and beckoned, "Come

on, Fluffy. What are you doing out there?"

Fluffy didn't answer, his pouty look getting more intense. By now all the cats were staring at him, curious what his deal was.

"Come on," the teacher insisted. "We haven't got all day, you know."

Just then, Fluffy opened his mouth. "I..I don't feel well. I think I'm just going home." He turned around just as Ms. Purrpurr walked to the door and flung it open.

"Don't be silly," she said with a stern tone. "If you were sick, you wouldn't have walked all the way...."

Suddenly, Ms. Purrpurr stopped talking and gawked at Fluffy. Everyone else could see him now. There he stood in the dark hall, knees shaking, wearing a pretty yellow and white polka dotted skirt. He turned his head away and immediately started to tear up. Ms. Purrpurr didn't know what to say in response to this peculiar sight. Unfortunately, all the other cats began to laugh and point.

"Boy, don't you look pretty today!" Calvin shouted.

"Wow, look at those sexy legs!" Snickers barked.

They all teased him, except for Romeo.

"Why are you wearing a skirt?" Romeo asked quietly, moving to the door.

Fluffy looked back toward his tail and stared

Chapter Thirteen

at the frilly garment that hung unattractively around his middle. "It's my person, Cassie. She put it on me. It belongs to her doll."

"Doesn't she know you're a male?" Romeo asked, almost insulted for his friend.

"Yeah, but since she turned six, she's become a monster." Fluffy leaned in close. "Don't tell the others, but she dresses me up all the time. I'm thinking of running away."

"Oh, don't do that. I think you look kind of cute." Romeo said, trying not to laugh.

Fluffy whacked Romeo with his tail as the two of them entered the art room. The other cats continued to giggle in Fluffy's direction, but Ms. Purrpurr kept it to a minimum.

Ms. Purrpurr gave everyone assigned seats. They were ready to begin but waited for Tabitha who apparently was running a little late.

Uncharacteristically, Calvin sat near his green blob of clay humming and tapping his paws. Something was different about him. It was almost as if he was in a good mood. Ms. Purrpurr and the rest of the cats couldn't help but notice.

Snickers, who could be nosey, asked, "What's with you, Calvin? Did you land a commercial or something?" Just then, Snickers started to lick himself inappropriately. The others made 'eeeww' sounds.

"Snickers!" Ms. Purrpurr scolded.

"Sorry," Snickers jumped, pulling his head

back up.

Ms. Purrpurr left the class to see if Tabitha was lingering outside. Perhaps she had forgotten that the group was meeting in the art room.

Calvin smiled and looked over at Snickers. "As a matter of fact," he began, "I actually had two auditions, and I didn't get either one." Then he laughed.

"I don't get it! Then what's with all the cheeriness?" Snickers snickered.

"Duh...yeah?" muttered Uncle Fred.

"Well, I heard on the news that the famous cat *Theodore 3rd* was brutally attacked this weekend by some cats in the city. His person got real nervous and wants to take him out west. Isn't that great? I only wish I could have seen that clean little body of his getting beaten up and twisted around." For a moment, Calvin went off into another world and slapped a sneer grin across his face.

Romeo instantly remembered what he saw from Grandma Crumb's window and realized why that poor cat looked so familiar. "Oh!" he shouted as the light went on. "Calvin, I saw the whole thing! Yeah, but he wasn't *beaten up*, beaten up. They poured garbage on him and rolled a...."

Just then, the door flew open. It was Ms. Purrpurr. She was panting and looked anguished and worried as she leaned against the door frame. All the cats sat up straight, curiously.

Ms. Purrpurr took a deep breath. "Tabitha isn't

215

outside. Waffles hasn't seen her either, but he did remind me that it's...it's...Monday! Come quick! We have to hurry!"

Ms. Purrpurr turned around and ran out the door. Behind her, she left a trail of dust and confusion.

Romeo leapt from the table. He watched his teacher hurry off and asked, "What's she talking about? What happens on Monday? Where's Tabitha?"

Fluffy jumped down. "It's the Pound! They *always* come on Mondays! Tabitha wasn't wearing a collar!"

A sudden shock swept over the cats in a way they hadn't expected. All of Mr. Shadow's warnings. All the talks about the Pound. Could they be true? Could the Pound *actually* take one of them away? Impossible. Maybe it wasn't the Pound at all. Maybe she was just late. After all, it was only a little after eight o'clock, and Mr. Shadow said that the Pound comes at twelve. But he also said that they sometimes make surprise visits.

Darla started to whimper as all the cats piled into the soup pot. Twinkle Toes limped behind. Down they went to the bottom floor where they found Ms. Purrpurr explaining the situation to Mr. Sox. She was hysterical. Romeo and the others ran to comfort her, though they were just as frightened.

"What can we do? What can we do?" Ms.

Life One

Purrpurr whined.

Mr. Sox sighed deeply and asked everyone to remain calm. They all listened as best they could and sat around him in a circle. Other cats in the room were now coming closer as well.

"There's nothing we *can* do," Mr. Sox unfortunately said. "The fact is, if the Pound got her, they got her. All we can do is wait and hope that she arrives soon." He petted Ms. Purrpurr softly on the top of her head.

The rest of the cats sat, hardly making a sound. They glanced at the door hoping to see Tabitha walk in. She didn't. Many thoughts swirled wildly through their heads. The image of sweet Tabitha being captured by those brutes made everyone sick to their stomachs. If she was captured, the chance of her returning was slim. Though she was still pretty with her white fur coat, she wasn't cuddly and cute any longer like a brand new kitten. Not many families would want to take home anyone older than a teeny-tiny kitten. Reality was, Tabitha would probably be killed within two weeks. All nine lives gone! Her friends felt hopeless.

"How about this, Mr. Sox," Snickers tried. "Maybe we can dress up like a human. You know, we'll all stack up together real tall and wear a mask or something. Then, we can buy her and take her home. What do you think, guys?" He looked around the room, but only found shaking heads.

Chapter Thirteen

"Nice idea, Snickers," Mr. Sox said kindly, "but, that's just not going to work."

"Maybe she was eaten by a giant rat," Uncle Fred suggested. Nobody agreed with that. "What? I've heard of giant rats before."

Suddenly, a voice came from behind. "There is one thing we can do." It was Queen Elizabeth.

Romeo whipped around and instantly felt ten times better. If anyone could help, it would surely be her.

"What can we do, Queen Elizabeth?" Romeo asked excitedly.

"Well," she went on, "I'm not making any promises, but I do know where Tabitha lives. I walked her home once when it was very late. She helped me that night. There were some alleys around, and she scared them away. I had a broken leg and was unable to defend myself. She's a feisty girl when she has to be."

Everyone seemed a little surprised because Tabitha was such a shy thing at school.

"Anyway, I can go over to her building and at least see if she's there. If she's not, then we can assume the Pound got her."

"Yes, Queen Elizabeth, you must go to her home and see what you can find. In the meantime, we will wait here. Hopefully, she'll show up on her own and this ordeal will all be over," Mr. Sox concluded.

Romeo pleaded to go with, but Queen Elizabeth asked him not too. She'd be back very soon and preferred he stay behind. Before she left, she whispered something in his ear when no one was looking.

"I've got a plan, kid," she said softly. "A plan for you, and a plan for Tabitha."

Romeo didn't have a chance to say a word because she was gone before he could respond.

"Wait!" he called. "What are you talking about?"

But it was no use. She was already heading out the door. Romeo watched her run off and felt the familiar pangs of being left behind. When he turned back, most of the others were huddled together. Darla and Ms. Purrpurr were still weepy. Others headed up to the Thinking Room to pray for Tabitha. Romeo grabbed a book from the floor and sat alone in the corner. He held it upside down and stared at the charred ceiling wondering what Queen Elizabeth would find.

Chapter Fourteen

Queen Elizabeth ran past Vittles, then Waffles. "I'll be right back! Not to worry!" she shouted as Waffles watched her tear down the street.

Outside, the wind was particularly harsh and bitter on this Monday morning. It slapped her body around like a kite.

Tabitha didn't live far away, only four blocks down 50th Street. As Queen Elizabeth approached Tabitha's brown brick building, she could see the shape of a young girl sitting on the stoop shivering from the cold.

As she got closer, Queen Elizabeth saw that the little girl was crying and holding something small in her hand. Her two long braids blew in the wind. The girl glanced up and saw Queen Elizabeth right away. She gave the cat a sad look that connected

 220

somehow in Queen Elizabeth's heart. Queen Elizabeth inched up to her. The closer she got, the more the girl cried.

Queen Elizabeth reached the stoop and sat next to the girl's little patten leather shoes. She nestled up against her cold leg and let the girl stroke her back. Just then, she heard a break in the girl's sobs. She was whispering in Queen Elizabeth's ear. "Find her," she said. "Find my kitty."

The little girl threw her hands over her face and wept. As she did, something fell to the ground. Queen Elizabeth looked down. It was a round, leather strap. A silver heart tag hung from one side. It read: *My name is Tabitha.* It was Tabitha's collar! Queen Elizabeth knew exactly what to do.

A rush came over her as she gave the girl a lick on her cheek and darted back to the Factory. Queen Elizabeth didn't see, but the sad girl waved goodbye holding Tabitha's collar in her hand. It was as if she knew.

Within moments Queen Elizabeth was back at the Factory entrance, safe and determined. She ran so fast, she was hardly able to speak. By the time Waffles undid all the intricate locks, she had managed to catch at least half of her breath.

Inside, everyone was waiting anxiously to hear about Tabitha. Their hopes had dimmed, for Tabitha had not arrived on her own.

Immediately Queen Elizabeth asked to speak

to Mr. Sox in private. Romeo and the others watched curiously. The two respected cats seemed to be arguing over something, but just what was unclear. After ten long minutes, Queen Elizabeth took off her own collar and handed it to Mr. Sox. His face look dour and serious. Queen Elizabeth had no expression, though was full of mystery.

She stepped into the middle of the room and made an announcement. All were silent.

"I'm going to say this once, and only once. We can assume Tabitha was picked up by the Pound. I am going to allow myself to get caught by them. It's the only way. There, I will find Tabitha and save her. I know it is dangerous, but it's something I have to do. She saved me once, and now it's my turn to save her. I'm a stick, and sticks help each other."

She stood tall and proud and spoke deeper than she normally did. Everyone was shocked by her plan, especially Romeo. As soon as Queen Elizabeth headed for the door, they all started whispering and gossiping among themselves.

She and Romeo had a moment before she left the building. Like before, Queen Elizabeth whispered something to him. "I'm going to do it, Romeo," she nodded. "Don't worry."

"But..." he grunted.

"When I'm there, I'm going to find out what happened to your brothers. You deserve to know." She smiled at him lovingly.

 222

Life One

For the second time that day, Romeo watched her leave. Again, he found himself in complete awe of Queen Elizabeth's bravery and kindness. Being the young cat that he was, he couldn't understand his feelings completely. He didn't realize it then, but he was quickly learning the meaning of respect.

Queen Elizabeth knew right where to go. She headed for the corner of 54th and 8th. It was a regular spot for the Pound. She would wait there no matter how long it took and allow herself to be captured.

As she walked to her destination, she began to feel nervous and alone. But once she put her mind to something, there was no turning back. Any time she doubted her plan, she thought of that fateful night when her life was saved by Tabitha's bravery. If it wasn't for her sharp, fast claws, who knows what would have happened.

When Queen Elizabeth got to the corner, she sat down and waited. Behind her was a dark alley. Strange moaning noises were echoing from it, along with some sort of mystical fog. She heard rattling and clanging and scratching. Still, her heart pounded louder than all those sounds put together.

She watched the feet for an hour or so as they rushed past on their way to work. The later it got, the faster the feet went. Monday mornings were always hard on the feet.

Queen Elizabeth's fur blew and twisted from the cold and heartless wind. No one stopped to pet

Chapter Fourteen

her. The people were in too much of a hurry. For the first time in a long while, she felt scared, really scared. Not like when the dogs were chasing her, but a lonely scared. She knew her plan was risky with consequences she would have to accept. She lay down with her paws over her cold nose as she shook and waited.

After a short while, the familiar gray van came sputtering up the street. Though she didn't see it immediately, Queen Elizabeth could hear its noisy engine and clanging insides. Then she spotted the black smog-cloud that surrounded the van from all sides. It rounded the corner and came to a screeching halt. The ghastly sight sent a chill up her spine. The door squeaked open and two plump legs stepped out. They splashed in the mucky slush that had gathered at the curb. Queen Elizabeth barely moved.

"What's with this one?" the guy with the fat legs yelled to another in the van. He had on dirty, old overalls and had bloody claw marks up and down his arms. "It's not even moving! He wants to go with us." The man knelt down next to Queen Elizabeth and stared at her with big, empty eyes. His breath smelled foreign and rancid. He smiled, though not pleasantly, showing off his three lone teeth.

"Put it in the truck and let's go," somebody yelled from the van. "I'm hungry."

Within minutes, Queen Elizabeth was being

Life One

thrown into a small wire cage. She put up a bit of a struggle to eliminate any suspicion and was immediately thrown in the back of the dreaded van.

Back there, she was not alone. Four other cats and one small dog, all in similar cages, shared the awful place. None of them had collars either and none were Tabitha. They all sat silently in the darkness and quiet and gently rocked with the motion of the van. Some of them were crying. Pangs of sadness and shame were overwhelming. The Pound was the ultimate humiliation, and these animals were already feeling its effects.

Along the ride, two more cats were picked up. One of them screamed and howled from the back of the van, hissing and banging on the sides of the cage. The louder he got, the more the drivers laughed. Queen Elizabeth tried to ignore the men by staring at the heavy clouds above through a tiny window as they tore through the city.

After a few minutes, the van stopped. They were at the Pound. The two men savagely yanked the cages from the back and tossed them onto the cold concrete floor. Everyone was jostled around. The dog was even hurt. The mean men immediately retreated to a large, pink box of stale, half-eaten donuts.

The cats and the dog were taken into another room. There, they were put into different cages. They were even smaller than the ones in the van. This room itself was very large, yet very empty. It made the tiny

Chapter Fourteen

 226

cages feel even smaller. There was a huge door at either end, and one metal desk sat at the far corner, though no one was at it. The walls were painted sad gray, even the cages were gray. There were several cats in this room, maybe twenty or so, and just the one other dog. The place was noisy. All sorts of mournful meows and howls echoed from every corner. Queen Elizabeth figured that Tabitha would be in one of the other cages nearby. Once settled, she would find her and plan their escape.

Queen Elizabeth was placed in a cage at the far left side of the dank room near the front door. It was the loneliest corner, for she was the only one there. Considering that most of these cats were probably alleys, Queen Elizabeth preferred this arrangement.

Throughout the day, the cats were checked on by some tired, disinterested woman in a tight, brown, polyester pant suit and blond wig. She fed the cats by throwing some crunchies into the cages as she sluggishly walked passed. Queen Elizabeth managed to get seven whole pieces, but they were actually very stale and foul tasting.

By nighttime, the lights were turned off and the two heavy, solid doors at the far end of the room were locked with bolts. There was some sort of alarm attached to the door leading to the outside. Behind this door, Queen Elizabeth could hear the sounds of constant barking. She wondered if those were the dogs that ate the cats who didn't get adopted. Hope-

Chapter Fourteen

fully, Tabitha hadn't met them yet.

After sitting and staring for a while, Queen Elizabeth had to close her eyes. It had been a very long and trying day, and she was exhausted. At that moment, she had to admit she had absolutely no idea how to escape this prison. She was concerned, yet hopeful, though she hadn't counted on the Pound having such secure doors and alarms. As ratty and rundown as the place was, the doors were highly advanced. She decided to take a quick nap before drawing up any plans.

Queen Elizabeth closed her tired eyes and quickly fell asleep. She dreamt she had been in the Pound for weeks and weeks, starving and alone in a room of dogs. The man from the van came in with an annoying laugh and dangled her by the tail over the pack of dogs. He started to lower her into their heavy jaws when....

She was suddenly awakened. In the cage next to her was a cat. They shared a thin wall and a few bars, though she wasn't able to see him clearly. He was rustling around. Queen Elizabeth wondered how long she had been asleep. It must have been a long time, for a sense of night was in the air. She sat and studied the cat out of curiosity and boredom.

He walked around his cage in tight little circles, then paused. With his back to Queen Elizabeth, he quickly turned. "Nice place here, huh?" he sarcastically said.

 228

Life One

Queen Elizabeth, who was still dazed and groggy from her nap, looked up. "Uh....yeah," she giggled. "It's great."

The new cat sat up straight near the part of the cage he shared with Queen Elizabeth. He looked at her through the bars. This time she got a glimpse of deep, dark eyes. He definitely seemed older than her, perhaps it was his heavy and hearty voice that gave it away.

"How long have you been here?" he asked inquisitively.

"Oh, just today," she told him after half a second of thought. "How about you?"

"I just got here."

"That's right. I forgot," Queen Elizabeth said embarrassed. "I didn't know they made pick ups this late at night."

"Oh, they don't," he said confidently. "I come in here now and again to see how the others are doing."

"What? I don't understand."

Suddenly, his tone grew deeper as he spoke faster. "Look, I know why you're here. You're trying to find a way out, is that right?"

Queen Elizabeth's mouth dropped as she squinted her eyes trying to get a better look at him. "Well, of course, I'm trying to get out. Actually, I have a...."

"A friend. You have a friend in here. Yes, you

are a very brave cat. Very brave indeed." Even in the darkness he had an aura of mystery and secrecy.

Again, Queen Elizabeth was shocked. "Why, yes, as a matter of fact, I do. But how did you..."

"Never mind that. If you want to get your friend out of here, you'll have to work fast." As he talked his shifty eyes scanned the dark grim room to see if anyone else was listening. It didn't seem that anyone was.

"But how? How can I get out? Do you know a way?" She was sounding desperate, yet excited.

"Yes, I know of a way. But first, there is something else you're here to accomplish. Some other purpose. Can you tell me what it is?" He asked with confidence.

By this point Queen Elizabeth had started to shake violently. She wasn't cold, rather chilled by the insight this strange cat had. She gathered her strength and spoke. "I am trying to help another friend find his family. They were all brought here together, all six of them, all young males. He doesn't know what happened to the others."

"I see. Now you must listen to me carefully. I'm going to help you and your friend get out of these cages and beyond that door." He motioned to the other end of the room by sticking his paw out between the bars. "There, you will talk to Beef, the dog you heard barking earlier. He's the watchdog around here and knows where everybody is."

Life One

"But...but... won't he hurt me? Why would he help *me*?" Queen Elizabeth questioned.

"He won't hurt you on one condition. He will have you pay him back with a promise. That promise is for you and him to discuss. Is that clear?"

Queen Elizabeth wondered if perhaps she was still dreaming. At a loss for any other plan, she decided to trust this mysterious cat. She gathered herself up and listened to what he said next.

"Now, do what I do and you will see how to get out of the cage."

He stretched out his paw and maneuvered the lock in such a way that it slid open. It took Queen Elizabeth two tries, but she was able to do it herself. Once free, she quickly walked up the antiseptic aisle of the Pound looking for Tabitha. There were cages on either side of them, stacked four cages high.

"Tabitha?" Queen Elizabeth whispered like a mouse. "Tabitha?"

"Uh, I'm Tabitha," blundered some heavy, male cat. "Get me outta this joint, doll?"

"You're not Tabitha. You're an alley." Queen Elizabeth snapped. As she did, other cats woke up. They got excited at the sight of seeing her walking around the room and started banging on their cages, getting louder and louder.

"What do I do?" Queen Elizabeth nervously called back to her new friend.

"Just keep looking," he said from his dark cell.

Chapter Fourteen

"Keep looking."

At the end of the room, Queen Elizabeth spotted two little paws sticking out of the bottom cage. They were waving slowly. It was Tabitha. Relieved, Queen Elizabeth ran over to her.

"What are you doing here?" Tabitha said surprised. "How did they catch you?"

"I'm here for you. Now, sit still and I'm going to get you out of there."

Queen Elizabeth jostled with the lock for a second before she finally got it open. She and Tabitha nestled together for a brief reunion, then stepped away from the cage. Their eyes caught many of the sad, scared-looking faces that surrounded them. Up, down, and around the entire room was one worried face after another, each whining and clutching onto their cage bars with hopeless paws.

"Don't look at them," Queen Elizabeth said to herself. "We can't save everyone." But the crying and whimpering was too much for her to take.

"Set them free!" she heard whispered in her ear. She didn't turn around to look, though she recognized the voice as that of her new friend. "But, be careful, some of them are alleys. Remember, you must hurry."

"All right, let's do it!" Queen Elizabeth said feeling a rush of energy come over her. She showed Tabitha how to open the cages. One by one the happy cats came pouring out, jumping down to their appar-

 232

ent freedom. They stretched and shook their stiff bodies. Some had been locked up for days.

Queen Elizabeth stood back for a moment and watched as Tabitha continued to free the sticks. Wanting to thank her new friend, she ran over to his cage, thrilled and grateful.

"Thank you, sir, for helping us, but, how do we get passed that door?" She pointed to the large thick door with the big alarm system on it.

"Yes, the door. It's very simple, really. See that large red button half-way up the side?"

She looked and saw the very button he spoke of.

"Well," he continued, "jump up and press that button. It will set off the alarm, but it will also open the door. You will have to move very fast through it. Within minutes, the guards will be here and not at all happy. Once outside, you can talk to Beef. Just let him know that you talked to me. He will try to chase after you guys at first, but don't worry, he wears a long chain. He can only go so far."

"Sounds risky, but thank you. And who should I tell Beef you are? I mean, what is your name?" Queen Elizabeth asked looking up into the cage.

"Remember, move fast! You won't have much time," he reminded her.

Queen Elizabeth paused a moment. "Why don't you come with us?" she asked.

"Because," he answered, "I'm needed here."

233

Chapter Fourteen

"I don't understand. Why *here?*" She looked around the miserable room. Tabitha had only let out all the sticks, leaving the alleys and the one vicious dog behind. Queen Elizabeth ran to her before getting the answer.

"This way, Tabitha," Queen Elizabeth pulled. "You have to meet this cat." She tugged Tabitha over to the cage where her new friend was.

But when they got there, his cage was empty.

"Who?" Tabitha asked. "You want me to meet who?"

Queen Elizabeth looked into the vacant cage. She was completely confused and frightened at the same time. "I don't know. He was just here a second ago. I swear."

"Come on, let's get out of here. Forget about him," Tabitha insisted.

She grabbed Queen Elizabeth by the ear and ran toward the door. Queen Elizabeth kept looking back at the cage. Just as she turned away for the last time, a soft purple glow flickered from the far corner of the cage.

Tabitha, Queen Elizabeth, and thirteen other cats stood by the back door. She explained about the alarm and the guards. She told Tabitha and the others to run fast while she stayed behind and talked to Beef.

"No, Queen Elizabeth!" Tabitha said scared. "It's too dangerous. He could hurt you."

 234

Life One

"He won't. Besides, I've come this far. I've got to talk to him."

Queen Elizabeth leapt up, and with all her might, pressed the red button. Just as she was told, the door swung open sounding the alarm. The noise inside the room was horrific as the alley cats left behind howled and wailed from the confines of their cages. Queen Elizabeth took one last look before heading for the door. She noticed that the male cat who jokingly claimed to be Tabitha was gone.

"Where'd that fat cat go?" she screamed at Tabitha in the midst of the chaos and commotion.

"I let him out," Tabitha yelled back.

"He was an alley!"

But Tabitha was already on her way and didn't have time to think, for she was practically trampled by the cats fleeing the door. Outside, Beef ran as far as he could on his chain after the escapees. When the dust cleared, two cats lay dead on the pavement from Beef's powerful blows. Within the hour they would be alive again and back on their way, as long as the Pound guards didn't get to them first.

By now Tabitha was out of sight, and Queen Elizabeth was the last cat to leave. Beef was huffing and growling and tugging at his collar. He was not very big, but very fierce and violent looking.

Behind Queen Elizabeth was the room of cages where other animals were still banging to get out. She knew she didn't have any time to waste. She

235

Chapter Fourteen

held her breath and walked straight up to Beef. With his big brown paws, he lunged and grabbed her tight, bringing her closer to his face. His long tongue was inches from her little head. Because of the cold air, smoky smelly puffs of breath exited from his angry jaws. He opened his mouth as if to bite her, when she screamed from his clutches.

"Beef! The cat inside told me you could help!" She closed her eyes tight, curled her body and didn't move. A moment passed, and her eyes opened. Beef was looking at her with his mouth now closed. He lowered her to the ground.

"What did he tell you?" Beef asked, tightening his grip.

"He...he told me that you could help me with something if I promised to help you."

Beef put her down on the ground. The night mist surrounded them as their eerie shadows stuck to the Pound wall. "Start talking," Beef grumbled.

Queen Elizabeth went on to explain the situation with Romeo and his five missing brothers. She reminded him that Romeo was a black and gray striped cat with a diamond on his back. Beef whispered something in her ear, causing Queen Elizabeth to drop her head low. She knew the truth now and would somehow find a way to tell Romeo that he would never see his beloved brothers again. But first, she had to go back into the Pound and release the dog that she left behind. That was her deal with Beef, and a promise was a promise. By now the guards had been alerted and were on their way. Queen Elizabeth only had seconds.

The big door was still slightly open, enough for her to creep back in. When she did, the caged alleys started hollering and roaring once again. She quickly found the jailed dog cage and told him he was getting out. From the other side of the room she could hear the faint sound of footsteps approaching. It was the guards. Her paws were quivering making it hard to open the lock. The dog was jumping up and down, anxious for freedom. Finally, the cage door opened releasing him. He ran outside to safety without even a thank you. The guards were very close now. Queen Elizabeth ran back toward the door. She could see Beef out there, pleased that she carried out her promise. Suddenly, a strong, angry paw shot out from the cage to her right and sliced her across the face. She immediately hissed, but the paw kept scratching her again and again, sending her into shock. As she collapsed to the floor, the paw hit her hard in the stomach.

"That's for not letting *us* out, you witch!" yelled the bitter, caged alley cat.

Because of the blow to the stomach, Queen Elizabeth lay dead on the Pound floor. A stream of blood dribbled from her mouth and soaked into her fur. By now, the guards were at the front door opening the lock with a vengeful urgency.

Chapter Fourteen

Just then, Tabitha came running back in the other door. She had hidden around the corner waiting for Queen Elizabeth to come out. When she saw her teacher lying on the hard floor, she ran as fast as she could to her side.

"Wake up! Wake up!" she cried. "Wake up!" Tabitha rocked and shook Queen Elizabeth, though it was no use. Tabitha knew she was dead. The little cat could see the front door slowly opening. The alley that had killed Queen Elizabeth hissed at Tabitha, about to swat at her too. Just then, Tabitha grabbed Queen Elizabeth's bloody neck with her teeth and pulled her away in the nick of time. She dragged the lifeless cat through the aisle to the far door. The alley cats flung themselves against their cage doors, hoping to see the two sticks get caught by the guards.

Little Tabitha continued to pull with all her young strength, finally making it to the back door just as the guards charged into the room. She yanked Queen Elizabeth outside, ripping her skin even more. Quickly, she pulled her around the corner into a dark place and waited quietly for the guards' next move. Luckily, the door slammed shut, and the guards never came out. "Beef will get 'em," she heard them say through the door.

Tabitha's heart pounded. She waited on the dark street for Queen Elizabeth to come back to life, unaware she was being watched by Max, the alley she accidentally set free. He eyed the two sticks from a distance. By the time Queen Elizabeth woke up, he was gone.

Queen Elizabeth opened her eyes slowly and focused on Tabitha. She carefully lifted her head. "Thank you," she said wearily. "Thank you."

"No, no, no!" Tabitha said in tears. "Thank *you*, Queen Elizabeth. Thank you." She threw herself down on Queen Elizabeth and held her with all the admiration in the world.

Chapter Fifteen

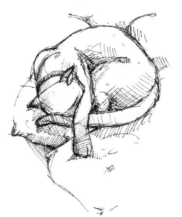

It was either very late at night or very early in the morning. The city was dark, yet showed faint hints of light. The sleepy neon signs and street lamps didn't do much but illuminate the dust that hovered around them.

Tabitha and Queen Elizabeth headed back to the Factory at a slow and haggard pace. The streets were empty, yet bursting with haunting images. Shadows followed them around every corner, and the hum of hungry cats vibrated passed every alley. Queen Elizabeth was tired and forlorn. She didn't say a word as the two continued on their way.

The Factory was a far thirteen blocks away. Tabitha made the decision they should take the subway. Tired, Queen Elizabeth agreed as they headed into the 6th Street station. After what they

 240

had just been through, the subway would be a piece of cake. Hardly any people were getting on the trains, and the ones who did were not very alert. Tabitha led Queen Elizabeth, as she was taught, to the far end of the platform. They jumped onto the last car of the train. After an uneventful ride, they reached the station nearest the Factory.

They walked the final block. Vittles was patrolling the entrance.

"You're here!" he yelled with relief. "Oh, I knew you could do it, babe! I knew it!"

Queen Elizabeth and Tabitha made their way down the long hallway into the rec room. A few cats were asleep on the pillows but most had returned home. Even Romeo was gone.

Queen Elizabeth flopped herself down on the first pillow she found. She quickly fell asleep, though not for long. Her sleep was restless and tormented. Reality had set in, and she now had to face the cruel facts that she had just become a niner. One more fragile life was all she had left. She had to make it an important one, yet a careful one. Unfortunately, the ninth life was usually the shortest.

Queen Elizabeth woke up about seven A.M. Tabitha was resting peacefully on a pillow nearby. It was a comfort to see her. Despite her new predicament, she knew losing her eighth life had been a worthwhile experience. She thought of the sad little girl who cried on the stoop near the sidewalk and forgot momentarily about her eighth death. She soon decided to wake Tabitha up and take her home to her family.

They quietly walked the four gloomy blocks again. Neither one had spoken much at all since they left the Pound. The only thing mentioned was another promise. Queen Elizabeth made Tabitha swear not to tell anyone about losing her eighth life.

"I don't understand," Tabitha said.

"I don't want everyone to worry about me." Queen Elizabeth added.

When they neared Tabitha's building, Queen Elizabeth once again saw the little girl from the stoop. She decided to stay back and allow Tabitha to walk the final steps alone. Tabitha ran to her person with more speed than she thought she had. She leapt into her lap sending the girl's tears far away. Queen Elizabeth watched the sweet reunion, then turned to away. As she did, she took one final look in the direction of the two friends and caught the eye of the little girl. The girl held onto Tabitha tightly, but looked directly at Queen Elizabeth.

"Thank you," she mouthed from the steps.

Queen Elizabeth blinked and walked away. Rather than going back to the Factory, she went home to see Gwen.

Later that morning, the hubbub around the Factory was that Tabitha and Queen Elizabeth were all right. Vittles told everyone the happy truth of their early arrival. Anxiously, all the cats waited for them to return for a victory celebration.

Tabitha walked in around nine o'clock after her people had gone off to school. Everyone greeted her with warm hellos and congratulations. They were all interested in hearing the details of how they escaped the horror of the Pound. Tabitha insisted on waiting for Queen Elizabeth before any story would be told.

Finally, at about ten-thirty, Queen Elizabeth showed up. She was still tired, yet put on a happy, glowing face.

"....and then," she explained to the huddled cats. "... the door opened and Beef, the large dog, sat there in the distance growling at us."

She told the gruesome tale with as much animation and charisma as a movie star. In fact, Calvin took mental notes on her delivery and body movements. Even though she described all the excitement and danger, Queen Elizabeth did leave out two crucial parts. She made no mention of her supposed *friend*, and purposefully left out her sad ending.

"How did you get away without a scratch?" Soot shouted.

"Yeah, was the dog blind or something?" Uncle Fred asked.

Queen Elizabeth looked at Tabitha and hurried for something to say. Truth was, she got her life back, which meant all her bad scratches healed the night before. Tabitha felt that Queen Elizabeth should tell everyone the truth. Still, Queen Elizabeth went on with her story.

"I was lucky, I guess. The dog put up a pretty good fight," she added.

Everyone cheered and whistled as the two heroes marched through the Factory. They were all amazed at the speedy escape, something they doubted was possible. Romeo was mesmerized by her story, but was dying for his chance to speak with Queen Elizabeth alone. What about his brothers? He had to know what she found out.

Queen Elizabeth purposely avoided Romeo most of the day. She dodged him at the rec room, at Roy and Yellowtail's, and even in the Thinking Room where she, herself, had personal thanks to give. Romeo finally cornered her as she was leaving to go home.

"Wait!" Romeo shouted. "Wait for me!"

Queen Elizabeth knew that she couldn't ignore him any longer. She bit her lip and waited for him to catch up.

They were standing near the second door of the building. Romeo was excited, yet nervous at the same time. He looked at her with wide, adoring eyes, hungry for any bit of information. He finally got up the courage to ask what had been burning in him all day long.

"That was some story, Queen Elizabeth," he shyly said.

 244

Life One

"Thanks, kid. Just don't get any ideas of your own," she teased.

"Oh, don't worry about that. So, uh, did you find out anything about my five brothers? You just have to tell me. Where are they? Do they miss me?"

Romeo looked up at her with the same innocent eyes he had the day they met. He was full of life and questions and wonder. It would break her heart to tell him that his brothers had all been savagely killed over and over by an alley. If it weren't for Dennis, he would have been taken too. She looked into those sweet eyes and couldn't do it. She had no choice in her heart but to lie. Still, it would be a difficult lie to tell.

"Come over here, Romeo," she motioned, pulling him to a pillow a quiet corner. "Let me tell you what I found out." Her face turned sad, and Romeo's glow began to fade. He knew the news would not be good.

"W-w-what is it, Queen Elizabeth? Where are my brothers?" he asked with a shake in his voice.

"You see, Romeo," she explained, "sometimes things happen in our lives that we just don't understand. Take your brothers for instance. Sure, they loved you and still do, but..."

"Oh, just say it!" Romeo blurted out. "Tell me, *where are they?*"

Queen Elizabeth stared him in the face, then quietly said, "I don't know. The dog said they were

Chapter Fifteen

all taken away and that you were somehow left behind. He heard they were taken far west, over the big ocean, and would never return. I'm sorry Romeo, but they're gone."

Romeo turned his head and looked the other way. He didn't want her to see him cry, though that's exactly what happened. It started with one tear, then another, until he was weeping his little heart out. He looked up at Queen Elizabeth and whined, "Maybe I could go find them. If they're out there somewhere, then I could find them, right? Right?"

"No, Romeo, it's over. There's no way you could ever find them now. There's a whole, big world out there. It would be impossible. Just know that they love you, and I'm sure that wherever they are, they're thinking of you right now."

Queen Elizabeth held Romeo and felt guilty for lying to him this way. She knew he deserved better, though she didn't have the courage to be honest.

After a little while, Romeo and the others went home, except Twinkle Toes. They all appreciated their homes a little more that night, especially Tabitha, who always wore her collar from that day on.

Chapter Sixteen

Max found Fidel around the corner and down the block. He was at Kitty's Cavern, a sleazy, cabaret hot spot for male alleys.

Max walked in and was immediately escorted to Fidel's table by Margo, one of the club's prize dancers.

"Here you go, Maxie," Margo said with a wink. "Where you been keepin' yourself?"

As she sauntered away, Max gave her a healthy pinch on her bottom and tossed her a roach from under his paw. An impressive tip.

Fidel was sitting with his gang at the table closest to the stage. He was puffing away on a pipe full of cheap tobacco. In front of him was a deep bowl filled with beer. Next to him sat Raven, his usual gal, though his eyes were fixed on Lolita, the

Chapter Sixteen

star of the show.

Above, Lolita pranced around the stage tantalizing all who watched as she floated between two feather boas. She swung and swayed driving all the males mad. To the side, a band played moody music on their homemade instruments as the club's patrons slowly got more and more drunk. Raven sucked on a cigarette butt she found outside, while her *boyfriend* gawked at the female temptress on the stage.

Max knew not to bother Fidel during Lolita's dance, so he ordered a beer and waited for the song to end.

As it did, Lolita left to a concert of whistles and a shower of roaches. Next on stage would be Muttle, the feline comedian. He was a short, stubby tabby cat with a funny looking expression on his face. He had an orange bow tie wrapped around his thick neck and silly squares of tinfoil attached as shoes. Rather than whistles and tips, he was brought on by a series of boos and hisses. Still, the show must go on.

"So, uh," he began, "did you hear the one about the cat that sat on a mat? It turned out that the mat belonged to Fidel, so he killed him."

The room was silent.

"Okay, so you didn't like that one, but you'll love this one. Did you hear the one about the stick who cut the cheese? It was Swiss cheese, so they sent him to Switzerland."

Life One

Again, the crowd was still.

Below, Fidel turned his attention away from the stage as Muttle continued to disappoint the audience. He noticed that his old friend Max had joined his table. Fidel gave Raven a lick and turned toward Max.

"What's new with you, Max?" Fidel asked taking a puff of his pipe.

"Funny you should ask, Fidel," Max answered with a menacing grin.

"Oh, do tell, do tell."

"All right, so last night I had the unfortunate pleasure of going to da Pound. Don't even ask me how I got caught up in dat situation. All I can say is, I'll never play Truth or Dare again."

Fidel laughed.

"Anyway, so I'm at da Pound and dis stick broad gets outta her cage, opens up her friend's cage and starts unloadin' all the sticks from the joint. Anyways, the friend was da dumb one of the group. You know there's always a dumb one where sticks are consoiyned..."

"Yes," Fidel agreed wide-eyed.

"So, the dumb one opens up my cage by mistake. So, we all gets up against da back door when the first broad opens dat door and we all go runnin' out. I woulda opened the other alley cages if da guards weren't on their way."

"Understandable," Fidel nodded.

Chapter Sixteen

"So's, I'm out there and there's this big luggy dog chasin' us around. Beef, you remember, Beef? He got a few of da sticks, but I gots away okay. Next thing I knows, dis broad starts talkin' to da dog like he's gonna help her." Max leaned in closer. "She starts talkin' about dis cat named Romeo and his five bros, see. She says Romeo's got a diamond thing on his back." Max sat down and allowed Fidel to soak in the information.

"Yeah, Max?" Fidel said shaking his head. "What has this got to do with?....Wait a minute, you say he has a diamond on his back? And five brothers? Could he be..? *Mr. Gamble* and all his sons had diamonds on their backs."

Max nodded his head again. "Yep. Remember da fun we had whit dem?" He rubbed his two front paws together and laughed to himself.

"Then, wait a minute," Fidel charged. "This Romeo is the same cat Bait is always talking about. It has to be." He thought hard for a moment over his bowl of beer. "He said he's one for us to watch. And the female, what was her name?"

"It was, uh...Princess somethin', or Momma somethin' or..."

"Queen Elizabeth? Was it Queen Elizabeth?" Fidel asked with rage.

"Yeah, yeah! Dat was it! Who's she anyway?"

"Never mind who *she* is. It's Romeo I'm concerned about. Romeo, the stick, is really Romeo

Life One

Gamble, son to those *traitors* who robbed me of my six alley males. They all got *theirs*, didn't they Maxie?"

"Dey sure did," Max said remembering the ghastly slaughter of the Gamble parents four months earlier.

"I *thought* we got all six boys too. Apparently not. They were born with traitor blood, demons from our own side. How come I wasn't told one of them got away?" Fidel grabbed Max by the fur of his neck.

"I don't know, Fidel, really I don't." Fidel released him from his clutches. "All I remember is all da boys went to da Pound, and Beef sayin' dey was gone. We was rid of all of 'em. I guess one of 'em was da wrong cat. When I got there, I do rememba one of dem bodies did have more of a moon than a diamond on its back."

Fidel boiled at his seat. He knocked over the bowl of beer spilling it onto Raven's fur. Immediately, she started to lick it off, getting more intoxicated as she did.

"Let me think. Let me think," Fidel said as he concentrated. "This Romeo character is walking around after we killed his pathetic parents and massacred his five brothers? And this woman he's with, she knowlingly freed all the sticks, but not a single alley? Well, sir, in my book they will pay! Yessiree, they all better watch their furry backs!" Fidel stood up and walked out in a tremendous rage. The thought of anyone related to the traitorous Gambles walk-

Chapter Sixteen

ing around free and clear burned through him like fire. As Fidel left, he knocked over three tables and two waitresses. Nobody chased after him, not even Raven.

Over the next month or so Fidel, sent many warning signals to the sticks, starting with another sign near the Factory. This one was placed in a nearby tree where the sticks would surely see it. It read:

Stix bEWarE.

Fidel iz mad,
and wil atack.
No one is saif.
Stix go hom.

Mr. Sox and the others were terrified by such a message. Still, Mr. Sox insisted that it was just a threat, and Fidel wouldn't really attack.

More threats were felt during that month in the form of other random messages left around the city, in the subway stations, carved into a few trees, and even at the fish market Roy and Yellowtail frequented. Still, more serious warnings were left at City

Life One

Park, where Fidel's new crop of young cats savagely killed a number of small rodents, leaving body parts and signs for the sticks to find. They said things like, *Dis will be yoo, stix,* or *stix- yor next!*

Mr. Sox still kept up his argument that these attempts were only meant to scare the sticks. That Fidel was going through a power phase and not to worry. Yet, Mr. Sox's confident facade was slowly breaking down as he, himself, began to question the constant threat from the alleys. Thus, panic swept over the Factory like a huge, burly blanket. The Factory was already under *real* black clouds, and now it was under one of a different sort. Until this rumbling passed over, no sticks went out alone. No one took the subway. And Mr. Sox placed the additional guards back at their posts, including Uncle Fred, who was the most frightened of all.

Despite the tension, life for the Factory cats was business as usual. Music, art, and conversation continued to bounce off every beam, even classes remained in session. Keeping an air of normalcy was important. Romeo and all his friends tried their best to put on happy faces as they prepared for their graduation from Stick School. It was only one month away. They had proudly gained a basic understanding of reading, which they would now practice in the outside world. Mr. Shadow had successfully taught them the ins and outs of the city and how to get around. Of course, Mr. Sox had done all he could to instill stick pride in their hearts. It was up to them now. They would be on their own after one short month. It even appeared that Uncle Fred would be part of the graduating class, though he was still trailing behind.

One calm Wednesday morning following a huge rain storm, all the young stick students arrived for their eight o'clock class. As always, Darla was in the litteroom. Uncle Fred had already been scolded for cleaning his butt. And Twinkle Toes was on time for a change, though he looked awful. His fur was messy and wet, and he smelled mildewy.

"What happened to you?" Ms. Purrpurr asked, inspecting a bump on Twinkle Toes' head.

"Uh, nothin,' babe," Twinkle Toes chuckled. "I was playing out in the rain this morning and I guess I bumped my head. Nothin' to worry about." He laid down at his seat and gave Ms. Purrpurr an unconvincing smile. When she walked away, his seeming smile turned low, very low. Romeo noticed.

"All right, class," Ms. Purrpurr began as she walked to the front of the room, her big belly wiggling around. "Before we get started, I would like to discuss your graduation."

"Yeah!!" all the cats cheered.

"Settle down, settle down," she continued, tapping her chalk against her paw. "You have one more month to go."

They started cheering and banging again. This time Ms. Purrpurr gave her signature *look* and put on her best teacher voice. The cats stopped immediately.

"Now, the graduation itself is always a big celebration. Uncle Fred, I'm sure you remember watching the last one, even though you did not get to participate."

Uncle Fred nodded his head in shame.

"As always," she went on, "the ceremony will be held at City Park. It will be very grand with music and speeches and shrimp."

A panic fell over the class. Should they be going there? What if Fidel were to attack? Fluffy immediately raised his paw waving it uncontrollably.

Ms. Purrpurr rolled her beady eyes. "Yes Fluffy? Do you have something to say?"

He put his paw down and answered. "Yes, Ms. Purrpurr. Is City Park going to be safe?" A dash of worry sprung from his voice.

The rest of the class, with the exception of Twinkle Toes who had fallen asleep, nodded in agreement.

"There will be absolutely no problems," Ms. Purrpurr explained. "We will have several guards with us that day, and trust me, Fidel won't do anything in a public park."

"I hope the old lady's right," Snickers whispered to Romeo.

After that, the morning went on as usual. Ms. Purrpurr worked with the students on sentence structure and poetry. Hardly a cat was good at writing

Chapter Sixteen

their own poetry, yet Twinkle Toes did seem to be the best, when he wasn't snoring away. He was selected to recite a poem at the graduation, not something he was particularly looking forward to doing.

During Mr. Shadow's class Calvin got up from his seat to leave early.

"Where are *you* going?" Mr. Shadow barked holding two large ropes in his paws. He was in the middle of demonstrating how to tie a knot.

Calvin looked around with a dazed expression. "Uh, Mr. Shadow, I have to go. I have a big audition."

"Again?" Mr. Shadow asked. "You've been on three this week, and you haven't gotten one job. Why don't you just forget about this acting foolishness?"

Calvin stood back, surprised at Mr. Shadow's attitude. "Well," he went on, "Lloyd's expecting me. I *have* to go."

"All right, go ahead," Mr. Shadow huffed. "But be careful out there. It's raining pretty darn hard. And don't walk down any quiet streets!"

"I know. Whatever."

Calvin left the room with an attitude as the rest of the class went back to knot tying. Mr. Shadow, being the clumsy guy that he was, knew how to explain the procedure, though he had yet to do it well himself. His big, plump paws tangled and twisted the strings, frustrating him to no end. He finally let out a scream. Fluffy had to demonstrate the actual tying to the class.

 256

Life One

He was good at it. Mr. Shadow fixed his sweater and stepped aside, pretending he had planned the lesson that way. Nobody bought it, but they let him think they did.

After school Romeo and Snickers were deciding what to have for lunch. Fluffy would not be joining them because he wanted to read in the library. He loved books on Egyptian history. Twinkle Toes also declined their offer to come along.

"Naw, guys," Twinkle Toes mumbled. "I'm just going home, I guess."

"Well, you can't walk alone, not with all the threats out there," Romeo said concerned.

"Oh, I'll be all right. Don't worry. I'll see you guys tomorrow." Twinkle Toes trudged sluggishly toward the soup pot. His fur was still damp, and he had begun to shake and sneeze from the cold. Romeo and Snickers looked at each other with worry.

"Come on," Romeo whispered. "Let's follow him. Something's not right." He swatted Snickers with his tail and raced ahead. Twinkle Toes was already gone.

"But I'm so hungry," Snickers whined, clenching his grumbling tummy. "Can't we eat first? Please, please, please, please, please?" Snickers looked up at him with the saddest eyes he could fake.

"Awe, come on! We'll eat later. Besides, I saw you chewing on that spider during class. You can't be *that* hungry," Romeo reasoned.

257

Chapter Sixteen

"Hmph," Snickers moaned as he was pulled away, rumbling tummy and all.

Twinkle Toes was far in front of them as he headed down the hall and out of the building.

Romeo and Snickers trotted through the rain getting wetter and wetter. No cats like walking in the rain, but in a city like this, they were all used to it.

Up ahead they could see Twinkle Toes, though he couldn't see them. He was getting farther away because Snickers kept slowing them down. He stopped at every pretzel and hotdog stand smelling the enticing aromas. Because of the rain, all the mice and bugs were hiding, but that didn't stop Snickers from chasing a bird who had paused for a drink of puddle water.

"Come on Snickers!" Romeo wailed. "What are you going to do, kill a bird right here on the sidewalk in front of all the people? We have to keep going! Twinkle Toes is way up there already." Romeo was losing his patience, while Snickers was losing his hopes.

Soon after, Twinkle Toes came to his building on 55th Street between 6th and 7th. It looked more rundown than most. Before he hiked up the rusted, fire escape ladder that rested along the side, Twinkle Toes looked down the street. Quickly, Romeo and Snickers scurried out of sight behind a bus bench.

Twinkle Toes then began his climb. He lived on the second floor, thus not a far journey. The building was surrounded by cracked windows and dead, drenched plants. Twinkle Toes entered a corner apartment complete with a small balcony piled with muggy cardboard boxes. The heavy rain had soaked them through.

As Twinkle Toes disappeared inside, Romeo and Snickers ran up to the building. They sat under the balcony where their friend lived and waited. Within seconds, they heard terrible shouts and screams coming from above.

"Where the hell has this cat been? Get outta here with those muddy paws!" some man yelled from the apartment.

Just then, there was a horrible crash followed by a loud, painful meow. Snickers flinched forward, but Romeo held him back. Then, another voice shrilled. This time it was a woman's, though she didn't sound very ladylike. "Bart, get that filthy cat outta here! I swear, he's sleeping out on the porch again tonight! And I don't care how much it rains!"

Another series of terrible noises came from that apartment, including breaking glass, hitting, kicking, hissing, and pacing footsteps.

Down below Romeo and Snickers sat together next to a newspaper rack. They had stunned expressions on their faces and nasty thoughts in their heads.

"Wow," Romeo said softly, "I had no idea Twinkle Toes had it that bad, did you?"

Chapter Sixteen

"Let me at 'em!" Snickers growled shuffling toward the ladder. "I'll show them who to talk to!"

"Stop it, Snickers! Just stop it!" Romeo interrupted. He grabbed Snickers by the tail and pulled him back toward the newspaper vending machine. In fact, he pulled him with such force that they both flew back and banged into the side of it. Atop the rack was a large puddle of rain water. It spilled all over their already wet bodies.

"Come on!" Romeo said shaking off some of the water. "Let's go. There's nothing we can do now. We'll get lunch." Romeo walked away with a disturbing knot in his throat. He would talk to Mr. Sox about Twinkle Toes. *He* would know what to do.

As soon as Romeo said *lunch*, Snickers forgot all about Twinkle Toes and his unfortunate home life. For the rest of the afternoon, he and Romeo enjoyed stealing yummy scraps from behind a nearby butchery.

Meanwhile, back at Smelly's bar, Fidel and Bait were carving out their next plan.

"I've got to get that Queen Elizabeth," Fidel said menacingly under the flickering red light. "It's her fault Smack and Tumble lost their 9th lives at the Pound. She should have let them out! Her royal highness has got to be taught a lesson. Besides, I could use a new ID tag, if you know what I mean." He dangled his collar in Bait's direction.

Smack and Tumble were two former alleys that

 260

Life One

Fidel had known for a long time. They had been good to Fidel. Because they were left at the Pound following Queen Elizabeth's escape, they endured several horrible, grisly deaths. Fidel blamed Queen Elizabeth.

"Well, boss," Bait grumbled. "I think you're doing a pretty fine job scaring those losers. You should see 'em. I mean, they've even got cats standing around that whole building of theirs. It's dumb though, because I don't go in from the bottom. They'll never be able to stop me." Bait took a swig from his brew then wickedly threw the cup, bursting it against the wall. Pieces of glass bounced around and smashed onto Thumbs, who was playing somber, jazz tunes from the corner. Bait ignored the broken mess and casually ordered another drink.

"What do you think you're doing?" Fidel thundered. Thumbs just kept on playing.

Bait erased his cunning smirk and suddenly looked very dumbfounded. "I, uh...uh.." he muttered.

"Never mind, never mind," Fidel said, rolling his eyes and gaining his composure. In an instant, he tapped his paw in such a way bringing his whole gang dashing to his side. Without looking at any of them in the eye, he snidely said, "Go clean up Bait's mess! We wouldn't want Smelly to kick us out." They did as they were told.

Smelly smiled at Fidel, then smirked when he turned away to fix the drink.

Chapter Sixteen

"I don't care what you have to do," Fidel said drowning in his beer, "but scaring them just isn't enough. Go to that Factory tomorrow and see what you can find out! See what that *Romeo* is up to. If he's anything like his father, then he's a coward too! Do it or else!" Fidel got off of his stool and knocked it to the ground. His crew again was there to clean up the mess as Fidel stormed out of the bar, vengeful and angry.

The next sound heard came from outside as two young mice pleaded for their lives. Then, one final, loud gulp and a loud belch.

Chapter Seventeen

The following day at the Factory, Romeo and the others eagerly waited for class to begin. Ms. Purrpurr and Calvin were the only ones who hadn't arrived yet. Everyone else was there, even Twinkle Toes who looked more worn out than the day before. It seemed as though he hadn't cleaned himself in days and had a sniffle that wasn't letting up.

Romeo hadn't decided whether to talk to Mr. Sox, or Twinkle Toes himself. Yet, he knew it would have to be soon. He didn't like seeing his friend unhappy and sick.

Calvin ran in at the last second. He flew through the door with a gusto and energy he never showed before. A huge grin slid across his face as he grabbed Darla giving her a big lick on the cheek.

Chapter Seventeen

"Gross!" Darla screamed, running into the litteroom.

Calvin continued to prance about the room without his usual morning attitude.

"What's with you?" Fluffy asked snobbily.

Just then, Ms. Purrpurr entered and everyone hushed down. Calvin stepped up to the front of the room. Ms. Purrpurr stared at him with inquisitive eyes.

"Yes?" she said sincerely. "Is there something you need, Calvin dear?"

Calvin looked out at his classmates. "I'd like to make an announcement," he proudly stated.

"Go ahead," the teacher said, "just make it quick. We've got a lot to do today."

Calvin cleared his throat and began. "Well, you are all looking at the new spokescat for Slimy Cat Snacks." He smiled big and wide and waited for an anticipated response.

"Huh?" Uncle Fred spit.

"I said," Calvin repeated, "I'm the new spokescat for Slimy Cat Snacks."

No one believed him as evidenced in their blase expressions.

"Yeah, sure," Romeo teased. "I have to admit, you had me there for a second." Romeo shook his head and laughed.

Calvin's jaw dropped to the floor. He leaned against the teacher's desk and sighed heavily, very annoyed. "Guys, it's true!" he snapped. "I'm really the new Slimy Cat Snacks cat. Really."

Snickers, who was an expert on cat food and their ad campaigns, wiggled his big body around in his seat and asked, "Yeah? Then, where's Theodore, the other Slimy Cat Snacks cat?"

"Dummy, I already told you, he and his person left the city. He got attacked or something. Jeez, don't you ever listen to a word I say?" Calvin snapped.

The class laughed to themselves, making Calvin more and more agitated. He could almost feel the steam spitting from his ears. His blood was hot like coals, and he was beginning to grit his teeth.

"Fine! If you guys don't believe me, then just come to the Crowman's Day Parade and see for yourselves," Calvin whined.

Joe Crowman was the city's mayor and had been for some time. About the only thing he did for the city was create the annual Crowman's Day Parade. On one special Sunday, it ran all the way down trendy 4th Street, drawing huge crowds from all over the city. The parade showcased many young performers, mostly school bands, drill teams, local celebrities, stuff of that nature. One year Dennis Crumb, who was in his school band, was actually supposed to play the tuba in the parade. He missed out because he stuffed six rotten bananas in the horn one hour before show time and couldn't get them out. But the parade's prize attraction was its balloons. Enormous balloons fash-

Chapter Seventeen

ioned after the most popular cartoon and advertising characters hovered over the city and floated past the buildings like giant clouds. They would bounce through the air as they soared down the street, bobbing into street lamps and passed office windows. They were attached to long ropes that teams of people down below carried. The balloons could be seen coming from blocks away and meant big publicity for the products they represented. It was a big celebration, just about the only celebration in this city.

"What are you talking about, Calvin?" Tabitha asked. "How are *you* going to be in the Crowman's Day Parade?"

"Yeah?" the others prodded.

Calvin stood back and gave a gloatful smile through his thick whiskers. "Because, you nitwits, *I'm* the new Slimy cat! So, you will see a balloon of *me* next Sunday flying through the air. How's that for news, eh?" Calvin checked his claws arrogantly on his right paw.

"No way! You're kidding?" Fluffy roared.

"Just see for *yourselves* next Sunday. In fact, the only reason I'm here *today* is to tell you twerps about it. I have to go home right away because *I* have to *model* for the balloon. The Slimly Cat Snack company wants to begin their new campaign with *me* right away, just in time for the big parade. So, I guess I'll see you *losers* tomorrow."

The way Calvin emphasized half his words

made everyone wonder. There's no way he was telling the truth. Or was he? Just the thought of somebody hiring him for anything was ridiculous enough. It made a cat want to abandon stick life and go live in the depths of Vent City. Well, maybe not.

Everyone chuckled a few minutes more about Calvin after he left, then went on with their day. They figured he just wanted to ditch class by resorting to that dramatic lie. And Ms. Purrpurr wasn't pleased that Calvin was missing school so close to graduation.

"He better plan on making up his work," Ms. Purrpurr mumbled to herself.

After the class said the pledge, they discussed the plans for graduation. Soon it would be time to start practicing for the ceremony. They didn't have to do much more than march in a straight line, but for young cats even that was a challenge. Tabitha was selected to be Ms. Purrpurr's assistant for the celebration, and it was understood that Queen Elizabeth would give a speech. Twinkle Toes was working on his poem, and the others would help paint the diplomas. The papers would stay in the Factory during the ceremony because of the rain and be hung on the rec room's back wall. That wall was already adorned with dozens of other proud diplomas reaching back to Queen Elizabeth herself.

As they planned for their big day, nobody noticed Bait sneaking through the rafters. He snuck

Chapter Seventeen

in through the fourth floor by way of a dead, twisted tree. The guards below never thought to check the trees. Once inside, Bait watched Romeo through a crack in the wall.

"I should just do away with him now," Bait said to himself, rubbing his front paws together. "Naw, Fidel would be upset if he didn't get to see for himself."

Bait sat up there all morning. He watched the cats through the slit as clownish impressions of them formed in his head. "Pathetic," he said to himself as he spotted Uncle Fred trying to pick his nose with his claw. "Unbelievable," he muttered as Snickers fell off his chair and farted in front of the whole class.

When he got hungry, Bait simply reached back and grabbed a few maggots from the open fight wound on his back and gnawed away. Unfortunately for his stomach, he didn't notice fat, juicy Octavian circling just five inches above.

What an idiot, Octavian thought as he spun his sticky web.

Later that afternoon after Mr. Sox's lecture on bus safety, the future graduates left the classroom and walked through the library. Once again, Fluffy decided to stay in and look at some ancient Egyptian pictures. He was drawn to the ones of cats. He often closed his eyes and imagined himself living in ancient Egyptian times in a grand palace alongside of a great pharaoh draped in golden tassels and furs. Around

Life One

him a harem of females would pop baby mice into his mouth. And below his body, a velvety, puffy pillow would be fluffed for him on the hour. He and the pharaoh would parade through the pyramids on jeweled-covered litter boxes filled with dusty, golden litter. Litter bearers would hold them high above the dusty sand and bowing crowds. Oh, how Fluffy loved to fantasize.

Romeo and Snickers kept an eye on Twinkle Toes who didn't mutter a word the whole day. He did his usual slouch to the soup pot, but this time Romeo stopped him.

"Twinkle Toes!" he hollered. "Wait up!"

Twinkle Toes looked behind and faked a smile. He turned his head trying to avoid Romeo and a potential conversation. Yet, Romeo caught up to him before he could walk away.

"Yeah?" Twinkle Toes asked without his usual charismatic touch.

"Hey, uh, do you want to get a bite?" Romeo asked.

"Come along with us, Twinkle Toes," Snickers tagged. "We're going to find some mice."

"Snickers will even let you have the fattest one," Romeo said teasingly. Snickers shot him a *no way* look. Romeo slugged the glutton in the back when Twinkle Toes turned away.

"I don't think so, guys," Twinkle Toes said. "I'm really not very hungry. I should get home. They don't like it when I'm out too long."

Romeo and Snickers looked at each other lost.

"Yeah," Romeo said nervously. "We wouldn't want to make them mad or anything, would we? *Would we*, Snickers?"

"Uh....no, no, of course not...who?"

"See you later," Twinkle Toes said as he slumped away.

"Nice going, Snickers," Romeo punched.

"What did I do?"

As Twinkle Toes walked away, something clicked inside of Romeo. He just couldn't sit back and let Twinkle Toes leave again. Without a second thought, words shot out of Romeo's mouth... "We followed you home yesterday, Twinkle Toes."

Twinkle Toes stopped, his back to Romeo and Snickers. He didn't move.

Romeo paused and took a step closer. "We, uh, heard them yelling and stuff. You know, you don't deserve that." By now Romeo was directly behind Twinkle Toes and shaking like a leaf.

After a second or two, Twinkle Toes whipped around and stared Romeo and Snickers in the eye. "I don't know what you freaks are talkin' about," he said angrily. "Look man, I said I'm going home, and I'm going home! Good bye!"

"B-b-but..," Snickers sputtered.

Romeo stifled him with his paw. The two cats watched Twinkle Toes leave. They stood there sad and afraid for their friend. It was at that moment Romeo realized how lucky he was to have Dennis, as peculiar as Dennis was.

"Come on, Snickers," Romeo said. "Let's go talk to Mr. Sox." Romeo pulled him back into the library.

"Just once, can't we eat first?" Snickers whined.

That afternoon Romeo and Snickers told Mr. Sox everything they knew about Twinkle Toes. How he was always tired and messy and just not funny anymore. They especially told him what awful noises they heard coming from his grungy apartment. Mr. Sox had suspected something was going on. Unfortunately, after talking to Romeo and Snickers, his suspicions were confirmed.

"What do we do, Mr. Sox?" Romeo asked.

"Well, Romeo, I think that you will have to wait."

"Wait for what?" Romeo continued.

Mr. Sox took off his glasses and put them next to his atlas of the city. "When Twinkle Toes is ready to talk, he will." He rubbed his tired eyes and sat down. "I just hope it's not too late by then."

Romeo and Snickers looked worried. They shifted their eyes around in their heads as they thought and thought.

"Too late for what, Mr. Sox?" Snickers finally asked.

Life One

"Well, it is possible that Twinkle Toes has already lost some lives. I suspect he has, due to the level of his fatigue lately. Like I said, when he's ready to talk, he'll talk."

Neither cat liked what Mr. Sox had said, but listened knowing he was probably right.

The next week, classes were filled with tons of review. Ms. Purrpurr had everybody read a paragraph out of a book and spell out an entire sentence in yarn. Uncle Fred almost got everything right, but spelled *dork* instead of *pork* and suffered many jokes for it all week long.

Mr. Shadow finally demonstrated some weaponry with his rocks and rubber bands, while Mr. Sox lectured on cat abuse. Twinkle Toes sat very quietly.

Everyone planned on somehow going to the Crowman's Day Parade on Sunday. They would either spread out over the sidewalk *(a big group of cats looked suspicious to the people)*, or they would all gather and hide somewhere together, as long as it wasn't in an alley. They would try this choice first. Queen Elizabeth knew of an abandoned toy store on 4th with big windows. It would be perfect. The nice thing about the parade was you could see it from anywhere down 4th. The balloons were high up, thus allowing prime viewing. From the Factory's third floor window, several cats spotted some balloons already being prepared for the parade. MayBell recognized Freud Fig from the Nature Show, and Soot swore he saw Hector

Chapter Seventeen

the Wine-O from the Wine-O Beer Company. So far, nobody spotted Calvin's balloon, but he claimed they were still working on it.

Calvin had been in and out of class all week, apparently taking publicity pictures and getting ready for the big parade. According to him, he would be sitting on the actual float below the big balloon with the producers of the Slimy Cat Snack commercials. They would be riding on a giant fish-shaped cat snack as the Slimy Cat Snack jingle played on a continuous loop. Calvin was beside himself with joy. On Friday, he even brought in a can of Slimy Snacks for everyone to share. He had to carry it over in his teeth.

The general mood at the Factory was high. It had been almost two whole weeks since the alleys' last threat. The sticks figured Fidel's power phase had finally ended. Thus, everyone's mind was free to focus on the parade.

Finally Sunday came. All the cats met at nine o'clock sharp, except for Twinkle Toes who didn't show. Queen Elizabeth led the way to the old, broken down toy store. Romeo, Snickers, MayBelle, Soot, Roy, Fluffy, Darla, and Tabitha followed. Mr. Sox, Vittles, and some others stayed at the Factory. Unfortunately, Uncle Fred was scheduled for guard duty. Many other cats were at their homes watching the parade from a window with their faithful people.

The nine cats slinked their way up 4th to Daddy Jack's Toys, though Daddy Jack was no longer. The front window had been broken by a bullet allowing some of the chilling air to sneak into the store. It also left a large enough gap for all the cats to slip through without much trouble. Still, they had to be careful because several pieces of shattered glass lay below.

Inside the store window, the cats sat inch deep in dust. Several decapitated baby doll heads lay about, mostly missing an eye or a patch of hair. They wore painted smirks and seemed to stare at the cats from every angle. In the corner of the window was a thick pile of scuffed plastic legs, which were once attached to the dolls. They lay there like in a weird graveyard, eerie and odd. As for the rest of the toys, their locations were unknown, and nobody was about to lurk around the creepy back room of the ghostly toy store.

"Ouch!!" Darla screamed when she crawled through the jagged hole.

"What happened?" Queen Elizabeth said turning quickly around.

Darla's back was bleeding, though not bad. A piece of the broken window snagged her fur. "Look!" Darla said, showing Queen Elizabeth her wound.

Queen Elizabeth inspected the area. "I think you'll be just fine," she said with a smile.

"Uh, oh," Darla said surprised. "The sight of blood always makes me have to go to the litteroom. I'll be right back." She grabbed Tabitha and found a nice spot for Darla to relieve herself. They were back shortly.

Chapter Seventeen

Outside, the sidewalks were filling up with noisy people. Family after family waited on the cold concrete for the festivities to begin. Most of the younger ones were pulling on their parents who scolded them to be quiet.

Then, a loud, deep roar of distant thunder startled everyone. They looked toward the noise in hopes that it was just a cruel tease. However, the marvelous balloons weren't the only things hanging over the city that day. Dozens of creepy, gray clouds were hovering as well.

The thunder growled again and again. This time it added to the musical styles of the Drippy High School Marching Band. The musicians were dressed in bright blue sequined jumpsuits, all of which were a little too tight. They were charging down the street, banging on their drums, led by their chubby mascot, Colonel Drippy. He was a short, fat man with big, slicked back hair. He twirled a baton to the static beat of the band, but kept hitting himself in the face with it. He even knocked off his fake moustache, though not many people noticed.

Two other cadets also led the band, each holding one end of a banner that read: Fifth Annual Crowman's Day Parade.

A wave of excitement floated through the crowd. Inside the toy shop, Snickers started jumping up and down causing the little bits of broken glass to dance around his paws.

Life One

"Stop that!" Fluffy charged. "I don't want glass flying in my face." He brushed the pieces away and pushed them toward Snickers.

Snickers looked at Fluffy sadly, then went back to his jumping. Fluffy just rolled his eyes and went back to looking out of the foggy window.

Just then, a woman shot up from the sidewalk, pointing and shouting, "I see one! I see one coming around the bank!"

Everyone leaned forward. They followed the direction of her point and spotted the very first balloon traveling up the street.

"Wow! Look at that one!" cried Soot with a grin bigger than Colonel Drippy's.

"Yep, that's a beaut," marveled Queen Elizabeth.

About four blocks away, the cats could see the leg of Mr. Chicken-Horse. He was a popular cartoon character who was half chicken/half horse. On the show he spoke sixteen different languages, but only when he was in the shower. Otherwise, all he did was moo.

The excitement rose as his leg, then his other leg continued to creep around the bank building. The giant hooves darkened the street and broke three office windows on that first block. A group of workers frantically pulled and tugged the balloon's ropes, guiding it through the city. The wind whipped and slapped the balloon around, making their job difficult.

277

Chapter Seventeen

Soon Mr. Chicken-Horse's butt was sticking out and finally his chicken head. The balloon moved slowly, yet not very steadily, still everyone cheered like it was a scoring touchdown in motion. It was magnificent. The crowd went wild. Up ahead the marching band continued to pollute the air with bad, off-key music.

When the balloon passed over Daddy Jack's Toy Shop, the cats inside watched speechless. For most of them it was their first parade and their first balloon. They had never seen anything so big before.

"I want to see another! I want another!" Tabitha yelled, jumping up and down.

Mr. Chicken-Horse was followed by a series of balloons, including Hector the Wine-O and Lilly Lint. Hector banged into Sammy's Department Store creating a big boom, though nothing was louder than the thunder that continued to rock the city.

"Hey, where's Calvin already?" Romeo asked.

"Yeah," Snickers said, "I bet he's not even in the parade. Why don't we go eat?" He turned and headed toward the opening in the window, when suddenly Queen Elizabeth let out a piercing scream.

"Oh my! Oh my!" she hollered. "I can't believe it! It's...it's...Calvin!"

Yep, she was right. The next and newest entry to the parade belonged to the Slimy Cat Snack Company. The fish snack float that Calvin had described drove along the parade route, and above, larger than life, was a huge inflated Calvin. He drifted down the street like a giant nightmare. His eyes were the size of taxi cabs, and the glare off his shiny teeth blinded those below. The Calvin balloon bobbed around in the wind like the other balloons did. As it wiggled and swayed, the funny expression on the balloon's face blurred and made gigantic Calvin look almost crazy.

For the first few seconds none of the other cats made a sound, then they all erupted into wild screams and laughter.

As the float came closer, they could hear the monotonous droning of the Slimy Cat Snack theme song. Its twenty seconds of pure musical torture was heard over and over again, surely deafening the real Calvin, who was now visible on the float. He sat beside a sign that read: *Slimy Cat Snacks. Slime is our business.*

"It's *really* him," Fluffy gagged, half sick. He stared at the balloon in complete shock. "Calvin was telling the truth. How about that!"

Everyone smiled and cheered for the city's newest celebrity.

"Hey, that's not Theodore!" cried a kid in the street as Calvin's float passed by him. "Mommy!!"

The cats ignored the people and continued to watch the parade. By now, another marching band

Chapter Seventeen

had come onto the scene. This one even worse than the last.

Soon Calvin and his balloon were almost directly in front of the toy shop. Calvin himself was walking in circles and chewing on the float's decorations. He didn't seem all that interested in finding his friends in the crowd, though they kept a close eye on him.

Then another rumble of thunder roared, followed by a tremendous banging noise. As Calvin's humongous balloon floated deeper and deeper into the city, a sudden popping sound exploded. In fact, it was so loud that all the people and cats and dogs, even the mice, had to cover their ears. After the initial bang stopped, everyone looked up to see what had caused such a blast.

"Look!" Fluffy yelled, pointing to Calvin's balloon.

Everyone looked to see the disturbing sight of Calvin's giant left paw deflating. It was an odd, morbid sight, only to be followed by something even more upsetting, Calvin's face was caving in. His eyes bunched up and his jaw suctioned his whole face together. Next, his entire butt collapsed. A mysterious hole in the balloon sent a forceful, whirling wind zapping though the street flinging people right off their feet until finally the whole balloon spit out its last gust of air. It hovered momentarily over the stunned and wind-blown crowd.

Chapter Seventeen

"What happened? What happened?" the people started shouting. Chaos grew as everyone ran. The mammoth balloon was about to drop.

"Run! Run for your lives!"

Calvin looked up and saw his wilted balloon body hanging overhead. It was surreal, to say the least. He leapt off the float and hurled himself out of the way. The fish snack float skidded to a screeching halt, flinging paper mache into the faces and mouths of the parade watchers. Then, the big plastic balloon mess crashed down to the concrete, knocking out two of the rope holders and one hotdog seller. The dead balloon lay on the ground covering nearly an entire block. People screamed and pushed and clawed their way out from under it. The cats at the toy shop were absolutely motionless watching the impossible scenario. Darla started to cry, and Snickers hid behind the old, broken register.

The big balloon had been shot down. No one knew how or why, but they knew just the same.

"Back to the Factory!" Queen Elizabeth screamed.

All the cats filed out of the toy shop's broken window and hustled toward the Factory. They rushed the door, spinning Waffles in a frenzy.

"Hold on! Hold on!" he insisted as he undid the series of locks. "Be patient!"

Once inside, the cats charged down the long hall looking for Mr. Sox. He had to know right away

Life One

what had happened out there. They couldn't wait another second to tell him.

Romeo found him in the library. He was standing with some other cats involved in a deep conversation. Immediately, Romeo interrupted him and gushed about the disaster at the parade. By now, the others had arrived at the library as well and shared their impressions of the fiasco.

"You should've seen it, Mr. Sox," Fluffy added. "It was like somebody blew up Calvin and stuck him in the sky."

"The people were screaming! Oh, my, how they were screaming!" Darla explained.

Snickers was covering his ears, hoping the ringing of the Slimy Cat jingle would stop pounding away in his head. To ease the pain, he started banging his head against the floor.

Mr. Sox listened to all the sad stories about the parade. He took off his glasses, rubbed his tired eyes, and sat down. He had a funny look on his face.

"What is it, Mr. Sox," Queen Elizabeth asked. "If you're worried about Calvin, I saw him run away. I'm sure he's just fine...."

"No, no," Mr. Sox interrupted. He stood up again and walked a few feet away. He then looked up at everyone and said, "Come with me."

Mr. Sox led them outside to the back. He stood quietly for a moment while he waited for everyone to huddle around. The earlier, intermittent thunder had gotten closer together and louder, and tiny specks of drizzle were beginning to fall.

Once everyone was gathered, Mr. Sox went on. "Well, I guess *this* explains what happened today at the parade."

He pointed across the street to an empty lot filled with old rubber tires and other worthless junk. In the center of it all was a very worn and withered spooky tree. Its bony, twisted branches hung on with their last breath. Romeo looked and saw what Mr. Sox was pointing to. There, on the bare branches was a new paper sign.

"Read it, Romeo!" Darla yelled from the back.

"It says," Romeo hesitated, "*Take that sticks!... signed, Fidel.*"

The puzzle had come together. Everyone was terrified.

Back on 4th Street, high up in the window of a run-down office building, sat Fidel, Bait, and Max.

"That was a good one, boss!" Bait chuckled. Beside them on the floor were two sling shots and some extra rocks.

Chapter Eighteen

Mr. Sox immediately called an emergency meeting with Queen Elizabeth and all the guards. They locked themselves in the library for hours. Nobody else was allowed in.

Back at the rec room, all the other cats sat around and worried together. A new layer of paranoia was sinking in. Fidel had crossed the line this time, and they could only wonder what he would do next.

"What if he tries to get one of *us*?" Roy asked clutching on to a pillow. "What if he rips our eyes out and cuts out our tongues!?"

"Don't be silly," Fluffy said. "He's not going to do that."

"Don't be so sure," Romeo mumbled.

"We should kill them all!" somebody yelled from the back of the room.

Chapter Eighteen

Just then, the hall door flew open and Calvin came swishing in. He was breathing hard as if he had been running for hours. His fur was a mess, and he looked ghastly. He stumbled melodramatically over to one of the larger pillows, unnecessarily knocking Snickers out of the way to get there. Throwing his body down hard, he let out a tremendous sigh. Everyone else watched unsympathetically.

"What's your problem?" Soot chimed, looking Calvin up and down.

Calvin cleared his throat like he hadn't in days. "What's my problem? What's my problem?" He glanced around the room at the cats as if they were all crazy. "Didn't you see what happened out there? It was my worst nightmare! I mean, imagine if a big balloon of *you* came soaring out of the sky flattening everyone in its path, and..."

Snickers couldn't hold his laugh in any longer. Biting his tongue wasn't working. Funny sounds came sputtering out of his mouth until he finally burst into a roaring bellow. Others followed, and soon all the cats were howling and rolling on the floor. Roy started imitating the dying balloon as it deflated and crashed down. He jumped off a table, first puffing his cheeks out real big, then sucking them back in. Calvin sat on his pillow with a disgusted look on his face. He rolled his eyes five times over in his head. Exasperated, he tapped his back paw and shouted, "Look! It was miserable, alright!"

 286

Life One

The cats laughed even louder. They were out of control. It was a nice change of pace from the worried paranoia they had been feeling all afternoon.

Just as Roy got back on the table to repeat the funny deflating scene again, Mr. Sox and Queen Elizabeth entered the room. They looked concerned and tired. Mr. Sox motioned for Queen Elizabeth to step forward.

All the cats froze in mid-laugh to listen, some of them still on the floor. Roy fell off of the table creating a loud crash.

"I'm alright," he said popping up. "Sorry."

Queen Elizabeth gave him an annoyed look and began. "Mr. Sox, Waffles, and I have had a trying afternoon." She spotted Calvin in the crowd, who seemed fine, though looking exaggeratedly humiliated. "We have come to the conclusion," she went on, "that no action will be taken against the alleys."

A sudden gasp rose from the crowd as she continued.

"True, they have succeeded in scaring us practically to death, especially with today's balloon incident."

Snickers started to giggle again, though he struggled to keep quiet. Romeo reached out and punched him in the side. That stopped him quickly.

"Anyway, the alleys haven't physically hurt any of us, and we do believe that Fidel is just making a big statement. You know him. He wants to make sure

Chapter Eighteen

we know he's around. If we were to attack him, what would that say about us? We are the non-violent ones. He can't take that away from us."

They all looked at each other. They knew she was right, but they still wanted revenge.

"So," Queen Elizabeth continued, "we are electing to ignore what happened today and just go on with our lives, all of them. Trust me, we agonized over this decision, but we feel it is best. Sticks are peaceful. We will *not* fight back. Still, we will continue to have extra guards around the building for added protection. Keep safe, as you have been. Avoid walking alone. Use subways only in emergencies. You know the routine."

Romeo raised his paw high.

"Yes, Romeo?" Queen Elizabeth called.

"What about the graduation? Are we still going to have it in the park?"

Queen Elizabeth looked at Mr. Sox, who nodded in her direction. "Yes," she said. "For those of you graduating next week, the ceremony will go on as scheduled. It has been a stick tradition for years to have it at the park. A few crummy letters and one popped balloon aren't going to stop us now."

Her speech was over. All the cats started talking among themselves, except for Snickers who was still chuckling in the corner. Romeo glanced over at Queen Elizabeth. The expression on her face didn't look as confident as her words had sounded.

 288

Life One

"Queen Elizabeth?" Romeo asked, walking over to her. "Are you sure we'll be safe at the park next week?" His eyes looked worried and concerned.

Queen Elizabeth looked down and reassured him, "Yes, Romeo, there is nothing to worry about. We will have a lot of protection with us just in case." She turned away and walked out of the room. Romeo didn't see her again until the next day.

Chapter Nineteen

The morning of graduation day had finally arrived. It was always on a Friday so everybody could come. Many cats spent the weekends with their people.

Romeo left Dennis and his 5th floor apartment extra early. He grabbed a quick bite of the tuna that Mrs. Crumb had left him the night before and dashed out the foggy window. He didn't even wait for Dennis' usual morning goodbye.

Since the balloon fiasco, Fidel hadn't harassed them. Perhaps that was good, perhaps it was not. The Factory cats were still very careful and very cautious, especially concerning the park. Mr. Sox had arranged for five guards to attend the ceremony, while keeping several stationed around the Factory. Because Uncle Fred was finally graduating, he was not scheduled for

Life One

guard duty.

Everyone met at City Park at eight o'clock. Mr. Sox and Queen Elizabeth were the first to arrive. They waited beneath an old stone bridge near the edge of the park. It was a pretty spot, one of the few in the city. There was a small stream nearby and lots of trees. The day smelled new, though not necessarily pleasant. Luckily, the rain had stopped from the night before, but the ground was all mushy and muddy. Every time Mr. Sox took a step, he got his paws covered in mud. He was constantly scraping them off on a big rock that lay nearby. Queen Elizabeth watched and giggled to herself.

Calvin was the next to arrive. He slowly walked up the muddy lawn to the stone bridge with a sad frown on his face. Queen Elizabeth approached him, lifting his chin with her paw. "What's wrong, Calvin? You're graduating today. You should be smiling."

Calvin brushed her paw away and stared off into the stream. He squinted his eyes and frowned bigger than before.

"Come on, Calvin," she said again. "What's the matter?"

"Nothing," he snapped, kicking a rock into the water.

Queen Elizabeth gave him a look.

"Okay," he said. "Fine. I'll tell you, but I don't want to."

"You'll feel better once you get it off your

Chapter Nineteen

chest," she assured him.

"Well, you remember the whole *balloon* thing?"

"Yes," she said slowly.

"Well, because the stupid thing broke, and because people got hurt, the company has to pay a lot of money, and well, Slimy Cat Snacks is out of business." He threw himself down into the mud and covered his face with his paws. Queen Elizabeth could hear him crying through all that fur and muck.

"There, there," she consoled. "It's going to be all right."

Calvin lifted up his muddy head. "No, it's not! Now I have to start all over!" He wailed louder and louder. Mr. Sox came over to see what was the matter. Queen Elizabeth told him what happened. Mr. Sox just rolled his eyes and sloshed away. Actors.

As Romeo walked to the park, he spotted Twinkle Toes up ahead. Romeo ran fast through the many feet to catch up to him. Twinkle Toes was standing on his hind legs in front of a donut shop with his front paws pressed against the window. Inside, a large woman with a broom came over and pounded on the glass.

"Scram!" she shouted. She had little bits of jelly stuck to the sides of her face.

Twinkle Toes plopped down and started to leave.

"Hey, Twinkle Toes," Romeo called. "Wait up!"

Twinkle Toes waited in the shadow of the large,

plastic donut that hung over the door. Romeo finally caught up to him and gave him a nudge.

"So," Romeo began, "today's the big day!"

"Yeah, whatever," Twinkle Toes moaned.

Romeo wasn't going to beat around the bush any longer. Not on this day. He stared long and hard in his eyes and said, "Look Toes, you can't fool me anymore. Now tell me, what's going on?" Romeo kept his gaze locked and didn't let go.

Twinkle Toes nervously shifted a bit, mumbled a few syllables, and huffed. This was it. He was giving in. "All right, Romeo, I'll tell you..."

The sad cat admitted what Romeo had already suspected. His people were beating him and making him sleep outside in the rain. They were hardly feeding him anything edible, and they hadn't cleaned his litter box in weeks. Sometimes he didn't even have litter. They had never been particularly kind, but ever since they both lost their jobs, they were taking it out on him.

"You've got to get out of there!" Romeo emphasized.

Twinkle Toes shrugged his shoulders.

"Tell me one thing, Twinkle Toes," Romeo said. "Have you lost any lives because of these people?" He was terrified to hear his answer, yet he had to ask.

Twinkle Toes turned his head away shamefully. He started to twist his right front paw nervously.

"Twinkle Toes?"

Chapter Nineteen

Twinkle Toes continued looking the other way. "All right, all right," he finally said. "Look, Romeo, don't tell the others, but yes, I...I've lost three lives."

"Three?" Romeo shouted in horror. "Three? Oh Twinkle Toes, we've got to get you out of there right now!"

The two cats walked to the park together. Romeo couldn't get the image of Twinkle Toes shivering in the rain night after night out of his head. And to think, he lost three lives already, and he wasn't even a year old. It was criminal.

At the park everyone gathered under the bridge. Romeo stuck with Twinkle Toes, and Calvin sat alone. They were all terribly excited. The big day had finally come. All their hard work, all those hours, and now their reward. It was particularly exciting to see Uncle Fred finally graduating. He stood the proudest. His fur nicely groomed, his breath didn't smell too bad, and he even brought Ms. Purrpurr a flower. Of course, it was wilted, but it's the thought that counts. Even though Uncle Fred could still barely read and had no other skills, for that matter, Ms. Purrpurr couldn't bare the thought of having him in class for another six months. Thus, she and the other teachers allowed him this day.

Fluffy stood in the middle of the cats looking dapper and confident despite the pretty pink panties Cassie had put on him. She cut a hole out for his tail and safety pinned the waist so they would fit. Fluffy felt like an idiot, but he did a good job of acting cool.

After a few moments more, the ceremony began. Everyone was silent as Mr. Sox stepped forward. When he did, a loud fart-like noise was heard as his paw squished into the mud. He cleared his throat and began.

"Welcome. Welcome. You have made it. You should be proud of yourselves." All the young students looked around at each other and smiled with pride. "Six months ago I met most of you for the first time at the Factory. I thought to myself, this is a great group of cats. They look smart and eager to learn. I was right. And to the cats who started late, good for you. You managed to work hard and catch up. You are all now officially cats of the Factory. Your diplomas will forever hang on our walls, and your opinions will always matter. I think Ms. Purrpurr and Mr. Shadow would agree with me when I say that you are ready to make your way in the big city we all call home. And no matter how tough it gets, how hard things seem, remember, you always have a safe place to go."

Romeo smiled in Twinkle Toes' direction as a silver bolt of lightning was seen in the distance.

"You have been well-taught," Mr. Sox continued, "well-prepared and well-trained. Remember, the city streets are never going to be easy, but now that you have the needed skills, they can be tolerated. Another thing, never, NEVER forget who you are!" He pointed to each and every one of them. "You are sticks! Sticks now and sticks to the end! Don't ever let anyone, especially an alley, say you are anything less! Don't forget how precious your lives are, each and every one of them! Now, without further ado, I want you to take your tails and move them from the left side of your body to the right side, a stick graduation tradition."

Everyone wiggled their tails. Fluffy had a bit of trouble because of his undergarments, though he was finally able to complete the maneuver.

"There," Mr. Sox said, "you are now Stick School graduates! Congratulations!"

The cats all cheered and threw leaves high into the air. They floated back down along with the rain drops that were starting to fall. Queen Elizabeth and Ms. Purrpurr rushed forward and gave everyone a big hug. Mr. Shadow stood back by a tree with the other guards watching every little thing. As he took a step forward to congratulate the graduates, he slipped and fell in the mud. His favorite yellow knit sweater got all dirty. He looked around, embarrassed to see if anyone had noticed. It didn't seem that they had. Everyone tapped each other with their tails and swayed, saying the stick pledge together one last time. After the celebration died down, Mr. Sox introduced Twinkle Toes. Nervously, he stepped forward to recite his poem.

Clearing his throat, he began. "Uh, they's asked me to think of a poem, and well, here goes...

Life One

'We're all smart now,
Even dear Uncle Fred.
I'm glad we all made it
And nobody's dead.
Stick School was fun,
But it's over now
So thanks to all the teachers
Who taught us somehow.'"

Twinkle Toes bowed and immediately stepped back with the others. Well, it wasn't Shakespeare, but it was poetry. He walked up to his friends and felt happy for the first time in a long while.

Queen Elizabeth ended the ceremony with a few kind words. Soon, everyone began to sing and dance together. They romped through the mud and kicked around pebbles. Uncle Fred was off busy chasing flies, while Darla spent half the morning peeing into the stream. It was a happy time, not just for the young students, but teachers and friends alike. Even Calvin snapped out of his bad mood.

Next, it was time to go back to the Factory for a congratulatory lunch. MayBelle was preparing the shrimp that Yellowtail brought over very early that morning. She had also filled the rec room with special decorations Tabitha helped make. All the paw-painted diplomas were laid out for everyone to see.

"Come on!" Queen Elizabeth shouted.

Chapter Nineteen

She gathered the sticks together as they started on their way. They had only traveled two feet when somebody yelled, "Everyone, quick, run!" It was Waldo, the photographer.

They looked at him with dazed, startled faces. Waldo was pointing to an area over near the bridge. All heads swung around to see what was happening. There, off in the distance beneath the golden bolts and drizzling rain, was the most deadly figure anyone had ever seen.

"What is that?" Darla screamed, clutching onto Romeo.

"It's...it's...Fidel!" Romeo hollered. "I think it's Fidel!"

Everyone stopped. Fidel and his gang of alleys were running toward the sticks through the dark fog. They crested the hilltop like a massive black shadow, ten of them, charging at full speed like a herd of wild beasts. In the cold air, their breath formed another sort of cloud that trailed behind them like ghosts. As Fidel got closer, his neon green eyes and rotten teeth pierced through the sticky haze. His collar with all the stolen ID tags clinked and swayed to the beat of his stride, as the wall of alley cats behind him grumbled louder and louder. They were approaching fast.

Frozen, the sticks stood like statues, still with some celebratory leaves on their paws and fading thoughts of shrimp in their heads.

"This way!" Mr. Shadow roared. He motioned

for everyone to follow him out of the park. They'd be safer on the streets.

The sticks darted away, the alleys quickly nearing.

"Go! Go! Go!" Queen Elizabeth shouted as the sticks ran passed her.

"Come on, Queen Elizabeth!" Fluffy screamed. "Let's get out of here!"

She didn't listen to him but stayed near the bridge making sure each and every stick made it out safely. Romeo heard her voice. Certain she was right behind them, he turned to see her still near the bridge checking the sticks off in her head as they each ran by to make sure no one was left in the park. But who was looking out for her? Fidel was closing in, mad and fast.

Romeo ran back for her. Mr. Sox tried to stop him, but it was no use. He wasn't going to let Queen Elizabeth get hurt, not again.

"Come back, Romeo!" Tabitha yelled with all her might.

Romeo charged into the depths of City Park, keeping one eye on his friend and one eye on the enemy. Fidel saw the perfect picture before him, two targets, unguarded and alone, while the other sticks ran far, far ahead.

Everything was happening so fast and so chaotic that Queen Elizabeth didn't realize how much danger she had put herself in. She saw Romeo and ran toward him. Her heart raced faster than it ever had before, her body sweating and shivering.

"Go the other way, Romeo!" she wailed.

Romeo kept racing for her, only feet away. By now, several of the sticks were nearly at the Factory. Once they started to run their adrenaline kicked in and they practically flew. But some of the others stood like lions at the gate, ready to take on their worst enemy.

"Romeo!" Queen Elizabeth blared through the wind as she took a flying leap in his direction. Romeo quickly turned away thinking she was on his tail. He ran like the wind. Queen Elizabeth was a fine athlete, but this time when she jumped, she tripped and slipped in the wet mud. She landed with a thump against a large rock, snapping her neck with a stabbing, sickening pain. She reached out a paw for Romeo, but he didn't see her as he sprinted for the street. She tried to scream but nothing came out.

As Romeo zoomed, he turned his head to see if she was still behind him. There she was laid out in the mud as a thunder bolt shattered the morning sky.

"Nooooo!" Romeo screamed as he saw Fidel take a soaring jump over the rock where Queen Elizabeth lay hurt.

Fidel roared as his faithfuls surrounded the boulder. In midair, Fidel's eyes filled with fire and his jaws opened wide. His claws were stiff and sharp and jetted out of his ratty paws like knives. In slow motion, he wailed and came soaring down on top of Queen

 300

Life One

Elizabeth. By the time she looked up, it was too late. She didn't even have time to shield herself. Fidel's gang moved in, blocking Romeo's view. A loud, gut-wrenching scream was heard, following a series of hisses and moans. Then, from deep within the foggy mist, everything went silent.

"Get off of her!" Romeo hollered. His blood was boiling as he instinctively ran back. He jumped on top of one of the alleys, digging his teeth into its neck. The cat let out a yell, and Romeo's fur stood straight up on end. All of a sudden, Fluffy came charging out of nowhere. He grabbed another alley and slashed him hard in the face. The cat fought back, attacking Fluffy with tremendous force.

"Steak! Candle! Get *that* one and bring him to me!" Fidel ordered his new cronies, pointing to Romeo.

By now, Snickers, Roy, Waffles, Twinkle Toes, even Tabitha came rushing back. They all courageously clawed and hissed their way though the ordeal. Two of the alleys were down, gasping in the mud. Fluffy and Snickers grabbed Fidel and pulled him off Queen Elizabeth. Romeo smacked Steak and Fish out of his way and ran to her side. Her body was covered in mud and soaked in blood. Gently, he lifted her head up, feeling a big bump where she hit the rock. All around him cats were screeching and fighting a nasty battle. Fur was flying, blood was spraying, and lives were in danger. Still, Romeo sat beside Queen Elizabeth, cradling her

Chapter Nineteen

head and brushing the mud from her eyes. He called her name, but she didn't respond.

"Queen Elizabeth? Queen Elizabeth?" he pleaded with desperation. "Wake up! We've got to get you out of here!"

Still, she didn't move. Romeo knew he only had seconds to spare before Fidel or his henchcats came back for him. He continued his efforts to revive Queen Elizabeth, shaking her and tapping her. Nothing worked.

Romeo feared that she was dead. No time to cry now. With his teeth, he grabbed her by the fur and started to pull her away.

Tabitha came running over. "What are you doing?" she screamed. "Come on! Help us!"

"No! I've got to get her out of here! She's dead! Her eighth life!" his voice quivered, low and mournful. He tried again to move her, but her body was too heavy for him alone to carry. "Help me, Tabitha! Help me carry her away!"

Tabitha looked around at the fighting cats and knew they had to move fast. Coldly, but for his own good, she yelled to Romeo, "No! Leave her! You have to! You don't have time to carry her! They'll get *you* for sure!"

"But I have to get her out of here! She's only got one life left now! They'll kill her dead! Now help me!" Romeo demanded.

Tabitha grabbed Romeo by the tail with her

Chapter Nineteen

teeth and pulled him away as fast and as hard as she could.

"What are you doing?" he growled at her, moving back toward Queen Elizabeth. "Leave me alone! I'll save her myself!"

"She's dead, Romeo!" Tabitha desperately cried. "She's dead! You have to leave her here!"

"I know she's dead, but she's got one more life left! I've got to..."

"No, Romeo!" she interrupted. "She's really dead!" Tabitha didn't want to say it, but she had no other choice. Only she knew Queen Elizabeth's secret. It was the only way to save Romeo. Her eyes filled with tears. "Romeo, she's gone! You don't understand, she lost her eighth life at the Pound. You have to let her go." She tried to pull him away, but Romeo didn't budge.

He stood in shock, staring blankly at Tabitha. Could this be true? Could this awful thing be true? Romeo looked at Queen Elizabeth, then at Tabitha again. His heart sunk as he crumbled to the ground.

"Noooo!" he wailed. "It can't be! It can't be!"

Tabitha knelt down beside him. "We *have* to go, Romeo! They're going to get us too!"

"They killed her! That *beast* killed her!" Romeo took one final look at Queen Elizabeth who lay bloodied and violated in the mud. Filled with rage, his eyes tightened and he began to huff. His anger flared in Fidel's direction as he darted through the muck. Fluffy was fighting off the beast, both already suffering several deep scratches across their faces.

"Come back!" Tabitha yelled to Romeo from the rock.

Just then, Romeo jumped as high as he could. He caught Fidel's eye, who braced himself for Romeo's landing. All four paws pounced on Fidel, crushing him to the ground. Fidel struggled to get up as some of the other alleys piled on top. Then, with a roar, Fidel erupted through the mass of cats like a volcano, grabbing Romeo and tossing him to the ground. Now Fidel was on top of Romeo and had him pinned down in a frightfully tight grip.

"Everyone get away!" Fidel screamed to his gang. "I want to do *this* one alone."

Fluffy charged forward. Fidel flexed his paw and hissed in Fluffy's direction. Below him, Romeo lay helpless.

"Come any closer and I'll kill him right now," Fidel snarled.

Fluffy stopped and slid back into the mud. The rain was getting heavier and the fog becoming thicker. All the other cats, sticks and alleys, stood and watched Fidel. Nobody knew what he would do.

"So, here we are!" Fidel huffed in Romeo's face. His breath was horrid, and he drooled angrily. "Queeny can't help you now, boy! Can she?"

Romeo wiggled his tongue and shot a spit wad into Fidel's eye. Fidel hissed and slashed Romeo

Chapter Nineteen

across the face with his sharp claws.

Romeo let out a wail and screamed, "Why? Why are you doing this?"

Fidel looked him deep in the eyes. His expression was satanic and his breathing heavy. Romeo could see every muscle in Fidel's body clench together like a thick rope. Fidel purred menacingly.

"Why am I doing this? Why am I doing this? That *friend* of yours killed two of my best alleys, and you, my little Romeo, are the product of two traitors! That makes you unworthy of living!"

"W-w-what are you talking about, Fidel?" Romeo wiggled to get away, but Fidel only tightened his grip.

"Didn't you hear what I said? Romeo the stick, ha! You are *nothing*, Romeo! Your parents were nothing!"

"What do you know about my parents?" Romeo shouted.

"They were *alleys*, you fool! Gutter-breeding alleys who betrayed *me* by sending their pathetic, precious males away to be sticks. Do you know what I could have done with six male cats? Do you realize what your *stupid* parents did?"

"That means... that...."

"Yes, Romeo. You are an *alley through and through*! Born to alley parents! You were supposed to belong to *me*!"

"You're lying!" Romeo shouted. "It's not true!"

 306

Life One

"Isn't it? That mark on your back, your father had the same one. I remember seeing it when I killed him."

"What?" Romeo's eyes bulged.

"That's right, I killed him and your pathetic mother too! In fact, I killed all your brothers! When they came back to life, we killed them again and again and again! Nine times each! You were supposed to be dead too! I particularly remember seeing your hopeless mother cry when we killed her last son! Pathetic!"

"Get off of me! Lies! All lies! Help!" Romeo struggled to get away. He kicked and clawed through Fidel's tight grasp. But all his struggling wasn't enough.

"Now it is your turn to die!" Fidel warned, raising his fierce paw high in the air.

Just then, a man was seen in the distance. There were two men, both cops on horseback. They started charging over to the cats. Fidel saw them and cursed the ground they rode on.

"Damn!" he grumbled. He looked down at Romeo, "We'll have to continue this later, my friend." And with that, Fidel swung his claw down fast slicing Romeo across the face once again. The claw didn't go in very deep, but the motion was enough to knock Romeo's head against the ground hard. Romeo's eyes rolled back in their sockets. Just as the policemen rode up, Fidel whistled for his gang and they all shot away in an instant. As a final insult, Fidel grabbed hold of Queen Elizabeth's collar. He tore off her tag and scurried away. The rest of the sticks hid behind a bush and waited to see what the cops would do.

From atop their horses they could see two cats lying on the ground, bloody and motionless.

"I guess it was just a cat fight," one of them said to the other.

"Yeah. It sure sounded like something bigger, though. Well, I'll call the Pound to get rid of these two. Come on, let's go." They rode off on their horses. Nobody noticed the eyes on the little mustang. They were bright purple.

When everyone was sure the police had left, Fluffy, Snickers, and the others rushed to Romeo's side. By now the alleys were far away. Fluffy immediately lifted Romeo's limp head. A sad look fell upon Fluffy's face as he looked up at the others mournfully.

"He's dead. Romeo's dead. Help me get him out of here."

Without a word, Fluffy and Snickers lifted Romeo's body with their teeth and pulled him out of the park. Everyone, not just Romeo, was wounded that day. None as seriously as Romeo though, nor as final as Queen Elizabeth.

They dragged Romeo down the pavement. It was a frightful sight seeing the cats pull his lifeless body through the crowded sidewalks. People stopped to look. Some kids pointed. One even screamed. But, most went on with their day, unaware of the tragedy that took place only minutes earlier.

Romeo's blood dripped on the concrete and streamed into the gutters. The sticks walked in a sad procession with empty expressions and angry hearts. Fluffy imagined Romeo playing and laughing on this very street just hours ago. Even though he would regain his life and be fine in no time, he would never be the same. What he saw and heard that day would haunt him forever. The sting of finally knowing the truth about his family. The horror of knowing his alley roots. Those emotional wounds would take more than a lifetime to heal.

But perhaps the hardest, most devastating news Romeo would wake up to was remembering the cruel fate that ended Queen Elizabeth's ninth life. As always, she died bravely helping others, something he would never forget. Her untimely death would pain Romeo forever.

Chapter Twenty

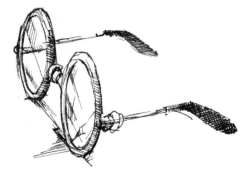

The sad news flowed through the Factory like a dark wind. Nobody could bring themselves to believe what had happened to Queen Elizabeth. It would be a long time before anyone would smile again. She was a bonefide hero. Waffles and Roy were sent back to the park to get her body. Romeo was whisked off to the medicine room, still dead. As anxious as everyone was to see him alive again, they felt saddened for his loss and the grieving that he would certainly endure. Would he still be the same happy, curious Romeo when he woke up?

Fluffy found Mr. Sox alone in the library looking worried and confused. The old teacher paced about the room, letting his glasses fall low against his nose. Fluffy asked him the difficult question that Romeo surely would ask later.

  310

Life One

"Yes, Fluffy. It's true," Mr. Sox said. "Everything Fidel told Romeo is true."

"But how, Mr. Sox?" Fluffy asked. "How could something like that be true? How could Fidel have killed his whole family? It doesn't make sense."

Slowly, many of the other cats entered the room and huddled in a bundle around Mr. Sox. He took off his glasses and sat down on an old wooden chair.

"Life is complicated, children. Strange, cruel things happen around here all the time. You will learn that in *your* lifetimes, over and over again. What happened to Romeo's family is unacceptable. And what happened today is a great setback, not just for Romeo, but for all sticks. Fidel attacked today, violently. This hasn't happened since Carnival's day. It is clear that Fidel wants a full-blown war. And that's *exactly* what he's going to get. He's gone too far this time." The wise cat turned and looked toward a window that had been boarded up long ago. "It will be a new world out there tomorrow, and I'm afraid of it. Our future now depends on *you*, all of you. *You* have to decide what that future will be, for yourselves, for your children, for sticks everywhere."

Mr. Sox put back on his bent glasses, walked out of the room and headed home.